ULTIMATE TOMBOYS

*By
Bunny*

Copyright @2021
All rights reserved.

Under International Copyright Law, no part of this book may be reproduced, distributed, or transmitted in any form by any means, graphic, electronic, or mechanical, including photocopy, recording, taping, or by any information storage or retrieval system, without permission in writing from the author except in the case of reprints in the context of the reviews, quotes, or references.

Printed in the United States of America

Paperback ISBN: 978-1-63732-746-3
Ebook ISBN: 978-1-63821-440-3

For details, email Bunny.Productions@yahoo.com

AGE IS NOTHING BUT A NUMBER

Live your life as you feel!

Bunny.Productions

I am honored to introduce you to Bunny's first novel Ultimate Tomboys. I have known Bunny for a few years now and I can vividly remember the day she told me about her book. It was around my birthday, and I was down in the dumps about getting older. Bunny told me, "Girl, cheer up. You're beautiful Inside and out. Age is only a number." She said that she was writing a book about women our age. I won't say how old, since, of course, age is just a number. She said that she
wanted to show the world that women are sexy and can kick ass at any age. The main characters in Ultimate Tomboys are certainly sexy and definitely kickass. However, I think that an important theme of the book is sisterhood.

As you read the book, you will meet characters that stand by each other and protect each other no matter what happens. Bunny's character development is amazing.

Her characters come to life. The women in this book come from many different backgrounds and unite to help a friend. Sisterhood is a bond of the heart. It transcends race. A real sister is one who loves you and accepts you with all your faults. Someone you might bicker with but will always have your back. These characters rely on each other and trust each other with their lives. This is not one of those books where the man rescues the woman. Instead, this is about strong women that take care of each other. That is a great message.   Ultimate Tomboys is one of those books that you just cannot put down. I am glad that I read it during vacation. I did not want to do anything until I finished the
book. Bunny's descriptive writing will have you seeing every scene as if you were there.

The plot twists kept me guessing until the very end. I am certain that you will find yourself drawn to one of the characters. Mine was Bonnie. Not really one of the main characters, but I really identified with her.
She is in the background for the most part but is the one who organizes everyone and keeps things together. I am already eager to read the second book to see what happens next!

Susan E. Schwab

CHAPTER ONE

Tex and Jordan are sound asleep in their beautifully decorated bedroom, the house was quiet, minus the rhythmic hum of the central air. One body, garbed in black-on-black clothing, crept up to the front door, jimmying the lock using special equipment to enter the home. After gaining entrance, a man gave a thumbs--up and two more bodies moved closer to the home, quickly and quietly.

It was a warm summer night around 11 pm, in Freebush, California. Upon entering the house, they went straight for the stairs, shining their small flashlights, ascending the stairs. As the leader reach the top step, he put his finger up to his chest indicating a sign for the others to stop. The others stopped on cue. The leader went towards the master bedroom door and put his ear to the door-all was clear. _The plan had gone well so far, and he didn't want to blow it during this last stage.

Hearing nothing that would alarm him, he turned and gave the others all clear to continue.

"On three," the leader whispered behind him.

"Gotcha" the number two-man responded.

When the leader raised up the third finger, all hell busted in the couple's tranquil night. Jordan and Tex were not only husband and wife, but they were also the number one undercover agents in the United States, the best.

Within seconds, the booming sound of the bedroom door crashing open disintegrated all slumber. Tex and Jordan found their king size bed surrounded by masked men with their pistols pointed in their faces. Reactive screams were caught up by Tex in her need to catch a collective breath, trying to decipher what was going on. Jordan just stared at the intruders with a mad as hell look, daring them to pull the trigger.

"Why the fuck is you in my house?" asked Jordan.

The intruder standing on Jordan's bedside raised his gun and smacked him on the side of the head. Tex gasped.

Assessing what is happening Tex figure out that they were being robbed or these men were there to assassinate her and her husband. But the latter seems not true. Assassins come in, do the job then leave. Something is not right about this picture. Jordan, as a man, was not taking lightly, the fact of someone has the nerve to break into his home.

"Fuck you" "Why are you in my house?" shouts Jordan.

A soft bang was heard, at the same time, a needle was jammed into Tex neck, she is out cold, while Jordan body lies halfway off the bed with blood running down his chest. The intruders looked around the room, then at each other, and exited the house just as quickly as they had entered.

***

Jordan's funeral was attended by over three hundred people. Tex sat on the first pew at the church's sanctuary greeting and hugging everyone who came to give their respect for the loss of her husband. She is wearing a white silk suit garnished with medium-sized pearls streaming down the front of her fitted jacket. She has on a large pearl and diamond brooch that sparked as she greeted guest. Wearing a white wide-brimmed hat with a white lace veil that covered her swollen eyes. White gloves that came up to her wrists boast four small pearls on the sides.
Her four-inch heels made her taller than usual, so she remained seated. Her large white purse was beside her, left open slightly, holding a program and envelopes given to her.
    To her left was her best friend, Bonnie, and to her right sat her boss name Deuce. He became the new boss of the agency the moment Jordan was pronounced dead. The agency's policy was well-stamped. The way the secret operations works, is that every job is filled, upon someone's death.
    In the spy business it is not safe to leave any holes, infiltrators thrive on weakness, and would not hesitate to take advantage.
    Tex really didn't know the man; she'd only heard of him. Nevertheless, she was in mourning and had more important things on her mind than who took over her dead husband's position.
    People began taking their seats because the memorial service was about to begin. Tex held up her veil to wipe her eyes. Her best friend Bonnie tapped her shoulder to check on her and Tex nodded that she was okay.
    The preacher got up and made his move toward the podium.
    "Ladies and gentlemen, we are here today to honor a great man who has gone on to his next journey. Jordan will be dearly missed by his lovely wife Tex, his colleagues and the world."
    "Amen!" and "Yes!"" were heard throughout the church.
    The preacher paused to allow the people to vocalize, and then continued.
    "Tex has asked me to keep this short for numerous reasons. Knowing Jordan, he wouldn't want to be cried over. Words he used all the time was, 'get on with life", a proud man. The preacher paused a bit to give an endearing look at Tex.

She returns the affection. "So, with that in mind", he continued, "we will begin with a hymn sung by sister Del Johnson.

Ms. Johnson walked from her seat towards the microphone, as the organ player begin playing. When she reaches the mic, she immediately starts humming, the sound shook the audience up. The singing note made people hearts weep. What a voice. Ms. Johnson starts singing the hymn, *"you'll never walk alone"*, at the end of the song, the whole church jumped up, clapping, and screaming. "Amen!" "Yes Jesus!" "She *sang* that song!"

Ms. Johnson climbed down the podium and starts walking towards Tex, reaching her side, she bends down and gives her a kiss on the check. Tex returned the gesture.

The home-going was over in fifteen minutes. The golden coffin with two long handles on both sides was rolled into the hearse and all who intended to make the trip, headed towards the cemetery. The procession was four cars, deep.

Bonnie, who was the only one sitting in the lead limousine with Tex. She studied Tex as if to see how she was holding up. Tex sat emotionless and seemed to only want to keep her eyes glazed on the hearse in front of them. As a courtesy, the limo driver had a cd of inspirational hymns softly playing throughout the speakers. Bonnie leaned forward a bit and said to the driver, "Turn that up a bit, please." The driver nodded and obliged. Hitting a button on the right-side door by her hip, Bonnie raised the partition glass, separating the driver from his passengers. Confident that what she was about to say next couldn't be overheard, her attention turned to her friend.

"I have some disturbing news".

"Today?" Tex said, incredulous.

"Yes, today," Bonnie said. "I'm sorry, but this has to come out now. I received information that leads me to believe that this death is a hoax."

"What?" asked Tex.

"A fucking hoax," Bonnie

"What kind of hoax?" Tex asked, trying to grasp what Bonnie was saying.

"Jordan is not dead," Bonnie answered.

"Bonnie, the damn body is in front of us going down the street," Tex said angrily while pointing towards the front of the limousine.

Bonnie lightly touched Tex on the shoulder, looking into Tex's eyes she said, "The casket was closed for a reason".

Bonnie took a quick breath then continued, "I need you to trust me when we bury that body up in front of us." Bonnie allowed Tex's confused silence to engulf them both. Then she instructed, "We will go back to the house and talk."

"Bonnie, you are fucking kidding me," Tex said.

"I kid you not and I would not have brought this up if I didn't believe it."

Sighing, Tex lowered her head and said, "We will handle this when we are alone."

"Okay," said Bonnie, who leaned back into the soft leather seat. At the grave site, before getting back in her limousine to leave, Tex hugged, and shook hands with colleagues and friends.

She told them she was quite tired and needed to rest. In front of everyone, like it was an impromptu decision, she asked Bonnie to accompany her home. Her mind was going a mile a minute. She knew deep down something smelled fishy, but she could not put her finger on it. Earlier, before the service began, she looked harder at the body in the golden casket. A wave of confusion ingulfed her. The body looked different somehow, some of the features were slightly off. She wondered if maybe Bonnie was on to something, to say the least, and now she was going to get to the bottom of it. She asked herself. Would Jordan do this? and why?

Bonnie has raised her curiosity and now she will get to the bottom of it. *'Why would Jordan do this?'*

***

A mystery man Jordan was. His birth name is Jared Lucas born on April 1st, a name he had not used for a long time, spent years erasing his past to become the man he so desperate want to be. He had surgery on his face to change his identity. His first kills were the nurses, he poisons them by bring them dinner. The doctor he blew up his car, just to keep the secret.

He hurried up and left from overseas.

Jordan practice walking different and altered the sound of his voice to complete the transformation.

Jordan was an only child. His mother died of leukemia when he was ten. His father was killed in a drug sting by his best friend when he was twelve. He lived in and out foster homes until he ran away at the age of fourteen, living in the streets or wherever he can lay his head.

Jordan saved all his money towards his destiny. Before he left the states, he shot and killed his father best friend who betrayed him and his son, then he boards a plane out of the states to begin his journey of becoming the KING. He is going to make his father proud.

***

Returning home after five years, Jordan needs to put his next plan in action.

He will join the best police force to get inside information so he can become the BIGGEST arm & drug dealer in the whole wide world.

The one difficult he encounters was changing his name and birth date because he didn't have the proper paperwork.

One day, it came to him. Flirt and date a clerk who can help him.

His 6'3 tall slim body with green eyes and chisel body made that part easy. Choosing the right clerk was a must.

Vivian a 5'5-inch black hair beauty caught his attention one day as he walked the court halls.

He starts becoming friendly with security guards in the area. He was coming once a week to get his papers in order. The court are giving free classes for entrepreneurs to get their businesses up and running.

Vivian walked by one day as Jordan was talking to two guards.

"Tell me about her" Jordan asked.

"Her name is Vivian" said one guard.

"What department she works in?" Jordan asks.

"Tough to get a date bud. A lot of guys tried and failed" one says as he snickers.

"Not looking for a date, looking for some help my man, I need some inside information, that's all" says Jordan.

"Yea, right, ok, she works with Judge Roger Taylor, I believe he helps with new identities, when someone been adopted and wants to change their birth name or some shit like that" says the guard.

The wheels are turning in Jordan head as the guard is talking.... yeeeees

His plan is coming into focus.

***

Back in her bedroom, Tex locked the door and put on some music. She loved Maria Callas, the best opera singer in the world. Maria was singing her signature song, an operatic song from Puccini's *Tosca.*

Bonnie poured a drink from a pitcher of water on Tex's side table and offered her one.

"No, I need a stiffer drink," said Tex.

Looking at her glass, Bonnie realized she could use a stiffer one too and went towards the bar on the left side of Tex and Jordan's bedroom where the murder had happened. She pulled out Hennessey and poured two drinks. She didn't put ice in the drink for Tex, as she likes it off the rocks, so to speak. She walked back over to Tex who was removing her jacket to get comfortable. She was gearing up for some serious business.

Taking the drink, Tex said, "Tell me everything."
-She walked back over towards the soft beige leather sofa in her sitting room. Bonnie followed her and sat beside on her left.

Taking a big sip, Bonnie sighed.

"Need that before you talk?" Tex asked.

"Yes, and another one." Bonnie had brought the bottle with her and was pouring another drink.

"When you are ready, my friend. I have never seen you like this," said Tex.

Shaking while drinking her Hennessey, Bonnie says, "I have never been like this even after everything we been through, this shit is bad. Shitty,"

"Out with it. I am burning up with curiosity," said Tex.

"Our old friend Myer came up to me downstairs in the basement of the church. I was coming out of the ladies' room when he was waiting for me by a side wall. He motioned me over with a hand signal. Immediately, I felt something was wrong. My blood started boiling," explained Bonnie.

"So is mine Bonnie, get on with it," says Tex.

"I will, just hold on."

Bonnie took another sip of her drink.

Tex breathed heavy, *she should have been an actress*, was Tex's thought about her friend.

"He gave me this flash drive and told me I needed to look at it as soon as possible," Bonnie continued.

"And that raised your blood? He always gave us information," said Tex.

Shaking her head, Bonnie said, "Not like this, this is different, distinctive. I sneaked out before the service started and drove back to our small command center.

Surprised, Tex said, "You did what?"

"I came to the command center, where it will be safe and put the flash drive in our secure laptop," said Bonnie. The information flashed before my eyes. Stunned, I return quickly to the service before you missed me. This is what I saw, said Bonnie as she cut on the laptop to display what the flash drive showed her. What Tex saw on the screen made her yell out loud.

CHAPTER TWO

"Lay Your Hands on Me" by Bon Jovi was playing in the background as two girls were dancing up a storm with a few young men.

The one with golden blonde hair was working two young things, one in the front of her and one behind her. The young men were drenched in sweat, trying to keep up with her. She was used to handling men, and she knew how to work it.

The other girl, hair light brown with loose curls, was only working one man. She liked to focus on one man at a time. That, way, she could pinpoint what was needed to get him in bed. After all, this was the mission on both the ladies' minds.

The music was pumping loud, and the dance floor was crowded. People were enjoying themselves at this new club that had just opened.
The owner made sure these sexy ladies were invited because they knew how to party and could work a crowd.

At the end of the song, the girls guided the three men out of the club into the parking lot. But only one of the men followed Blondie.

"Oh well, his loss," said the blonde one.

The four bodies reached the motorcycles in the lot. Suddenly, Blondie pulled out her gun and shot the guy standing by the light brown hair lady.

The body hit the ground hard. The other guy stared in disbelief.

"What the fuck?" said the lady.

"Sorry, meant to tease him about kidnapping him" says Blondie.

"Sorry my ass, I was going to fuck him. I am going to take your man."

"The hell you will," said Blondie. "I am horny as shit," laughing the whole time.

The young guy looked at the body on the ground and the two ladies battling it out over him. He didn't know whether to be afraid or to be happy, he gets to fuck two women at the same time.

A deadly drunk patron walked out the back door of the club with his drink in his left hand. The drink was spilling because he was walking wobbly, failing to keep his balance. Finally, he stopped trying to walk, and attempted to hold his body, upright, adjusting his eyes to the sight in front of him.

He put his empty hand up to his eyes, wiping at them to gain clarity. He was so drunk; he missed a couple of times before his hand reached his eyes to improve his vision. Looking hard, he saw a body on the ground, two beautiful ladies arguing, and a young man watching the scene intensely.

"Shit," the drunk whispered. Then he looked down at his hand and noticed his drink. Still staggering, he got the glass up to his lips to take a sip.

Adjusting his eyes one more time, he said slurring, "See no evil, say no evil," then he turned around and went back into the club. His glass was empty due to the combination of sipping and the way he was holding it. No one noticed him.

Blondie walked over and grabbed the young man's arm. "Come on, you have two horny bitches to fuck tonight. This is going to be a threesome."

He didn't argue because he didn't want to end up like the other guy. He went willingly with the blonde and the brunette followed behind them.

Beep, beep, beep, beep.

Both ladies went for their cell phones. Looking at a message, it read "88-tango," astonished looks washed over their faces.

"What the....? We haven't seen this signal in over a decade," said the blonde.

Looking at her cell phone, the light brown hair one said, "Yeah ten years, ten months, ten days, and ten minutes."

"You were always precise," said Blondie, keeping count down to the last second.

"It has saved our asses more than one time," She said.

"True that," said the blonde one, shaking her head.

The light brown hair one replied to the message by pressing the U.T.T #1, on her cell phone keypad. The blonde pressed U.T.T#2.

Looking at the guy, the blonde said, "Sorry, no threesome. We have to go."

"Maybe next time," said the light brown hair one.

Weighing her options, the blonde said, "Maybe a quickie."

"No, we have to go, this is serious," said the light brown hair one.

Shaking her head to indicate, she was right, the blonde said, "Let's go." They went towards their motorcycles, put on their helmets, and flew down the street, leaving the young guy standing there, dumbfounded. He didn't know what to do. Should he call the police? After all, there was a body on the ground. *Oh hell no. he* sprints to where his car is, jumped in, and screech off-*fast*.

***

A beautiful black woman with flowing dreadlocks was on the highway twenty minutes away from a ladies' workshop that, she felt like she desperately needed to attend. Her psyche was shot to hell. The radio in her black convertible Mustang covered her thoughts in soft music, making the ride calming. It was a beautiful day, and she had the top down, allowing her shoulder length dreads to blow freely in the wind. The Black Mustang's silver rims have the words 'Cobra' printed on them. She had the word "Cobra" added to the trunk. The rest of the car was all black inside and out. There would be no two-tone for her.

The combination of the wind blowing, and the music blaring were getting her into the right mood when she arrived at the workshop, which was called "Women Get Yourself Together".

She teaches math at a Baptist school and one of her fellow teachers suggested it would be a good idea for her to come to this seminar. It was about becoming a stronger woman and she thought it was a good idea because she had been down lately about life, especially since losing her boyfriend. She arrived at the church and parked. She walked in and was greeted at the door by a lady who gave her a program and guided her to a registration table.

"Hello, my I have your name?"

"Tyler"

"Last name"

"Just Tyler" she replied.

The greeter handed her a nametag, along with a tote bag stuffed with materials. She guided Tyler to the tables set up for a continental breakfast. They have donuts, bagels, muffins, pastries, and fruits like bananas, grapes, oranges, and apples. Other table contains cream cheese, with chunks of different types of cheese with crackers. To the left of that table is coffee, tea, water, and hot chocolate to drink.

She didn't want anything to eat, so she just grabbed a cup of coffee.

She took a seat inside the small room that was decorated with flowers and a podium in the middle. Speakers were playing soft gospel music. People were introducing themselves to each other all throughout the conference room. One lady came by and handed Tyler a sheet of paper. She looked at it as it was handed to her, and gave the lady a polite smile, but didn't fill it out.

The lady, who was still standing by her, tapped her on the shoulder and offered her a pen.

Shaking her head, Tyler said, "No thanks."

"Please, you must, everyone is obliged", said the lady.

"Not me" said Tyler.

"The information only for attendance purpose" said the lady.

To get rid of the lady, Tyler wrote down her name but a phony number. Smiling the lady moved on to the next person. The place was beginning to fill up.

Soon the reverend of the church appeared by the podium. Applause broke out.

She welcomed everyone to the workshop and led them in prayer. After the prayer was over, more women were let into the room. The workshop was full of women from a variety of races and backgrounds. Everyone was dressed casually. There was a strong unity in they were sisters. The reverend introduced the speaker of the day.

Linda Collins enters the room with loud applause.

Miss Collins was dressed in blue jeans, a red turtleneck, along with navy blue boots.

She had brought along a Bible, a paperback book titled *Women Who Love Too Much*, and some notes.

Miss Collins came out strong. "Ladies, you are Queens! Our Jesus died on the cross for us to be Queens. I don't know about you, but I belong in the royal Kingdom."

The place went wild with women clapping, stomping, and yelling in agreement.

"Sisters of faith, yes, I mean all my sisters of different races. I am a Queen! Are you?" Asked Miss Collins.

"If you are a Queen, stand up and yell, ***"I am a Queen!"***

Bodies jumped out of their seats and yelled, ***"I am a Queen!"***

After the noise quieted down Miss Collins asked, "Why are you suffering so? "Why are we pining for men who have no job or are not available?" The speaker paused for a moment to let the question sink in, while she scanned the faces in the audience. "We are better than that".

Let them go. When you have faith in God, He will send you that man. I know you ask yourself all the time, 'How come God gave you so much love and no one to receive that love?' Because ladies, He is saying, 'Give it to him first,' and you shall rejoice. Why is it so easy for you to give your love to someone who doesn't deserve your love? Well let's stop here and examine this problem. Sometimes it started when you were a young child. You didn't get hugged, never told you were loved, and you close those actions away. Yes, as a child you can mentally block away hurt.

So, unconsciously, you start giving people presents, money, clothes, and anything to get their love you so desperately crave. You give it your all and never think about yourself. You sacrifice yourself for that love you crave. But what you don't realize is that these deep feelings made you come into contact with takers. Believe me when I say this. You don't like good men. They are boring."

Miss Collins was on a roll. She had been talking about ten minutes, non-stop.

"Why? Because you are used to the drama and that's all you know. Ladies, you are Queens with a capital Q".

Tyler bowed her head in agreement. Her coworker was right. She did like this workshop and she would thank her the next time she saw her.

Tyler went back into the moment. Miss Collins had worked herself into a sweat.

"Those people will never love you like you deserve. Ladies hear me! It doesn't work. All those people are doing is using you. Let's wake up!"

Laughing, Miss Collins said, "You know women are horny. We love our holiness to be satisfied. You know what I mean by holiness right?"

She received clapping, laughter and shouting. "Yes!" and "Go girl!" were heard from her audience.

"Well, there is nothing wrong with getting ours, but ladies use it wisely. It is a precious jewel, a diamond in the rough. Don't give it away to just any man. Listen to me, ladies. The men already know it is a precious jewel. Why don't you? To them we are the land of the discovery country. They get to discover the woods, or should I say the forest. That is exciting to them."

Miss Collins looked out into the audience.

"I hope I am not offending anyone."

Approval was given by the ladies.

Miss Collins continued, "You give your holiness only to the one who deserves it. Now I'm going to end by telling you a story. I want everyone in here to know I was one of those women. I met this tall, brown, good looking, good smelling guy. We dated a while, when one night we decided to give our souls a treat".

Laughter came from the audience. She had everyone's attention.

"Ladies, this guy is *F-I-N-E*," she said as she threw her head back. "After dinner, he took me to an expensive hotel overlooking a large body of water with sun setting, shimmering on top of the water. It was pure paradise. I put on my sexy lingerie and sprayed on my sexy perfume because my holiness was on fire. When I came out of the bathroom, he was standing by the door with his clothes on. I said to myself, 'what the hell is going on?' He looked me up and down then took a deep breath. 'Oh, oh' I said. My gut was telling me something is wrong. He looked at me with sad eyes and said, 'Baby I can't do this'. My heart dropped right then and there. He continued by saying, 'I am married, and this is not right.'"

Miss Collins put her left hand on her hip with her right hand in the air and showed the ladies the emotion of a sister who was about to lose it. The women in the audience were once again up clapping, yelling.

"Go on sister! We know, we know!" was heard from the crowd.

With anguish displayed on her face, she said, "I could have killed him."

Laughter, clapping, and shouts of "Amen!" filled the room.

It seemed like it took the women in that room ten minutes to calm down.

They were all feeling her pain and have experienced and knew someone else who had experienced what Miss Collins was talking about.

"There is nothing like a horny woman on fire who has just been turned down."

In her element now, Miss Collins went on with the program.

Tyler could not believe so many women of different races experienced the same pain.

Coming back to the moment, Miss Collins said, "I said to him 'what you mean, no?' He said, 'baby, this is not right.' Then he started on that *male* talking. 'I like you a lot. I love our talks and our laughs. But this is not right.' I thought to myself he must be *insane*. He is talking all this nonsense when he should be throwing down. He must have read my mind or saw the steam coming out my nose because after saying that he opened the door and tried to get the hell out. Have you ever seen the two-hundred-yard dash in the Olympics? I did it in two seconds."

Bodies raised up and high fived each other amongst the laughers.

Miss Collins put her hands up to quiet the crowd then said, "Before he could get his body out the door, I had closed it."

The place was screaming.

"Wait, wait, believe it or not, I still wanted him. You hear me? I said, 'Not now baby, don't do this.' I was begging this man not to go. You know I did that 'tears in my eye' move." Many of the women listening nodded.

"He softly pushes me aside and said, 'Baby I have to go' and he left. Ladies I was mad. I tore off the outfit I was wearing and ran into the bathroom. I tried to scrub off the perfume. I worked myself into an uproar.

I called him every name in and out of the book. By the time I was finished my heart was beating fast, my skin was sweating, and my eyes were red from crying. I got myself together to leave because you don't want to walk out a hotel messed up, after all we do have dignity. I could not sleep well that night and the next day I was still mad. The next night God came to me in a dream. He told me what I could not see that night. The man was right. You are a jewel and don't throw it away on a no good or married man. Now this is the moral of this story. God intervened because the man couldn't reach me".

She stopped and looked around the room to make sure her message would be heard loud and clear.

Then she said, "I was about to degrade myself by giving my holiness to a married man who couldn't give me anything back. He is not the one. You are a Queen. I was saved by the grace of God. Ladies, stand up and say, 'God is good!'"

Everyone stood up and repeated "God is good!"

"Thank you for this opportunity today. *You all are Queens*".

The women all gave her a standing ovation.

Miss Collins sipped some water while the applause died down. She had felt the energy in the room.

Tyler's cell phone gave off a special beep. Immediately, she rose from her seat and went into the hallway to open the text message. It read "88-tango." With a stern look on her face, she typed U.T. # 3. She turned and headed toward the door.

"Miss is you okay?" asked a host at the event who saw the look on her face.

"I'm fine" said Tyler. "I have to leave," not stopping her stride.

To stop Tyler from exiting so quickly, she ran behind her and asked, "Are you sure?"

"Yes," said Tyler. "I need to leave. Trust me, this is wonderful. I just need to leave".

Satisfied, the host stopped and went back inside. Reaching her black Mustang, Tyler jumped in and sped off down the road.

***

Flash bulbs were going off left and right. The model is five feet eleven with golden skin is working the showstopper outfit. It is a silk peach colored dress that flows as the model walks. It gently crumpled around the body of the model with the hem ending at her calves. The model was wearing six inches pumps of the same color and material. Large, round, diamond earrings were hanging from her ears and four diamond bracelets were dangling on each arm as she walked.

The smile on the model's face was contagious as she walked the walk to the end of the runway and back behind the stage. She got a standing ovation.

A lady is running around the back with a grin wide as an ocean. She is a success. She has brown hair that is up in a ponytail, flawless make-up with skin that shines from head to toe.

As a young teenager, she began making her own outfits and received many compliments, so she decided to make outfits for her family and friends. The most valuable asset to any designer is a sense of timing. Knowing when to bring out the right design that will capture the world is a skill that one is born with. The clothes have to be exceptional and fresh season after season. It is a small miracle to accomplish this year after year. She has done this now for about four years straight.

In her element, this was her best of the four years. She was hugged and kissed by everyone backstage. Her assistant came backstage to grab her because it was time for her to make her entry. In the backstage area, he helped her maneuver into the lift. She took a deep breath and smiled back at her assistant.

The assistant, with tears in his eyes, watched her descend from below the stage with smoke raising as the audience clap with thunderous applause. Her name was in lights behind her. *TEG'S FASHION HOUSE.*

With a huge smile on her face, wearing beige pants, a dark brown silk shirt, a brown and tan silk scarf around her neck, and five-inch heels, she walked the walk. Her brown hair was flowing like a fan was blowing it. There wasn't a fan, but the way she walked exuded confidence.

The ten models who had been modeling her life's work followed behind her one at a time as "Teddy's Jam" by Guy played in the background. Flash bulbs and video cameras explode in a frenzy.

Teg was glowing in the spotlight. Her eyes had tears flowing in sync like clockwork.

The models had formed themselves around her for the audience to get another look at her designs. She had planned the whole scene out beforehand. Planning was her number one trait and had served her well over the years.

When she came backstage, her assistant, had a look on his face, holding her phone towards her. Looking at the phone, she saw a special message icon that has not been seen in years.

She looked at the message that said only "88-tango."

Shaking, she answered the text by pressing the number four, followed by UT, closed the phone, and looked toward her assistant and said, "I have to leave now."

He kissed her on the cheek as he handed her, her keys, and her purse.

"I will take care of everything".

As she was getting into her car, he said "Good show, the best!"

She smiles and close her door to her all-white convertible Rolls Royce and drove off.

***

Tex received the four replies with a sigh of relief. She turned to her longtime best friend Bonnie and said, "The Ladies are on their way." Smiling, Tex walked into the Command center with Bonnie following her. The *'Ultimate Tomboys'* are on their way.

CHAPTER THREE

Two motorcycles roared up to the side entrance address that was given in the text. The ladies cut the engines and removed their helmets. Blonde hair came from one and light brown hair from the other felling down to their shoulders in a in slow motion. The twins have arrived, Travis and Tyson. Not biological twins, but best friends since birth. Their mothers were best friends who happen to have their daughters at the same time, day, and year.

Inseparable, nothing, nothing comes between them.
Travis spoke first. "I wonder what Tex wants."
Tyson said, "I hope it's trouble."
"You know Tyson, we are getting a little too old for this shit."
"Speak for yourself. I have at least ten more years in me. My body is like a woman half my age."

Tyson stepped off the motorcycle and flexed her arm muscles.
Laughing, Travis got off her bike and put up her right arm and said, "Gotcha" friend, we are in our early forties, with furious minds & bodies."

Incoming headlights caught the lady's attention. instantly, Travis and Tyson hopped back on their bikes, trying to make out what was heading their way.
Relaxing, Travis put one leg up on the handlebars. Slowly, one of their hands push back their jackets, for easy access to their special diamond studded Taurus PT940s glock guns.

It was a white Rolls Royce with a moon roof that was coming down the road at a high speed.

Tyson said, "Damn, Tex is entering in high class."
"Not my type of car, like sporty ones, with some serious cams" said Travis.

The white Rolls Royce stopped about twenty feet in front of the ladies, windows dark.

Teg removes her gun from the pocket on the driver side of the door, and put it in her pocket.
Car engine was turned off and a bejeweled shoe hit the payment.
Keeping eyes on both ladies in front of her, she emerges completely from the car.

They knew instantly that this was not Tex.
The woman didn't appear to be a threat, so the twins didn't pull out their weapons.

Teg looked at the ladies and smiled. The code word was said by Teg "Tomboys". The twins relax more, this person is a Tex agent.

Simultaneously, Travis and Tyson said "Ultimate" in response.

Teg walked towards the ladies with her white fake fur coat flowing behind her.

Extending her right hand, the woman said, "Hello, my name is Teg."

The twins didn't take her hand. They just gave her a nod, taking her in up and down.

Tyson did the introductions. "This is Travis, and I am Tyson." Teg brought her hand down with a slight shudder of the head.

Tyson, still sitting on her bike, was dressed in brown ripped jeans with knee-high brown boots,
a tan pull-over tee shirt, and a soft brown leather coat.

Travis, leaning back on her bike with her right leg up on the bars, had on navy blue jeans that were ripped near the knee, navy blue ankle boots, and a light brown jacket with a navy-blue collar. Under the jacket was a sleeveless T-shirt with the words *Butch Cassidy and the Sundance Kid* printed on the front. Their jackets were an homage to Robert Redford and Paul Newman.

Travis asked Teg, "Do you know what's going on?"

"No," answered Teg, "I receive the text and…."

A loud roar was heard by all coming up the path, another vehicle. All heads turn simultaneous to investigate.

Travis said, "Listen to the roar of the engine. Those cams are singing!"

Teg sighed and said, "I am more refined."

"I see," Tyson said, smirking towards the white Rolls Royce.

The loud engine was getting closer and the vehicle lights were getting brighter. The car shining in all black with bright lights.
Travis and Tyson each put a hand in their jacket pocket to retrieve their special ten-round capacity,
 mother of diamond Taurus PT940 guns.

Teg stepped a little to the left of the twins and pulled out her twelve-round capacity,
Para-Ordnance. It was silver with a black handle and had special night sight attached. The twins noticed her move in their peripheral vision. The Cobra black Mustang came into view. Its engine was cut off and a lady, exited the vehicle.
 On each hip she held a gold-plated knife, with a press of a button, she could open and close them at will.

She stood by the driver's side of the car and looked at the three figures in front of her.

Smiling, she said softly, "Tomboys?"

Three voices said "Ultimate."

"And you are?" Teg asked.

"Tyler".

Teg reached out her hand first. "Nice to meet you. I am Teg."

"Nice to meet you," said Tyler. Looking towards the two other ladies, they gave her their customary stare.

"Down, girls," said a familiar voice coming from the doorway of the house.

All four heads turned at once towards the sound of the voice. It was Tex, and Bonnie stood behind her.

"Ultimate Tomboys, welcome," said Tex.

"Hello, my ladies" said Bonnie.

Walking inside the resident, Bonnie guided them towards a large hallway with shiny wooden floors. Nothing was said because all were busy checking out the place, as most undercover cops do instinctually. Tex was grinning.

She could sense the girls were as sharp as she knew they would be. She had made the right choice picking these four for her secret mission. Experience and wise agents. Wisdom and skills are a huge must for this to be successfully.

"This way ladies, I want to introduce you to each other." Said Tex.

"We have met," said Tyson.

"Not like it should be," answered Tex.

Turning around towards the group, Tex stopped. "Look Tyson, no shit from you.

Remember, I will not stand for it."

Before her twin Travis could say anything, Tex pointed towards her and said, "You either."

The twins had a reputation for being lethal with attitude.

Travis put up both her hands to declare innocence.

Tex answered her gesture with, "Bullshit."

"What?" said Travis.

"Not another word," said Tex in a profound tone.

Teg and Tyler looked at each other, gesturing…what.

"Let me introduce you ladies, starting with blondie and her side kick" says Tex laughing.

Bonnie giggle with her

"Who's the side kick?" ask Travis.

"You are, I am the brilliant mind" said Tyson.

Travis gave her the middle finger.

"Ok, for the other two agents, these ladies are called the twins, I am sure you have heard about them but never met" said Tex. "Blondie name is Tyson, her best friend is Travis". They have known each other since birth.

Tyson said sarcastically, "We are well known."

Travis nodded her head.

"Yes, you two are," said Tyler, sarcastically.

"Always so cheerful?" asked Tyson.

"Or cutting? Travis asked.

"I try to be," answered Tyler.

Ignoring the banter, Tex continue. Ladies this is Tyson and the other agent working with you three is Teg.

"You girls remember Bonnie?"

"Yes, hello Bonnie," said Teg, walking up and giving her a hug.

Bonnie said, "Nice to see again. You look great."

"Thank you," said Teg.

"Hello Bonnie," said Tyler.

Bonnie looked at Tyler and said, "Baby, you look much better since the last time I saw you. I am proud to see you look this way."

"Jesus, I am going to throw up," said Tyson.

"Not on the carpet. I paid a fortune for it," said Tex, sarcastically.

Travis laughed.

"Still a comic," said Tyson.

"I see you still have that attitude?" says Tex.

"Actually, it is better. I have been helping her," said Travis.

"Oh, the bad sheep helping the other bad sheep. Where is the guard?" Tex said, smartly.

"Not needed," said Tyson.

Aware that Tyson liked to get the last word in; Tex ignored her for the moment and looked over at Teg, who was sitting on the chair removing fake lint from her clothes.

Tex remarked, "No dirt in this room, Miss Dainty."

"I like that name. I think I will use it myself," said Teg smugly.

She started mouthing the title "Miss Dainty" softly.

Everyone in the room laughed.

Snickering Tex said, "Another wise ass."

"Come on Tex, that is why you love them. After all you have raised them since they were teenagers. They are not going to change now. They are the best," said Bonnie.

Looking at Bonnie, Tex said, "True, but I wouldn't say that in front of them and definitely will not take shit off any one of them."

"Oh god, now I am going to vomit," said Travis.

"For the love that all is holy," said Tyler.

"I see a comedian you are not," said Tyson pointing to Tyler.

"I see one twin jumps the other's response, how unique," said Tyler smartly.

Before Tyler could finish her sentence, Tyson tried to jump up, but Travis held her down with a stiff arm around her waist.

Travis whispered in Tyson's ear, "We will get her later, not now."

Tyson relaxed, but rolled her eyes at Tyler.

"Slow your roll, ladies," said Bonnie.

"Do we have a problem here, ladies?" Tex asked.

"No problem, we can work this out," said Teg, looking at the three other Tomboys with a smile.

"Everybody's a damn comedian," said Tex.

"We have covered everything else, so why not?" said Tyson joking.

That broke the ice, and everyone laughed.

"Now that we have cleared the air, Tex needs to talk," said Bonnie, sitting on the green suede sofa by Travis and Teg. Tyson was sitting in a big green suede high-top chair alone with one leg over the arm rest.

"I called you all together because we have a mission," said Tex.

"Goodie, I haven't had much action lately," said Tyson.

"I don't know if I am up to this. It has been a long time since I've been in the trench," said Teg.

"I need you Teg, or I would not have called you," said Tex, giving her a stern look.

The twins, Tyler, and Bonnie looked at Teg.

"I didn't mean I would not help, Tex. You are my girl, but it has been a long time. That's all," said Teg.

Tyler said quietly, you might stumble at first, but it will come back to you. Tex & Bonnie chose us four for a reason, we are the best.

"I ... just don't want to be the one who messes things up," Teg replied.

"If that were the case, you would not be sitting here," said Tex.

"If she is afraid, I don't want her here. Shit, she might get our asses killed," said Tyson.

"Shut up, Tyson. This is my show," said Tex angrily.

Tyson put her hands up to surrender.

Tex took a deep breath and said, "Ladies, I have a situation here. A hoax has been played, experienced agents are needed, I don't have time to wipe young noses. with all your talents, this mission will be a success."

"They still have it," said Bonnie.

"In spades," said Tyler.

"Ace of spades," said the twins in unison.

Tex was pacing in the area where the agents and Bonnie were sitting.

She had everyone's attention.

Slowly she begins talking "I thought my husband was murdered, but it has come to my attention that it is not true."

A surprised look appeared on all four faces.

None of them saw this coming.

Bonnie start handing out materials as Tex continue to talk.

"Some people have helped my husband set up this hoax. After a full investigation, it came to my attention that the body that was buried was not my husband and that I was supposed to die at that so call house burglary.

They were good but not great. Sometime after the viewing and before the service, the bodies were switch. Unbeknownst to all he had a bag with the medicine Propofol, a drug that is used during operations to put patient asleep, attached to his left leg for viewing of the body. During the service, the casket was closed through out. He made a fatal mistake and Bonnie caught it on film.

Travis, Tyson, Teg, and Tyler all gasped.

Putting a finger up, Tex said, "Wait, you haven't heard the true diabolical nature of the plan yet. That motherfucker had some of his goons try to take me out about a month ago.... again."

"Fuck," said Travis, jumping out of her seat.

Tyson followed, withdrawing her gun from her waist, saying, "Boss, no more, we ready now."

Teg has a disheartening look on her face. Tyler shook her head in disgust.

Putting both hands up in the air, Tex said, "Calm down. We will have our revenge."

Bonnie pulled up a video file on the screen, "let's start by looking at this film."

It began with three masked men entering Tex's old house. One came up the stairs while the other two checked out the bottom half of the house. They were noticeably quiet and knew what they were doing. It wasn't long before the Tomboys saw enough to know that they were professionals.

All the men had their guns out, prepared for action. The one that went upstairs, checked out each room, slowing opening doors, while the other two check out the bottom half of the house. The man upstairs became agitated because it looked like their intel was wrong.

"The lady should be in the house. Anything?" one of the guys radioed to one upstairs.

"No," said the voice that came back over the radio.

He mumbled, "Shit." He pulled out a cell phone and said into the receiver, "Boss, no one is here." One couldn't hear the other voice on the other end, so there was a pause until the unseen man stopped talking. Then the man on screen said, "We looked everywhere."

Whatever the other person said, it made the guy bob his head up and down.

Within a few moments, he snapped his cell phone closed. By this time, the other two guys have joined the one upstairs. Disgusted, he saw one guy leaning by a dresser smoking a cigarette. He walked over and smacked it out of his mouth.

"No one is here to smell the smoke," said the guy.

"They can come back later, stupid, but I guess it doesn't matter. Jordan told us to tear down the walls because she can be hiding. He told me where the attic and other hiding places are," said the leader.

Bonnie stopped the tape and Tex said, "That is how I knew he was alive.

"Tex, I don't mean any harm but that is not enough proof that your dead husband Jordan is behind this or that he is even alive," said Tyler.

"Good point, Tyler," said Tex, smiling at her. "But let's keep going. Resume, Bonnie," said Tex.

Bonnie pressed the play button and tape continued.

"He said it is very important we don't fuck up, and if we don't find her, make this look like a robbery," said the leader. All three were wearing masks over their faces.

"Where do we start?" the other guy asked.

"Anywhere, this man will kill us if we are not successful" says one of the guys.

"Jordan was married to this lady he wants us to take out" said the guy.

"Jesus, this is his wife?" one guy asked.

"What the fuck do we care? He is paying fifteen thousand" said another guy.

The atmosphere in the command center became heavy. You could smell the fury in the air.

Tyler, who was growing impatient and wanted to know more, asked Tex, "Where were you?"

"Lucky for me, I stayed over Bonnie's that night, we were having a girl's night.

"They were lucky, you were not there, those fuckers would have been crucified you are the golden one" said Bonnie.

"True that," Tyler agreed.

"And if they had succeeded…. said Teg.

"We would have hunted them down as the shits they are and gladly put them out to pasture" said Tyson.

"With no luggage," said Teg.

"No luggage?" Tyler asked confused.

"Balls," said Tyson.

Tomboys, nasty little fuckers…. I like' Tex said, "Ladies, you need to realize something here, this could be your last mission, we can all died, Jordan and his soldiers are lethal.

Bang, bang.

All eyes went back to the screen. The guys were throwing things around and ripping the place up.

They threw clothes all over, turned over furniture, and pocketed a few items. They were in the house a total of twenty minutes and then all three masked men left through the back door. The screen went static after two minutes.

"The cameras cut off when no movement can be detected," said Bonnie, explaining the static on the screen.

Putting her hand up in the air, Tex said, "Wait, a little something is at the end of the tape."

A man who was about six-three was walking slowly across the screen. It was night, so you could only see a silhouette of a body. His body was moving like a cougar, swift and graceful. You could feel his energy through the screen, strong charisma. The trained eye of a super spy could pick up on what he was doing. His movements were deliberate. He was looking to his left and right, casing out the area. He was holding a gun in his right hand.

With his left hand, he quickly popped the lock on the door and went inside. He was in about two minutes, according to the clock on the lower left-hand side of the screen. He came out in the same quick, graceful way by which he had entered. Whatever made him go inside, either he didn't find it, or he had it hidden on him. Suddenly, the screen froze.

The man had turned his face towards the main camera and his face was clear on the screen.

"Jordan, you bastard," said Tex.

Heavy gasps filled the room.

"That's why you moved?" Tyler asked.

"Yes, with a heavy heart" said Tex softly.

"Ladies, what I am about to tell you is deep, deep cover. Bonnie and I have a secret camera located over here in this beautiful picture."

Tex pointed to a large forty by forty picture of a purple painted vase with white roses and green leaves, some hanging down near the bottom of the vase. Upon further inspection, one could notice that the frame was a darker purple.

"What it records goes back to a secured camera computer in Washington, D.C.

The recording can only be accessed from that location.

Right now, you four do not need that information, but believe me when time comes, the film will be delivered to you".

All nodded.

Almost whispering, Teg said to Tex, "This must be hard. The man you loved for years is trying to take you out. My question is why?"

"Good question, I am thinking the same thing," said Travis. "Jared, now Jordan stole over twenty million dollars from the bureau along with drugs and guns from the evidence room over a long period of time. He was so good no one detected it was him. He was so good most of the money, drugs and armor never made it to the evidence room. It was taken from the criminals outright, just never reported. The criminals didn't say anything because that would shorten their sentences.

But you know in real life someone gets mad because they have been ripped off, so they begin talking. By that time, he had been doing it well over a decade.

For some of the guns, I found fake purchase orders from different sheriffs, captains, and lieutenants whose names were on receipts. I tried to track some of them down, but they were either dead or I couldn't find them."

Everyone wanted to ask *the* question but didn't know how.

Tex, sensing this, chuckled and said, "No I didn't know until after the death, but I did find some money hidden in the attic and took it. Fuck him, and his crew".

Everyone laughed.

Smiling, Tex moved on by saying, "Bonnie went to the house and removed the tape to edit it like the guys that Jordan had sent to kill me stole the money. It was hidden in the attic by an old trunk in some bags marked for charity."

"That was what exposed the charade," said Bonnie.

"Like that fuck would ever give to charity," said Tex.

Everyone chuckled and laughed.

"Assholes. I was sure Jared was not going to be pleased when the guys didn't come back with the money. So, Bonnie and I waited for Jared to come back to retrieve the tape, then we set the house on fire.

Snickering, Bonnie said, "He came that night if you can believe the balls."

"Uhm," said Travis.

Tex continue "He knew to act fast before I came back from wherever I was and before he tried to kill me…. she held up three fingers.

"What stopped him the third time?" Teg asked.

"Guessing, I will say the burning of the house. The rules are if a high official's house has been broken in and or burned down to the ground, the bureau lets you relocate and changes all your codes and personnel information in the main system. Only level ten has the new information and there are only two level ten officials at a time."

"You think we can find and talk to at least one of those guys?" asks Tyler.

"Dead," Bonnie repeated.

"After they screwed up this job, Jordan would have or had someone kill them. He hates mistakes and they made a terrible mistake by not killing me" says Tex.

"So, he dies"? asks Teg.

"He dies" says Bonnie.

"So, we can get a little taste?" Tyson asked.

"I got you covered along with the mission cost," said Tex.

"How much?" asked Tyler.

"None of your business," said Tex.

"Bite me," said Tyler.

"Consider it done," said Tex, smiling.

"Girl, you know better to go after Tex like that," said Travis.

Tyson and Travis gave each other the Tomboys' handshake.

"Cool, teach me?" Tyler asked.

"When we finish here," said Travis.

"Don't forget me," said Teg.

"Can't forget Miss Dainty," said Tyson.

"Remember, The Ultimate Tomboys," said Tex.

Smiles came across all faces.

"Ladies," said Bonnie, "You will have no contact with anyone at the bureau or other police divisions. It is especially important that you four stay anonymous."

"Yes, your contact is only Bonnie and me. I will keep the bureau off of your trails," said Tex.

"Where do we stay?" Tyson asked.

"Here, for right now, this place has the command center. Tex and I will live together to watch each other backs somewhere else secret" Bonnie answered.

"Teg, I need your expertise on the computer software," said Tex.

"This girl can get into any system," said Bonnie.

Teg waved her fingers across her chest with pride.

"Tyson," Tex said, "We need your expertise in interrogations but not too ... hard, okay? Less deaths, the better. It means no poking around by other police divisions."

Pretending to pout, Tyson said, "No fun."

"We'll find out a way for you to have fun, my friend," said Travis.

Smiling, Tyson liked that, and the twins did the handshake again.

"Ladies," said Tex.

Travis and Tyson put their hands up to surrender.

With a stern look, Tex waved her finger at them.

Four hands went back up again.

Teg laughed and said, "This is going to be fun with these twins."

Looking concerned, Tyler asked, "Do we have any intel on Jordan and his soldiers, like where he is?"

"The bastard has a 'cave' in Herr, California, about one hundred miles from here. Can you believe it? He stayed close by," said Tex.

"He needs to. That way he can keep up with what is going on," said Travis.

"Baby, he can do that anywhere. The man has connections," said Bonnie.

"Yes, he has spies in all police divisions and civilians' life. I know because I have the same. All good agents do," said Tex.

"Yeah, we have ours," said Tyson.

Travis nodded in agreement.

"You ladies are still in deep?" Teg asked.

"We teach others," said Travis.

"Yes, and they will be teaching us some combat moves. I haven't been out in a long time but as you see I have kept fit and damn ready for action," said Tex twisting her body around.

Tyler sitting quietly was thinking, *'I heard about these twins, they are lethal, bad asses'*.

"Let's take a break and eat ladies," said Tex.

CHAPTER FOUR

Tyler was walking behind the group. She nudges, Tex to slow down.

Tyler says, "You know the twins can't be control."

"Yes, I know, but they are good really, really good. They saved my life ten years ago. It's a story I can't get into right now. They will always respect me," Tex answered.

Tyler started to object.

Tex held up her hand to stop her and said, "Their methods are on the harsh side, yes, but they know when to pull back."

"I hope you are right," said Tyler.

Tex turned to face Tyler and said, "Trust me honey, you will want the twins on your side, not against you. They are loyal."

Sighing, Tyler remarked, "Only to each other."

"No Tyler, they will be loyal to this entire group."

"It's hard to tell," said Tyler.

"They are just testing you and your toughness. They will kill for you and protect you for a lifetime, sweetie."

"I will always trust you, Tex and Bonnie, those two, its going take some time. Teg seems to be cool.

"Okay," Tex said, smiling. "At the end of this mission, you will have a different picture of the twins."

Inside the room, Travis says to Tyson, "cut the shit, leave the girl alone."

"Why are you protecting Miss Holier Than Thou?" asked Tyson.

"She is not 'holier than thou, give her a chance" Tex believe in her, so we should too".

"Still mad, because I killed that guy," said Tyson.

"Right?! You didn't have to shoot my man."

"He was not your man."

"Okay, my fuck for the night. Still, that was wrong."

Teg in the command center listening to the twin's conversation, were speechless. Bonnie, who also was listening was not surprised.

Teg, who just met them, couldn't believe the conversation she was hearing.

"I'm sorry, I'm sorry," said Tyson.

"Thank you," said Travis sarcastically.

"She is still Miss Holier than Thou," said Tyson, getting in the last word.

Travis gave a heavy sigh.

Bonnie giggle under her breath, thinking, *'bad asses'*.

A nice spread of chicken wings, small hot sausages, biscuits, coleslaw, a plate of cheddar, American, and white cheeses surrounded by crackers, a plate of raw vegetables, and various drinks, including wine, water, tea, and coffee.

Travis was at the computer, looking up information. Tyson was beside her, helping her to get into a secret file that contained personal information on Jordan. Both had plates of food and drinks beside them.

Teg and Bonnie were at another computer cross referencing all phone calls received and made on the secret phone that Tex and Jordan used.

The numbers were encrypted, but with special software contained only on this laptop, they can cross reference all numbers, nothing so far. Tyler and Tex went to the table to get something to eat and drink.

Tyson, who loves to push the envelope, looked up and said, "Did you two finish making out?"

Travis laughed and so did Bonnie, who knew Tyson was joking.

Tex just gave her the finger, but Tyler looked at her with astonishment.

"How could you say something like that?" asked Teg.

"Because most bitches don't have any respect for others," answered Tyler.

Throwing her head back to laugh, Tyson remarked, "Oh…I knew you weren't holier than thou."

"God told me not to take anything off anyone and to do unto others as they do unto me," said Tyler.

Nodding, Travis said, "So true, I read that in the Bible."

"When have you read a Bible?" joked Tyson.

"Just the other day, when I was waiting for you at the tanning booth," Travis said seriously.

Tyson put up her hand to wave off the remark and said, "Whatever."

"Enough," said Tex. "Let's get back to the matter at hand."

Bonnie was giggling through the whole exchange. Teg was bewildered.

Tex sitting down with her food knew this group will accomplish this mission, they just need to gel and figured each other out.

Tyler walked over towards the twins. She had been eyeing something since they arrived at Tex's house.

She decided it was safest to ask Travis, "Hey Travis, what do the double Ts mean on your left arm? I understand the U.T. with the navy-blue star because we have one like that, but you and Tyson have two Ts." Travis stopped what she was doing to answer Teg.

"Tyson & I were given permission by Tex years ago to put an extra 'T' for 'twins". "known each since birth".

Tex interrupted, "Everyone one in this room will be friends for life. *"Everyone."*

Teg was still working on her laptop, half listening, but keeping her ears opening.

"Bingo, our first clue," said Teg.

Everyone crowed around Teg's laptop to see what she was talking about.

"A Felix Johnson's name keeps appearing connected with Jared, I mean, Jordan" said Teg.

"Felix Johnson is dead" said Bonnie.

"Almost five years by now" said Tex looking perplexed.

"Oh, I see know, it does say he is dead" Teg announced.

"Was there a body found? asked Tyler.

"Body never found" said Tex.

"oh, a body was found and identify by somebody…....Teg click some buttons on the key board name…. Deuce said Teg.

Bonnie & Tex, how well you know these guys?" asks Tyson.

"Yes, Deuce is my boss and Felix were my husband, Jordan best friend" said Tex.

"Well, says Teg, he is alive going under the name Paul King."

All in the room froze.

Tex look at the screen as a picture came up on the screen, it was definitely Felix, who is clearly alive because the picture is dated three months ago.

Tex thinking *'What hell is going on here.'*

Bonnie has a sober look on her face. She says to Tex, "This been going on longer than we thought, do you think Jordan help Paul fake his first death?"

"Bonnie, I think this thing is bigger than we thought, Tomboys, today news is telling me our mission is bigger than thought. It just went to level four.

"Are we ready to complete our mission?" Tex asked.

"Hell yes," said Tyson.

"I am in," said Travis.

"Me too," said Teg.

"I'm in" said Tyler.

"With-it" said Bonnie.

"This is our first real lead. Let's follow the path Jordan and Paul have given us. It says here that he is a big football fan," said Tyler.

"There is a game in town this weekend," said Tyson.

"It's a championship game. Surely Paul will be there," said Teg.

"And I have great box seats," said Tex.

"We have a game to go to, Tomboys!" said Travis.

"Rah, rah!" cheered Tyson.

Looking at each other, Tex and Bonnie both exclaimed, *"Mission on!"*

37

CHAPTER FIVE

"It's first and ten at the twenty-yard line," a voice over the speaker announced.

A loud roar went up from the home crowd in the stands.

It was a championship game that if the home team won, they would go to the Super Bowl. It would be the first time in this town's history that their football team would be going to *the* main game. The weather was perfect for a football game, around seventy-five degrees with a light breeze.

The crowd seemed possessed. People were jumping up and down, yelling, singing, and losing their minds. It was so loud, the quarterback for the home team had to quiet them down so his offense could hear the play he called. The crowd quieted down, only to leap to their feet again when the wide receiver ran twenty yards for a touchdown. It put the home team up fourteen points with only eight minutes left in the game. The crowd, as well as both teams, could sense what was happening.

It was much harder to quiet the home team's crowd for the extra point.

The home team's kicker just shook his head and signaled for his teammates to get into formation. Ready to kick, the kicker put one finger in the air to silence the crowd. The crowd temporarily quieted until the ball sailed right down the middle of the goal posts. An unbelievable amount noise waved around the stadium.

Felix aka Paul was at the ballgame. His suite was next to the ladies. The suites were divided only by a glass partition. It was so clear that if one weren't looking hard enough, one would think that it was the same suite. Tyler has a pair of binoculars that were designed to see far and take still pictures when she pushed a special button on the side. By this time, she had taken over one hundred pictures of the game. She didn't know what would be used so she just snapped away.

She keyed in on the suite to their left most of the time, being careful not to be noticed.

Of coarse Paul and his friends doesn't know the Tomboys. There was a timeout on the field and the home team's band took the field to lead the crowd in their fight song. The whole place was up and singing. The scene was surreal.

The players came back on the field from both sidelines and the visiting team had the ball. The crowd was yelling, *"Defense! Defense!"*

The Tomboys blend in with the other patrons in a suite that held twelve people.

Concentrating mainly on all club suites near him. The suites colors are navy blue and silver. The high back leather chairs were dark navy blue a star in the middle of the back rest. Six seats in the first two rows.

Behind the leather chairs was a bar with six silver high top chairs. The sitting area in the back held two silver and navy-blue leather couches facing each other, with a silver color steel table holding snacks of different varieties.

At the end of the suite was another bar with running water and a steel counter that was holding the silverware, cups, plates, and other condiments.

Beside the counter a steel middle-sized refrigerator held the cold drinks - beer, water, and sodas of different varieties. A single unisex bathroom was located near the door to the suite.

Another table to the left of the entrance contained hot and cold food, including chicken tenders, hamburgers, and Italian sausages, along with brown rice, french fries, and rolls.

Two thirty-five-inch color high-definition flat screen TVs were hoisted to the left and right of the first row of seats, positioned for everyone in the suite to easily view either or both of them.

Travis was a huge football fan. She was in heaven. She played the part of entertaining the group surrounding the girls so they could concentrate on their assignments.

She had drilled the girls on what goes on at a football game, how to dress, and how to act to blend in with the crowd.

"Second and thirteen due to a holding penalty," the announcer broadcasted over the loudspeaker. The crowd was hollering.

"Defense! Defense! Move them back!" yelled a guy in the suite.

The scene in the stadium was intoxicating. Everyone was into the game.

"Time out," said the referee, pointing to the visiting quarterback, who signal a time-out. for team. He didn't like the look of the defense he was seeing.

The crowd, who knew the play as well as the home team, started yelling on one side of the stadium, *"We know that play! We know that play!"* while the other side of the stadium yelled, *"Take them out, defense!"* during the time out.

Felix was enjoying the game, not realizing he was being watched.

During the time out, the tv station stayed live at the game. A camera person moved the camera around the stadium to show the people at home what was going on live at the stadium.

A person watching at home sprung up out of his chair to look closer at the screen. *"What the fuck!!"*. He saw something that made veins in his head elevate.

He ran back to his chair to grab his phone off the side table. Pacing while the number is ringing, when the person answer he said, "Felix, leave the fuck now". Then hung up saying **'Shit.'**

Tyler reached over and whispered in Teg's ear, "I know that lady beside Felix from somewhere, can't put my finger on it yet". She snapped several pictures of the lady.

The sudden fast movement in the suite beside them got Tyler and Teg attention. Felix and the lady were leaving fast. They both wonder what was going on. Tyler hurried and took more photos. One of the patrons in the same suite with Felix is a guy name Arnold. The ladies didn't know him. He was mysteriously taking pictures of the scene inside his suite and sometimes the game. He never thought to take pictures of the people in the suites surrounding him. He concentrated on where he was. He recognizes the man sitting a row in front of him but needed to do some intel because he couldn't remember why he remember him. Bad luck.

Tyson was quiet. She was enjoying all the sweet candy on the field. It didn't matter to her what color uniform the candy was wearing. She thought *Travis is right, this is heaven.*
Men wearing tight pants running up and down the field, falling all over each other were making her drool at the mouth. She kept a napkin in her hand, often wiping her mouth just thinking about what she could do to any one of them.

'Hell', she thought to herself, *'the coaches and assistant coaches are not bad either. The young ones will be better. She was a cougar with a capital C'.*

Tyson bent her head towards Travis and said, "Is that sweat on their asses?"

A lady sitting to Travis' left laughed. She had heard the remark.

"Yes, they sweat a lot during the game," answered Travis.

"My golden retriever is heating up," said Tyson.

The lady to Travis' left raised her hand and told Tyson, "Girl, give me some props. I am on fire too."

Tyson reached over Travis and gave the lady a high five.
Both were on their fourth beer and were in another world, a man's world, to be exact.
Travis shook her head at the two, then got up to move next to Teg, who was sitting on the first row of leather seats.

The lady moved over next to Tyson and both toasted their cup of beer.

Travis asked Teg, "How are we doing, friend?"

"Something just happens, Felix & a lady just bolted, fast."

"What you think that meant?" asked Travis.

"Not sure, hope we weren't made."

"They don't know us, it's something else."

Teg going over the film in the camera, speaks up, "Look, got a call, see his lips moving".

"Who is the lady he is signaling?" asked Travis.

"I don't know, Tyler thinks she knows her, said Teg.

"They bolted fast in different directions, sent Tyler to follow him," said Teg.

"Oh, that is why she left the suite."

"Yes, a few seconds ago she texted me back on my cell phone. The guy is on his phone walking fast. She is down the hall watching his movements. She said the lady disappeared.

"The game is almost over, so get all you can," said Travis.

"I am well ahead of the game. I have a lot. This was a great idea," said Teg.

Travis, return to her seat, while Teg took more video & pictures of the scene at hand.

-By this time, the lady and Tyson had got very friendly, alcohol does that.

Tyler returns to the suite, whispering she lost him in the crowd, Felix was looking around scared, and she was afraid of being spotted, so she backed off.

"Two-minute time out," announced the broadcaster.

The lady went to the bathroom and Tyson whispered to Travis, "What's going on? Any intel?"

"No, but both bolted out here. Something is up. Teg has some great material. We are going back to the command center and analyze the material," said Travis.

Before Tyson could reply the announcer said over the loudspeaker, *"Whoa, an interception! The game is over! We are going to the Super Bowl!"*

Balloons and confetti filed the air. The crowd was losing their minds, hugging, and kissing each other. Some were yelling, stomping. and running up and down the aisles. The place was a mad house.

"Super Bowl!" was being chanted throughout the stadium.

No one cared that five seconds were left on the clock.

The home team's backup quarterback came onto the field behind the center.
He said a few words that were not audible and kneeled down for the final seconds to tick off the clock.

The home team's players threw off their helmets with joy. Some ran to the sidelines and picked up their little children and brought them back out onto the field.

It would be trophy time in thirty minutes. Some players on the opposing team were sitting on the bench with their heads down. Others were walking slowly with their heads down.

They had come so close. Three points stopped them from the big game. The coaches and assistant coaches had removed their headsets, as they were not needed anymore. The game is over.

Arnold who no one notice left the club suite quietly, not knowing he had made a bad mistake.

Tyler sitting along, thinking…. *'Where do I know her'*.

Looking at Tyler, Teg says "Clear your mind, who she is will come back to you".

Moving next to Tyler "Yes, meditate, it works for me," said Tyson.

"You meditate?" Tyler asks startle.

"Okay, due to my nature, I deserved that question, but I do meditate," said Tyson.

"I'm speechless" said Tyler.

The ladies started exiting the suite.

"What about the ceremony?" the lady yelled across the room.

"Catching it on cable," said Teg pulling Tyler behind her.

On the elevator going down, the ladies talked about the game.

"Travis, you were right, Football guys are hot" said Tyson.

"Tight pants and all," said Tyler.

"Oh, Miss Religious gets horny?" laughs Tyson.

Rolling her eyes towards the sky, Tyler said, "I get around, believe me, I can get handled."

Travis, says "I'm glad I didn't see any one of you girls running behind one of the male players."

"Were they wearing underwear?" asked Tyler.

"No, just a jock strap," answered Teg.

"Oh, my Jesus. My nipples are hard," remarked Tyson.

"Freak," said Travis.

"Number ninety-four was running all over the field tackling everyone. I will take him and his father," said Tyson.

42

"His name is Ware. He's a good tackler. I took some pictures of him for entertainment," said Teg.

"I like you girl, did anyone notice his football stance, how he bent down on one knee barely touching the field and the other straight up with his chest bending forward?" said Travis.

"Don't forget the cheerleaders kicking their legs up like that. You get pictures of that?" Tyson asked.

"Ugh," said Tyler. "You like women too?"

"Baby I go all the way. Is that a problem with you?" asked Tyson.

"To each her own. I was just asking. Who am I to judge?" said Tyler.

"Good, let's keep it that way," said Tyson.

"Girls, we have been doing well. Let's not spoil it," said Teg.

"I'm okay," said Tyson.

"A Tomboy," said Travis.

"One who is about to pluck some candy," laughed Tyson.

Everyone laughed. The elevator opened. All walked out.

The Tomboys climbed into a mid-sized black Hummer. Tyler was driving with Teg in the passenger seat and the twins were in the back.

CHAPTER SIX

Clunk, clunk.

The barbells hit the floor. Tyson had just finished doing arm exercises with a four-pound barbell.

Tex was sitting in a chair doing leg lifts, "Ladies, that was indeed Felix, the pictures shot at the game. Astonished to see him alive and on video tape. Blowing my mind".

"And Arnold, an agent in the same booth as Felix" says Bonnie.

"Is he working with Felix? asks Teg.

"Maybe, maybe not" says Tex.

"I put nothing by that snake, Tex" says Bonnie. "I am going to look into what he is up to."

"Do that my friend" says Tex.

"I know the girl but can't remember where" said Tyler with hand on chin.

"It will come to you, don't worry" said Teg.

"How was he supposed to have 'died'?" Travis asked, gesturing quotation marks with her fingers.

"He was shot in the heart during a robbery," said Tex.

Amazed, holding up her hand, Tyler asked, "Did you see a corpse?"

"No, remember his body was ID by Deuce," said Tex.

"Found out later the body was cremated," said Bonnie.

"Ashes to ashes, dust to dust," said Travis.

"I wonder whose body really got burned," asked Tyson.

"Hell, if I know" said Tex.

"No doubt, someone innocent," said Teg.

"Or someone who was already dead, and they split the ashes between the two," said Bonnie.

"Ugh," said Tyler.

"Hey, I've been meaning to ask you. How long can they stay under, when given the drug Propofol?" asked Tyson.

"They can stay under safely may be an hour" said Tex.

Bonnie finishing the sentence said, "Or an hour and a half."

"What about this guy name Arnold who is he?" asked Teg.

"An agent at the office, looking to advance" remarked Tex.

"A weasel" says Bonnie, "Seeing him in the photos let Tex and I know the bureau might be onto Jordan" says Bonnie.

"Or the little shit is up to something on his own, advancing at anyone expensive is his motto, ladies look for him at all times" says Tex.

"Let's get back to the bastard who tried to kill me and know I find out his best friend is alive".

"Oooh, so tough, no love lost here," Tyson said, jokily.

"Not when I cried and thought someone had killed my man," Tex said harshly.

"Boss, at least you survived the attack," said Tyler.

"Yes," Bonnie interjected.

Pointing her finger aimlessly, at no one particular, Tex answered angrily, "Fuck him. I do have many questions that are unanswered like how he fooled me all those fucking years."

"Language, please ladies" jokes Teg

"You can't fake love for that long. You two were together for over ten years. It had to be something," said Tyson seriously.

Tex gave a quizzed look, then said "Something is shitty here, and we need to find out what the hell is going on,"

For the next few seconds, there is a deafening silence in the room.

Tex leaned forward in her chair, looking down at her hands, and said, "I will always love a part of that man. But I can't figure out for the life of me why he did this. I need to know and punish anyone who helped with this hoax." Looking up at the ladies in the room, she added,

"Even if Jordan dies."

All looked at Tex, whom they had known for decades. She never talked like this.

Tyson, who loved and craved action smiled. She was about to get busy.

Travis changed the subject and asked Tyler, "Have you remembered that lady who was beside Felix?"

"No, I can't put my finger on her. I know the face, but it has had some altering done."

Tex walked over by the treadmill and picked up her purple briefcase. She unzipped it and pulled out a purple folder. Purple was Tex's favorite color.

Walking back over to the Tomboys, she opened the folder and passed out some Intel with pictures.

Looking at the pictures, sudden the girl name came to Tyler.

Jumping up, she yelled, "Sharron Cox, she is a hooker I knew in my low times! She used to walk the streets until my pimp found her and put her up into an apartment, so she could get high-paying clients. She was always ambitious."

Tyson could not let this pass. "Miss Holier than Thou used to be a hooker or street walker? Guess you *can* get yours."

"The operative word is that I *used* to be a whore," answered Tyler angrily.

Tyson went for Tyler's throat. Tex jumped in between them.

Travis and Teg just looked at each other and shook their heads.
Teg gave Travis a look that seemed to ask *can't you help control her*? Travis returned with a look back that seemed to say *no, never since we were kids*.

Both decided right then and there to let Tex handle the situation.

"Look," yelled Tex. "This is uncalled for!"

"This bitch doesn't get off facing me," yelled Tyson.

"You called me a hooker," said Tyler.

"What do you call selling your body?" asked Tyson.

"Making money. Unlike you, giving it up like a Happy Meal," said Tyler.

"You gave your money to a man. At least I kept my money!" yelled Tyson.

Tyler was trying to get close to punch Tyson in the face. Tex sensed the move and moved to block her hit.

"Tyson, I am contemplating kicking your ass," said Tyler.

"Oh, Miss Holy is going to kick my ass," Tyson said, half-laughing, throwing a punch.

Tyler ducked to miss the punch and said, "You need God in your life and maybe you would not be such a bitch."

"Oh," said Travis, shushing up her face.

"That changes the whole dynamic," said Teg.

Travis gave her a look of *what*? Travis stayed out of the fray. She had to pick and choose her battles with Tyson.

Tex thought for a moment to let them get it out of their systems, but she knew deep down each would fight until someone was not breathing and she needed both girls for this mission.

Tex stood up tall and put both her arms straight out to push each girl back and said, "Let's stop this party or each can step."

Each looked at each other hard like boxers do at a weigh-in.

Tyler turned and went back to her chair.

The rest of the eyes were now on Tyson. Would she give up and stop?

Travis knew she would, but she would have to get the last word in, so she would win.

Tyson came back with, "This is fucking surreal."

Throwing up her hand like she was waving off someone, Tyson walked back toward the work out bench.

Travis thought, *'Good, this is ending'*.

Tyler let it slide. She was beginning to figure Tyson out, all bite, but deep down, a teddy bear. She was satisfied with defending herself. It made her look good in front of the group.

Tex said firmly, "This cannot go on. We will never be successful in our mission if every second you four at each other's throats."

Travis and Teg gave her a look declaring their innocence.

Ignoring their looks, Tex said, "No one is on the sideline. We all must work together so these blow ups will not happen again. Matter of fact, I want Tyson and Teg to come up here and hug."

"Never," said Tyson.

"Ever," said Tyler.

Tex said nothing but gave a look that could kill. No one moved.

Sighing, she let the gesture go. It wasn't necessary at the time.

Softly, Teg said "Can we get back to what is at hand?"

"Yes, let's go over what each person's part is needed to get this mission moving," said Travis.

"I am on point and ready," said Tyson, who had figured out she had pushed the envelope too far this time and needed to cool it. She would get Miss Holy later.

Tex went back to her folders that were beside the workout bench on the floor, examined them, and said, "The first thing we need to find out is where Jordan and Paul are located. I am sure they are surrounded by a security system and bodyguards."

"Wait a minute Tex, said Bonnie, "Arnold was in that suite for a reason, do you think he is on to Felix or/and Paul? Can we assess the bureau files and see what he is doing?

"Noted" said Teg.

"Do Felix or Jordan have any habits? We can start there," said Tyler.

"Sports, along with beautiful women, are Felix's Achilles' heel, it was stupid of him to come to a public place" said Tex.

"He was in a private suite," said Teg.

"True," said Tyson.

"Still, look what happened. We spotted him. If he makes a move like that again, I want you Tomboys to take him down. Kidnap him and bring him to me quietly," said Tex.

"I will take on that project. He will not get away again," said Tyler.

"I will help you," said Travis.

"Tomboys for life," said Tyler.

Looking at Tyler, who was looking at her, Tyson said, "Tomboys for life."

"For Life" says Teg.

Bonnie smiled.

"Loving this ladies" said Tex.

"I would like to start with Sharron, I will go to my old grounds and look her up. Maybe someone knows how to reach her," said Tyler.

"Tyler, can you handle that scene?" asked Tex, "That was a tough time in your life. You almost died."

"I need to conquer my demons to survive in life. I can do this, Tex," answered Tyler.

For a moment, Tyson felt maybe she had made a mistake. Maybe Tyler wasn't a cold bitch.

"Tyler, once you get her information, let me handle Sharron. I can come in as a fashion designer, what woman doesn't love fashion" said Teg.

"Thank you, Teg. Tyler, this is best. I'm not saying you can't handle this, but I feel more comfortable this way. Remember, you left a bad aura. People could be still looking for you.

Teg is not known, and she can get closer to Sharron and whomever we need. This situation is furious, and I am sure people would kill to keep it hidden. Trust me, no one goes through all this trouble for nothing," said Tex.

"Let's take the Hummer and get started," said Tyler.

"Not until I shower. I'm sweaty," said Teg.

Tyson covered her mouth, to stop the inevitable words from coming out.

Everyone laughed.

Since the gym only had two showers, Tyler and Teg went first.

Tex had messages on her cell phone she needed to return, so she headed to her desk in the left corner of the gym.

Travis slid over to Tyson and said, "You have to calm down. I love you with everything I have, but please let's work together. We will not have to work with these girls forever."

"Okay, but she is such a holier than thou person. She makes me feel like I am dirt," said Tyson.

"Personally, I think she admires you and wishes she could be you," said Travis.

Smirking, Tyson asked, "You think that?"

"Yes, she sees how tough you are and wishes she could be the same. Plus, Tyson, I sense this girl has had a troubled life growing up. Let's be more kind to her, okay?" asked Travis.

"I sensed that when Tex asked her that question about whether she could handle that assignment. So, I will calm down, but if she comes at me ever again … lights out on the broad," said Tyson.

"Fair enough," said Travis.

Tyler came back into the room and said, "One of the showers is available, ladies."

"You go," Travis pushed Tyson. She didn't press the issue and left the two of them alone.

"Thanks," said Tyson as she brushed by Tyler.

"You are welcome," said Tyler.

Travis looked at Tyler and said, "Everything will be okay."

Tex could be heard in the background saying, "I need that information on the down low or heads will roll."

CHAPTER SEVEN

Sirens wailed loudly in the background. Smoke was going upward toward the sky. People were scattered about, talking, and getting directions of what to do. Some people were crying or holding their hands or handkerchiefs up to their noses, so they could breathe fresh air. The air was polluted with smoke, gas, and an extraordinarily strong odor of dead bodies due to an airplane that had crash landed in a large corn field. All the passengers, including the flight crew and pilots, had died on impact.

The fire department chief had his crew looking for the black box that contained the pilots' voices on the final leg of the crash. This was a tragedy. All three hundred people died. Women, men, and children of all ages and nationalities were amongst the fatalities. The fire department chief would never get over looking at small bodies in a plane crash. He was glad he was going to retire this year.

The National Transportation Safety Board had their people there, ready to take control of the flight data recorders as soon as they were found.

The fire department chief informed them that the flight was carrying a second black box. The NTSB advised the chief that as soon as they were found, both would be taken back to the lab to be decoded.

The team at the site included four NTSB aviation specialists, technical advisers from the Federal Aviation Administration, and other officials from Knox Airlines, the company whose plane had crashed.

The plane had taken off from California that evening about three hours after the football game. The chief's assistant walked up to him and gave him a copy of the passenger list. Copies of the list were also given to the NTSB, FAA, and Knox officials. Listed beside the number eighteen was the name of Felix Johnson, which no one knew was a significant name.

He was dead. He had been holding the program he had brought at the game.

The program was half burnt up and wet, lying beside his body in the field.

Bodies passed by the officials all zipped up in black body bags, the kind that bring back soldiers whose bodies were not intact. It was a nonstop flight to Miami, Florida.

Putting the pieces together, aviation safety analysts came to believe that this plane went down because a bomb was aboard.

The conditions of the runway and crash site, as well as the information provided by the air traffic controllers, made them believe plane exploded suddenly.

Not an incident cause by human error or a mechanical failure. Weather was not a factor. It was eighty degrees with no wind. The pilots had good visibility and no objects were in the way to cause a crash. The two engines from the plane had separated and were at least four miles apart.

The tip of the left wing was in a thousand pieces, unable to ever be put back together. The main landing gear was still in the up position, which meant the pilots never pushed the button to bring the landing gear down for an emergency landing. The site showed the fuselage broken in two places. Everything here smelled of a bomb on board this plane.

Bombs on commercial planes were a major concern of the NTSB and FAA.

Mass chaos was reported back to the chief, who had at least eight eyes and ears spread out all over the scene. He wanted to know everything that was going on. He had to cover his and his department's asses.

Heads were going to roll for this incident and he and his department were not going to be on the receiving end. He told all his crew to report anything and everything, no matter how worthless they thought it might be. When put together, puzzles always give the correct picture.

The people who owned the large farm told the local sheriff that they had heard a loud explosion and ran outside to see a plane that was in the sky with fire balls in the back, as high as they ever seen, headed toward their field. They told the local sheriff that they thought that the plane had instantly exploded in the air.

The male owner of the farm said that his ears were still ringing from the explosion. He lightly tapped his ears to stop the ringing. The lady farmer told the sheriff that she knew no one had survived that accident. She had told her son to run back in the house to call the authorities. They were thanked for their information and asked if they would be available to answer more questions if necessary. Both shook their heads yes. The sheriff moved on, but the farmers sat down to watch the scene. It was better then what was going on the house at this point.

Other people who lived in the surrounding area began to arrive, asking questions and watching the scene.

"Jesus," one said, "Some families are going to be in much pain."

"Over two hundred died," answered the male farmer, who got the numbers wrong.

"This was a huge crash, and I don't think they can identify the bodies," said a female.

***

Back at the "cave", Jordan was informed that the mission had been accomplished.

"Good. Paul was stupid. I can't believe he would have taken a chance like that and went to such a public place. A football championship game or not, it was a stupid move."

"Do you think this will bring heat here considering the government will investigate the crash? A lot of people died." Radio asked Jordan.

Jordan answered, "No. Remember, Paul has been dead for over five years and plus, that is not even his real name."

"Okay, boss. I gotta go now. It is time to do check-ins".

Jordan just waved his head to indicate "go," and went back to reading his paper.

Radio left the room.

Jordan knew he had to be extra careful. The agency was not stupid, nor was Tex. He hated to leave her, but he could not take the chance. He loved her, but he also loved another.

***

Back at the crash site, the chief asked his assistant if he received the 800 number, so he could give it out to people who needed information.

"Yes chief, the number is 1-800-AIRLINE."

A piece of the plane's wing had landed about one mile from the crash. Attached to the wing was a tube of nitro that, for some reason, didn't go off as planned.

Unbeknownst to the person who attached the bomb and his handlers, the wings had a hidden number to help identify the part if a crash occurred. When a special light moved across the wing, the number corresponding with a specific plane would be revealed. This was only known by the highest authority in the airline company. This special area of the wing also picked up fingerprints.

CHAPTER EIGHT

A folder was thrown on the desk, creating a loud thud. This was the worst disaster in the last decade. Over three hundred people died in this terrible plane crash. I have been in this business a long, long time and can never get over losing so many people in one incident," said Deuce.

Deuce, the new boss, took Jordan's spot immediately, because the bureau never waited for a body to go cold to replace a recently vacated position. Jordan was well loved, but business must go on. Spy businesses never have any holidays.

His assistant Arnold said nothing. He was saddened that so many people had lost a loved one. In addition, his mind was on how he could fill the assistant position he was in on a permanent basis. The bureau told him he would temporarily fill the position until a replacement could be found. He wanted this position badly because it was a climb toward his goal of one day becoming the chief of the bureau. So, he went along on everything that Deuce said or did. However, if Deuce did anything, he thought would stop him from climbing, he would not be afraid to go against him. He went about things quietly, of course. One must never ruffle feathers in this business. There are long memories of past traitors and he cared not to get on that list. He would volunteer to do any extra work that was needed. In other words, he would be available. After all, the bureau was his life. He had no girlfriend or family. Every night, he went home to a frozen dinner or sometimes he treated himself to a hot, prepared dinner at a restaurant.

The secretary walked into the office and handed Deuce another folder with large letters on the front saying, "For Your Eyes Only." Deuce took the folder and thanked the secretary, and she left the room.

Deuce opened up the folder, moving swiftly through the pages, and handed the folder to Arnold saying, "Would you put this folder on Tex's desk? This is her field."

"Sure, will we be meeting for lunch at the same time?" Arnold asked.

"Yes, we need to have our fun. God knows this place will drain the air out of your lungs if you let it," said Deuce.

"See you around one o'clock," Arnold said, as he was leaving the office with the folder under his arm.

Once he left the office, Arnold made an abrupt move sideways, went into an empty office, and closed the door for privacy. He opened the folder and looked at the files. Nothing alarmed him, it was just some paperwork about the airplane crash. Specifically, the papers were the passenger list and status reports on the investigation from each of the different agencies.

The passenger list that contained the name Felix Johnson didn't set off any alarms.

He had no idea that this guy's real name was Paul King, who died years ago, and he was Tex's husband Jordan's best friend. After xeroxing copies, he put the papers back in order in the folder and left the room, walking toward Tex's office.

***

"Bitch, I know you are not in my face," said Tyson.

"I see your blue eyes, bitch," said the informer.

Tyson hauled off and smacked the shit out of the guy. He went down hard, and blood started coming out of his mouth.

"I know you take drugs, but you better get sober fast, motherfucker. I will take you the eff out," said Tyson.

The other three Tomboys were watching by the side of the Hummer. Nobody was better at getting information than Tyson, so they were going to let her work.

"What's his name?" asked Tyler.

"Blackie," said Travis.

Blackie held his mouth, trying to stop it from bleeding, and said, "I can't believe you hit me."

"Next time you will stop breathing, and for you to jump? You must be insane."

Tyson kicked Blackie in the side. He rolled over in pain.

"What do you want? Yeah, all of you B's," Blackie asked, spitting blood from his mouth.

Teg stared at him. No one called her a bitch, especially a low life, and got away with it.

Travis said softly, "Down, girls. He is not worth it. Besides, he is our best informer. Tyson's just ruffling him up a little. You know, just to keep him in line. He is on our payroll."

"Why is he playing hard?" asked Teg.

"Believe it or not, he and Tyson have a thing. Both like to push your last button," said Travis.

Laughing, Tyler asked, "So she will not cause him bodily harm?"

"No, she will not, but she'll leave some bruises and blood behind," said Teg.

"Learning fast, huh?" said Travis, laughing.

All three Tomboys were watching the action as they were talking.

Tyler had her hand on her knife, ready at any moment to use it.

Travis saw this and said, "Cool it."

Tyler relaxed and removed her hand from her knife that was shining brightly.

Tyson had reached over and smacked Blackie again and said, "Start talking."

"I can't if you keep hitting me," said Blackie.

He was panting. His mouth was swollen up and his tongue was having a hard time moving.

Tyson said nothing but reached to her side and brought out her gun, aiming it toward Blackie's knee.

Seeing the gun, Blackie put up both hands and said, "Okay, I will talk. What do you want to know?"

"I am asking about a guy named Felix" said Tyson.

"I know a lot of guys named Felix. Give me some more information".

"He's the meanest, bad motherfucker around here, hangs out with a guy named Jordan," said Tyson.

A look of fear came on Blackie's face. He never, ever wanted to hear those two names together. That meant death. He didn't know them but had heard unbelievably bad things about them.

"Jordan who? I don't know anyone by that name," Blackie said with agitation in his voice.

Tyson pulled back the trigger on her gun.

"Okay shit, just thinking his name will get me fucked up and saying it will get me killed. Those guys don't play. Look, my understanding is Felix was killed two years ago. That is the rumor. No one went to a funeral or saw a body or anything," said Blackie.

"He is alive. He has been spotted," said Tyson.

"Fucking go on and kill me, because that motherfucker has spies all over the place," said Blackie with a puzzling look on his face.

"Where?" Tyson asked as she shot a bullet close to Blackie's knee cap.

Jumping, he said, "I heard near Herr, California. It is not easy to get to. He has the whole four-mile radius locked down."

Tyson walked over toward Blackie and hit him beside the head.

"What the fuck? I answered your questions!" said Blackie, holding his head where fresh blood was running down his face.

"Next time, answer faster," said Tyson.

Blackie looked toward the other three Tomboys, who didn't say anything or move an inch.

He looked at them with sad eyes that said help.

They answered by returning glances that said *your ass*.

'Cold bitches', Blackie was thinking.

He knew he was fucked and had to start answering questions or his ass was on the line.

Blackie was sure that Tyson and Travis would not harm him. He wasn't sure about the other two, especially the one with the dreadlocks.

He had noticed she went for her shiny knife. He wasn't sure what they might do.

The two ladies that he knew, their reputation was tough and lethal, and he planned on living another decade at least.
Blackie told the girls about the area called the "cave" and he described the place like a scene from the Godfather movies.

He said, "It was one way in and one way out. To the left of the street are row houses, about six on each side, and when you reach the end of the street, that is where the 'cave' is. It is a large house that is protected by a tall tower where guards can see you coming at two miles before you see them. The place is on twenty-four hours, seven days a week protection. You don't go there unless you are invited or uninvited."

As he said that last line, he gave them a look and said, "You know what I mean. You will not see the sun again ever. *The* man who is the boss never leaves the 'cave.' My understanding is that everything he needs is there and they bring everything to him. On the down low, I heard he has a secret underground escape route if needed."

Travis spoke up for the first time and said to Blackie, "You know a lot for this to be a secret."

Blackie looked at her and said, "I normally keep my mouth quiet, but you four are not letting me have that privilege, are you?"

"How do you know this information?" Tyler asked.

"A little birdie told me," Blackie answered.

"The little fucking birdie's name?" Teg asked.

Holding his head and wiping blood off his face, Blackie answered, "I'm so confused. I can't remember anything. Bitchy here is beating me down."

Travis, Tyler, and Teg laughed.

Tyler tossed him a towel to help wipe his face.

"Keep going," said Tyson.
Blackie wiped his mouth gently with the cloth that Tyler had given him. He had figured out she was the one that was gentle but still tough.
He would play on her for his life if this turned bad.

"It's a lot of flat land surrounding the area. All trees and grass have been cut for maximum protection."

Teg asked, "For all this information, you must have been there."

"No, I know someone who goes there to play poker when he is invited."

"When is that and who is that?" asked Tyler.

"Normally, once a month, but the guy doesn't really talk about it. He was drunk one night at a friend of mine's house and was talking. Before he left, he was shaken and crying, begging us not to say anything about what he said. Those people will kill him and his whole family if they wish. We promised him nothing will be said."

"How many people were at the house?" Teg asked.

"Just eight including the guy, I think" said Blackie.

"What are their names?" Teg asked.

"Melvin, Big Boy, and Chuck, oh Chuck was killed in a drug raid two weeks ago. So, it is only three including Tom," said Blackie.

"That is only three names," said Tyler.

"I don't know the other names and Melvin didn't say them either," said Blackie.

"Can you get the other names?" asked Teg.

"Maybe Big Boy might know but Melvin will never talk," said Blackie.

"He will when we finish with him," said Travis.

Blackie just looked at her. She scared him; there was something about her that smelled tough underneath but soft on the outside. In his experience, that meant bad vibes.

"We need to meet Melvin," said Travis.

"Come on ladies, I will die. Do you understand?" Blackie was pleading by now. "I will die."

"We will be discreet. No names will be said," said Tyler.

"Look, anything you say will tip them off and people will give you up so they will not die," said Blackie.

"I said no names will be given out," said Tyler sharply.

"We know how to do our jobs. We have been in this business decades and still alive. We will not get you and your friends killed, but if you come up with some more information, we want to know," said Teg.

"This information better be right because my boss will have my ass in ten seconds and I will have yours in one," said Tyson.

"It's good," said Blackie, shaking. The interrogation was ending, and he was wondering with the Tomboy's stern faces if he would live to see another day.

Teg threw a cell phone at Blackie and said, "This is an encrypted number you can call from anywhere and be safe." Pointing her finger at his face she said, "And don't give the number to anyone."

"Okay," said Blackie. "Oh, you ladies might want to know that Flex Johnson is going by a new name.... Paul King".

The four Tomboys turned and walked toward the Hummer, got in, and drove off.

Blackie cut on the phone and saw one word. Tomboys.

He questioned if one eight hundred went before that and if he has to go through a voice active screening to get through. *'Clever'*, he thought.

Hell, he was thinking about asking to join their group, four babies and a dude.

Getting up and wiping his face with the towel given him; he was thinking that he would be on their side because when the shit hit the fan he wanted to be on the winning side. He knew shit was about to hit the fan.

It always does in this business and he was a very smart man. Tyson did rough him up a little, but it could have been worse. He would wear his bruises with honor. Of course, he would tell everyone he was approached by three fuckers trying to rob him and he took out all three.

CHAPTER NINE

Tyler was standing out in front of a house with a broken-down fence and gate, yelling Melvin's name.

"Girl has guts," said Tyson.

"More than she shows," said Teg.

Travis was standing with the girls by the Hummer, parked in front of the house.

Melvin, who was six-feet-two and weighed about three hundred pounds, came balling out of the house with his arms swinging, yelling back, "Who is the fuck calling me out like this?"

"Your worst nightmare," answered Tyler.

"Looks like a nightmare that is about to be put to rest," answered Melvin smartly.

Tyler stepped up to Melvin and hauled off martial-arts-kicks that put his ass to the ground.

"Like I said, your worst nightmare, motherfucker," Tyler was up in his face on the ground with her knife at his right temple.

Tyson loved the whole scene. *'Tyler is a bad ass after all',* she thought.

The Tomboys motto is never interfering unless needed.

"Bitch, if you didn't have that knife in my face, I would whip your ass on this front lawn," said Melvin.

Tyler laughed and got up, throwing her knife to the side, and bucked Melvin in a way that said *let's get it on.*

Melvin looked at Tyler, who was about five-four, weighing about one hundred and twenty pounds, as an easy target. He came after Tyler, who kicked the hell out of his diaphragm with her right foot. As he was bending over, she drop-kicked him in the face with her left foot. Melvin didn't go down but grunted and emerged from the ground with a distracted face. He was going to kill that bitch now.

By this time, three other people had come out of the house. One guy, around eighteen, had a large beer in his hand, drinking it and laughing, because he knew Melvin was going to kick this bitch's ass. He had seen Melvin in action before.

Melvin's woman yelled, "Kick her ass, baby!"

Travis, Teg, and Tyson went into cover mode in case the people decided to make a move toward Tyler.

Tyler gave her a quick glance that said *you are next*. She back down after looking Tyler in the eyes.

When Melvin punched Tyler and she went down, his girl went bad again and started yelling, "Hit her again! That's right baby, give her another one!"

Tyler jumped up with both feet at the same time and countered Melvin with a straight-out cross jab to his left cheek. Melvin instantly went to hold his jaw. Two teeth and blood spattered out his mouth.

Tyler countered with another jab to his right cheek. *Crack*. She had broken it.

Tyson yelled, "Go girl, whip his ass!"

The women moved closer to the action and Travis moved in closer to Melvin's girl to get her attention.

"What are you going to do, old bitch?" yelled the girl.

Travis didn't say a word, she just slowly walked toward the girl while she was still talking shit and slapped her so hard the girl was out before anyone could see the slap.

The other two bodies on the lawn took four steps back.

All the sudden, they realized this was serious and these ladies could kick their asses. The girl lying on the lawn had not moved. She was knocked out cold.

Travis reached down and put her hand on her throat. After a few seconds, she got up and turned to walk back toward the other Tomboys.

She said softly, "She is alive, just unconscious."

"Shall we leave her like that?" asked Teg.

"Yes," said Travis. "She is their problem, not ours."

Melvin got in another hit and Tyler's cheek swelled with black and blue bruises.

She touched the blood running down her face and licked her bloody fingers.

Tyler smiled at Melvin. With a puzzled look, he looked at her, thinking *'what's wrong with this bitch?'*

Tyler started yelling a loud sound and went flying toward Melvin. With blinding speed, she went to attack him in sections, the face, then the torso, then the private area. Within seconds, Melvin was on the ground crying in agony. Tyler landed back on her feet with her body in a martial arts stance.

The other lady that was watching the scene had ran into the house and was on the porch pointing a gun at Tyler.

Teg raised her weapon that contained a silencer and took the girl out by hitting her wrist that was holding the gun. She screamed and let go of the gun. Her wrist was bloody and swelling.

The young guy who had the beer, dropped the beer bottle, and put his hands up. Three of his friends had been attacked in the last four minutes. He was not about to challenge these fine, sexy, hot women. Obviously, they meant business.

The girl on the porch yelled, "She shot me! She shot me!"

Tyson ran up on the porch and removed the gun that she dropped.

Teg and Travis dragged Melvin's body to the Hummer and threw it in.

Tyson looked the young guy up and down said, "You need to take care of your friends."

She then turned to join the others in the Hummer, and they began to drive off down the street as she was closing the back door.

The young man watched with his hands still in the air. Slowly, he glanced at his friend on the lawn, passed out, and then to the friend who had been shot and was still yelling.

He decided he better get the hell away from this scene, so he started running.

"Punk ass," yelled the girl on the porch who then ran into the house to call for help.

A neighbor who was hiding behind his curtains saw the whole exchange, smiled and said to him, "Those punks finally met their match. Hopefully, those foul, nauseating, noxious people will leave for good. Good riddance."

***

The Hummer came to a slow stop and Melvin's body was thrown out the back hatch.

He landed extremely hard on the ground. He had a lot of explaining to do, including why he thought it was okay to hit a woman. But right now, the Tomboys needed some more information on the "cave." Tyson wanted to go after him, but Travis stopped her and told her that Tyler deserved to finish this one.

"True that," said Teg.

"No problem," Tyson answered.

Tyler came out of the Hummer with attitude. She was going to fuck this guy up after getting the information they needed. Tex had taught the Tomboys to never take things personally, but she would disobey this rule as soon as she got what she wanted.

She walked up to Melvin and said to his face, whose body is lying on the ground. "I am going to forgive you because people can get out of hand and start smelling themselves. You know, thinking they are all important and stuff. Know what I mean?" Tyler asked with a stern look on her face.

Melvin, getting a grip on where he was, said nothing. He was in the woods with four crazy bitches. He shook his head *yes,* letting Tyler know he understood what she meant.

Teg was on the phone talking to Tex inside the Hummer, away from the action.

"Tex, we found out that Felix is going by the name Paul King by Tyson and Travis' informant. Right now, Tyler is interrogating Melvin, who was at one of the card playing games, for more information."

"Okay, when you finish come back to the command center. I have some important information," said Tex.

Teg asked, "Is the information something we need to know now?"

"It can wait, but not for long. Come in as soon as possible," Tex answered.

"Be there soon, Tex," said Teg.

"Oh, um, Teg. That guy Melvin, you know what to do," said Tex.

Tex hung up.

She left the Hummer and walked over to Tyson, who was eating an apple and enjoying Miss Holy getting down and dirty.

Travis was recording the scene with a special video camera for later use.

Teg told the girls, "Tex wants us back as soon as possible. She has some news for us."

Travis and Tyson nodded *okay*. Travis yelled to Tyler, "Get on with it honey, and don't forget to leave our calling card!"

"Melvin, we need to know about Paul, and don't say you don't know him because we have on good authority you do," said Tyler, as she made a cut in his arm with her knife.

Melvin hollered. Blood was running down his arm.

"I don't hang with Paul. He doesn't have people like me around. He sees us as a low life if you know what I mean," said Melvin.

"He had you up to the 'cave' to play poker, I was told," said Tyler.

"Just one time. He was in a good mood and the place was empty. He was showing off if you ask me, like he was the big man and shit, but everyone there knew he wasn't. The big man was not there."

"How long were you there?" asked Tyler cutting him again on the arm.

"About four or five hours. I lost track. We were getting high, drinking, and playing poker."

"Any conversation you wish to pass on?" Tyler asked sternly.

"The man might be an ass, but he is not stupid. Nothing was said that can go back on the street."

"Describe the place," asked Tyler.

"We came in through a long, back, dirt road. I remember the street was not well lit up. I'm thinking if you didn't know your way, you will get lost. Also, it was not a place easy to escape from, a little spooky for my taste."

"When you arrived, what and who did you see first upon entering the house?"

"A large room set up for playing cards. A bar was set up for drinks and beside it was a table with snacks of all kinds of food. One of the other guys who were there remarked, 'Just like last time'."

"What did he mean 'just like last time'?"

"Lady you don't ask questions in that type of environment, you go with the flow," said Melvin.

Tyler understood.

"Melvin, I need some good information and you are not telling me anything."

"Bullshitting," said Tyson.

Looking over at Tyson, Melvin remarked, "I swear on my children's life, I don't know anything to tell you."

"Just talk. We will make that decision," said Travis.

"It is not for you to decide, just talk," said Tyson.

Tyler sensed Melvin was holding back. She cut him again, across the face.
Melvin screamed, "What the fuck is that for? I'm talking! more would be worse than if Paul found out. I heard the horror stories of his interrogations and the bodies that were never found".

Tyler tried one more time. This man was going to die right here if he didn't talk.

Melvin was on his knees now holding his bloody face.

Tyler bent down to his level and said, "I feel you are holding back, and things are about to get ugly. Give us something that will help us get to Paul."

Crying now, Melvin said "Okay, one night, I was at the main house and a police cruiser came to the main gate. The guards shot up the car pretty bad."

"Did they kill the officers inside? Wait, how many were inside?" Tyler asked.

"It was two of them inside the car and no they didn't shoot them. They were instructed to miss on purpose."

"What else?" Tyson asked.

"I don't know anything else," Melvin said.

"I am tired of this, shoot the fucker," said Tyson.

"Wait. Melvin, talk or die," Tyler yelled.

Teg was standing with a look of annoyance on her face.

Travis was by the Hummer, listening, and looking out for any intruders.

Melvin mummed, "I heard Paul called the Mayor and complained about the intrusion and the Mayor called the captain of police to advise him that he was on government property and to never send a police cruiser up here again. Paul was bragging he have superpowers over the Mayor."

"Did, the so call man of the house come home while you were there" Teg asked.

Looking her straight in the eyes, Melvin answered, "No."

"What else, Melvin? This is nothing" said Tyson.

"Another guy in the room laughed and said, 'Yeah, with over one hundred thousand greenbacks.'"

All laughed. They knew what he meant. The mayor was on the take.

"Damn, you can't trust anybody," said Tyson.

"You know Melvin, we, the Tomboys are not boo-boo, the fools," said Teg, who walked over to Melvin and shot him in the head.

"What the fuck, Teg?" Tyler asked.

"Tex advised me to take him out because the boys could be on their way." She then walked over to Melvin's body and started searching for any Id's or information, she looked under his balls.

"Gross," said Travis.

"Nice set of balls," said Tyson.

"Dead ass balls," said Tyler.

"Look a ring vibrator around his penis" Said Travis.

"I knew, I heard something, thought it was a recorder" said Teg.

Turning around she said, "Oops, some kind of sex gadget."

Freak, getting it on, in broad day light" Tyler says disgusted.

"Damn, Teg," said Travis.

"He was going to die anyway" said Tyson.

"Following orders" said Teg, looking innocent.

"No shit," said Tyson.

Melvin's body was on his back with both legs under his body.

"The police will think it was some kind sex act that went bad" said Tyler.

"Next victim?" asked Tyson, walking to the Hummer.

Travis chuckled.

"I am going after Sharron," Teg answered, ignoring Tyson's remark.

"We need to go to the jail. That is where most information is," said Travis.

"Remember, we need to see Tex first," said Teg.

"Off we go and, by the way, good work Miss Holy," said Tyson.

"Fuck you, Tyson," said Tyler.

With her arms up in the air, Tyson answered, "What? I am being real."

Sarcastically, Tyler said, "Whatever."

Teg and Travis chuckled.

CHAPTER TEN

"Paul King aka Felix Johnson is out of the picture," said Tex, throwing a folder down on the desk. "He was taken out by a plane crash. It looks like Jordan's handiwork."

"He would take out a whole plane to kill one person?" asked Tyler.

"Yes, he would, and he did," answered Tex.

"Where do we go from here?" Teg asked.

"You killed Melvin, who never told us who else was in the room for poker night," Travis said.

"Are we leaving bodies, ladies?" asked Tex, sternly.

"Not the usual amount," answered Tyson, smartly.

"You said, you know what to do" Teg answered bewildered.

"Melvin was a snitch, he had to go. But let's keep the body count low, it brings attention" said Tex.

"It's okay Tex, we were careful," Tyler said.

"Girls, I can't stress this enough – no unnecessary dead bodies," said Tex sternly, waving her finger.

"Sometimes dead bodies send messages," said Tyson.

"Tyler and Tyson don't fuck with me. This is important," said Tex.

"No fucking with the boss," answered Tyson.

The Tomboys laughed.

Tex didn't return their laughter and gave them all a stern look.

They straightened up and got serious.

Bonnie, who had been sitting in the back not saying a word, rose up with folders and a usb in her hand, and went to the front of the room and began talking.

"This mission is bigger than we thought. We are going to have to take a one-hundred-and-sixty degree turn and start peeling this mission like an onion, one layer at a time. We have to re-examine everything we have so far. That plane crash was no accident. Innocent people were killed along with Paul because of what he knew. Someone was cleaning up and getting rid of the problems."

"Smells like Jordan's shit" said Tex.

"Yes, Jordan is behind all of this. Paul either had information or did something really terrible for a whole plane to be taken out. Paul could have been killed by any of Jordan's men. The question is, 'who is Jordan sending a message to?'" said Bonnie.

She walked toward the computer in the room and put in the usb, a snowy picture emerged on the screen.

"Girls, that body up there is Jordan. This was sent to me this evening," said Tex.

"Anonymous?" Teg asked.

"Yes, but for what reason? I already know Jordan is alive. It's...like someone is trying to get under my skin or they are sending me some coded message," said Tex.

"We need to find out who is really sending this and why," said Tyson.

"It's' someone close to the action, Jordan is no fool. But what that person wants Tex to do is the real question," said Bonnie.

"How did you receive this information Tex? I thought the agency changed everything about you," Travis asked.

Heads snapped toward Tex. That was an incredibly good question.

"Sent to my office at the agency marked 'For your eyes only...,'" said Tex.

"Maybe that sneaky bastard, what's his name? asked Tyson snapping her fingers.

"Bonnie is watching Arnold," said Tex.

"With both bad eyes," said Bonnie, putting on her eyeglasses.

All snickered.

Tyler directed her question to Tex, "You think maybe Arnold knows Jordan is alive? Because if he does, then he is using you somehow."
Teg, sitting by Tyler, nodded her head in approval.

The twins looked at Tex for an answer.

"Ladies, right now, I don't have that answer, he is such a weasel looking for any way to get promoted, Bonnie is having him watch, He has been in my office per my secretary leaving material. I instructed my secretary to carefully copy the material then put it back on my desk, like I haven't seen it," said Tex.

"Yet he keeps sending you information," said Tyson.

"No doubt trying to get to see how Tex will respond to the information," said Travis.

"Ladies, I am four steps ahead of Arnold. Don't worry, we have a plan for him, don't we, Bonnie?" Tex asked.

"Sign, sealed, and will be delivered," Bonnie answered.

"Naughty, naughty...tisk, tisk, so devilish," said Tyson.

"Never mess with real pros," said Bonnie.

"Amen," said Tyler, raising her glass of wine in Bonnie's honor.

Teg, Tyson, Travis, and Tex followed suit and held their glasses up to Bonnie.

"I will accept," said Bonnie, and all took a sip from their glasses.

Tex smiled at her friend, who missed her calling. She would have been a great agent.

"Do Arnold and Jordan know each other?" Tyler asked getting back on track.

"Arnold was not on Jordan's level, so they hardly had contact, but knowing how ambitious Arnold is, he knows some things about Jordan," said Tex, "My only concern at this moment is getting Jordan.

Our only chance is his one downfall: poor judgments, not always thinking things clearly out before putting it in action. Ladies, listen, he is exceptionally good, but he is human. I have gotten him out of a lot of troubles before. All we have to do is guess his next step and we will have him."

"That will not be easy. Jordan is surrounded by very loyal people," said Bonnie.

"And the ones that are not loyal will be taken out, as you see," said Tex, pointing at the folder with the plane crash information.

"Seems like any way he can," said Tyler.

"So, it is written, so it shall be done," said Travis.

"No hard feelings?" asked Teg, regarding the casualty she created.

Looking at Teg, Tex answered, "None at all."

"Let's get to work. This is what we need," said Bonnie.

***

"Hey, take your hands off me. I know my rights. I didn't touch that man. He attacked me first. Hey, I said take your hands off me!"
The police officer paid no attention to the man he had handcuffed and was walking him toward a cell. The young guy had been mouthing off since he handcuffed him and put him in the back seat of the patrol car. His mouth had been moving non-stop.

He just kept going on and on, as he was doing now. This time, he had a bigger audience that was watching his every move and listening to what he was saying.
Jordan, there at the station to visit a friend, watched the scene like everyone else.

The guy was kind of comical. He was twisting his body in different ways and his mouth was running like a race car motor. The officer was having a hard time getting the guy towards the cell. Another person was already in the cell, getting a little annoyed because motor mouth was coming his way.

The officer was at his last wit with the guy. When they both arrived at the opening of the cell, he took off the handcuffs and pushed the guy in and slammed and locked the cell gate.

The guy gave back, saying, "You didn't have to push me, punk."

The officer sighed and turned and walked away. He was about to give that guy a serious ass kicking, but he needed his job, and he wasn't worth the aggravation.

"Hey man, bring down the noise. You are making things worse for you," said the other guy in the cell.

"Fuck them. I am not afraid of any of them," said the loud guy. He said this as he was pointing to the men in uniform on the other side of the cell gate.

"You are locked up. What do they care? Besides, you are killing my ear drums with your loud noise," the other guy said.

Turning around for the first time since entering the cell, the loud guy said, "Sorry man, I was just pissed at them," gesturing toward the uniforms.

The other guy gave an okay sign. He then stood up and put out his hand and said, "My name is Pete, nickname Pie and you are?"

The other extended his hand to shake Pete's hand and said, "My name is Rodney, Radio is my nickname, nice to meet you."

"You have a mouth on you, my friend," said Pete.

"Yeah, hence the nickname Radio, I used to get my ass beat all the time by my parents, but I see I haven't learned from that," said Rodney.

Both laughed.

Jordan, still watching from afar, walked away to visit his friend upstairs.

He made a mental note to himself to have those two checked out. They might be of use later for his special project. He did ask the officer on duty at the front desk for their names.

The officer answered, "Pete Brown and Rodney Moss. They both are twenty-five years old."

"Thanks," said Jordan. He turned and hit the elevator button to go upstairs. The elevator arrived, two people came off, and Jordan stepped in, looking at the two guys as the door closed.

CHAPTER ELEVEN

Police were called to the scene by an early morning jogger who found a body floating face down in the water. The body seems to belong to a man in his forties. The body had been floating in the water for some time, and at first glance, it appeared he was wearing only a pair of black jogging shorts. When the divers pulled the body out, they realized that the shorts were originally white. Tests will be needed to determine the cause of death. Due to the nature of the death, the information released has been limited. The police would only provide that the body was a man and while they had an ID, they were not at liberty to divulge any information.

The body was taken away in a zipped-up body bag that was placed on a stretcher. A member of the news staff overheard the captain trying to contact the family. He was using speaker phone but was unaware that anyone else could hear his conversation. The voice on the other end of the phone call advised the captain that the wife was unable to come to the phone because in reaction to hearing about the death of her husband, she was under heavy sedation.

The captain asked if the wife would be available tomorrow because he had some urgent questions. He knew the severity of the issue. The body belonged to a federal agent and he would be in deep shit if he didn't receive answers soon. "Unable to confirm," was the respond he received. The captain was not amused. "Thanks," he said to the other person and hung up the phone.

Following that exchange, he pulled out his own cell phone and speed dialed a number, "Jack Anderson, please." He was put on hold and he started pacing back and forth, waiting for Jack to come to the phone. He didn't notice the technicians around him setting up cables and equipment to send out live news. There was a journalist from a rival newspaper posing as a technician.

He wasn't doing a good job pretending to be a technician, because he was paying more attention to what the captain was saying and the news being reported to the captain from the different people under him, who kept coming and going with new information about the scene.

Suddenly, the captain said, "Jack, we have a sticky situation here in Nelly Park. That body belongs to an upper-level federal agent, I meet him before at an event."

The answer came back, "Holly crap" so loud it could be heard through the regular phone speaker, as the captain was no longer on speaker.

Next day, at his kitchen holding a newspaper the captain was furious. 'Those damn reporters. Damn magnates. There is no anonymity in this world."

***

Tex, reading the same article, shook her head, no doubt in her mind that it was more of Jordan's handiwork. He was cleaning house, but why? Did he know something was up? Was he on to her? She took a bite of her toast with grape jelly and then took a sip of her coffee. The Tomboys must work faster than she thought. Instincts were telling her Jordan knew something. She just hoped she, Bonnie, or the Tomboys hadn't made a mistake and tipped him off.

***

Blackie had read the same article and knew there was more that wasn't said. The word on the street was low key, but people were saying the man had been taken out. Some gangster was taking credit for the killing, but he was street smart. He knew they would not have lived to brag if they had done it because this man was a high-level federal agent. The agency would have been on their asses right after the body was found. Blackie paid no attention to the bragging, he was just looking for key information, and anything he could use and pass on to the Tomboys.

He picked up his teacup, took a sip, and kept reading the rest of his paper.

***

Deuce, looking over papers and going through memos on his computer, realized something was going on behind his back. He summoned Arnold to his office.

Arnold arrived within minutes. He had information for Deuce that he knew would be of value and would aid in helping him look good in Deuce's eyes.

The first thing Deuce said when Arnold entered the office was, "Something stinks. My agent instinct is ringing like the Wall Street bell."

"I am with you on that, boss. I have something you and I need to check out," said Arnold.

He gave Deuce the folder he was carrying upon his entrance to the office. Deuce opened it and saw there were a lot of memos and papers.

He passed it back to Arnold and said, "Give me the short version." Arnold loved hearing those words. He loved to be the one giving out good news. After all, he wanted to be important to the agency and his boss. In other words, he was a kisser up.

Arnold started by saying, "This person's name is Blackie, a low-level hoodlum living on the south side of town."

"What do I need with a low-level hoodlum, Arnold?" Deuce asked.

"Boss, the guy knows some information about the agent found in the river," said Arnold.

"Like what?" Deuce asked.

"Who murdered him," Arnold replied.

Deuce looked stunned.

Arnold said, "I have his exact address...."

Deuce rose up from his desk, stopped Arnold mid-sentence, and said, "tell me the rest on our way to Blackie's location."

Arnold rose up from his chair in Deuce's office and followed him like a puppy out of the office. They passed all the agents and secretaries at their desks. Some eyes were watching them leaving the area. Someone softly, says, "Kiss ass motherfucker…" Another set of eyes watched quietly, not saying a word. She picked up her cell phone and sent a text.

Arnold and Deuce entered the agency's garage and climbed into a beige Honda Accord four-door. Arnold was driving. Both were dressed in regular black slacks. Arnold was wearing a beige polo shirt with his three buttons clasped up to his neck. Deuce was wearing a black sweater, pulled over the head. Their gold badges were hidden in their pants pockets.

The address was about forty-five minutes away. It was in a bad neighborhood and many tenants could smell law enforcement from a mile away. Deuce and Arnold took precaution and brought along their service weapons.

They came upon 444 Good Manner Rd., parked the Honda Accord, and went into the building for apartment number 4. It was located on the bottom floor of the twelve-apartment complex. Music was coming from the other side of the door. Blackie was dusting down his furniture. He liked for his place to be spotless. Dressed in a T-shirt and short sweatpants, with a silk rag on his head laying down his perm, he was singing the words to the song, *'I'm bad, I'm bad, you know it.'* His body was swinging to the beat of the music. He loved Michael Jackson.

He stopped cleaning at sporadic moments to dance to the music when the song hit certain beats. *'And the whole world....'*

A red light above his door lit up. Someone just rung his doorbell, stopped him from singing.
Blackie went to his peephole and looked out, then went to turn down his CD player.
'Who is this?' he wondered. He knew by the look and the smell coming from under his door that it was the po-po. Through the peephole, he saw a badge was being held up by one of the men. Blackie didn't give a fuck about that. He had rights as a citizen; he doesn't have to open his door unless they produced a warrant.

Opening the door, but leaving the chain attached, Blackie asked, "Men, how may I help you?"

Arnold spoke up and asked, "Are you the person who goes by the name Blackie?"

"Depends, who is asking?" said Blackie.

"Law enforcement is asking," said Arnold, who produced his badge again.

Looking at the badge, Blackie pointed his finger at the badge and said, "That doesn't mean anything here."
"It means a whole lot by the law," said Arnold.

Deuce was standing by Arnold, not saying a word, simply watching the exchange with a curious look.

Angered, Blackie said, "You have a warrant?"

"No, but if needed, I can get one," Arnold said smartly. This guy was getting on his nerves because he expected people to respect law enforcement.

Deuce knew that would not happen. These kinds of people see law enforcement every day and don't give a damn.

Smiling, Blackie said, "Well motherfucker, I suggest you get one." He then proceeded to close his door.

Deuce put his foot in the path of the door to block it from closing and said softly, "Blackie, look, this is going wrong. Let's start again. My name is Deuce, and this is my assistant, Arnold. We need to ask you some questions, that's all. No harm intended."

Blackie looked at Deuce and said, "Well call your dog off, because he has no rights here. He doesn't pay rent here and you can remove your foot out of my doorway."

Deuce did as he was told, and Blackie backed down.

"You gentlemen can come in, but I am not promising to answer any or all of your questions."

"Thank you," said Deuce, entering the apartment. Arnold followed behind him with a stern look on his face holding a soft leather black briefcase. He dared this man to treat him and the boss in this fashion. Noticing Arnold's look, Blackie said to Arnold, "Are we jumping today?"

Arnold stared Blackie down. Blackie returned the stare down and repeated, "Are you jumping today? Because we can go down if need be."

"We are top brass guys. We don't go down to police stations" said Arnold.

"Not a police station, stupid. I meant you and I go down. Me kicking your ass on my property," said Blackie, indignantly.

Arnold bolted toward Blackie to take him on. Deuce stepped between the two.

"Cool it guys" said Deuce, looking at Arnold. Blackie stood with his hands in a fighting pose.

Relaxing his stare, Arnold said, "We don't need to go down to the station, as you say."

"Good, because I will, and can go, to the nth degree if needed. Law enforcement or not, I have been down and dirty with many men and women who thought they could come on my property and disrespect me. I am not afraid to die and will fight to...."

Holding up a hand, Deuce stopped the conversation and said, "Everything is cool. Your name is Blackie, I assume?" asked Deuce.

"The one and only," replied Blackie.

"Mr. Blackie let's start over. May we sit down?" Deuce asked.

"Have a seat, gentleman," Blackie said.

Arnold caught the use of gentle*man* instead of gentle*men*, but he let it go.

Deuce and Arnold took a seat, side by side, on Blackie's orange leather sofa.

Arnold pulled out his small recorder and asked, "May I?"

"No, you may not," Blackie said smiling.

He saw that Arnold had an attitude problem and he was not in the mood to go downtown to the police station and have to wait in those piss-filled cells to be released by his lawyer. Well, it was his cousin, a somewhat lawyer. He was good for getting him out on bail until court dates come.

Arnold put the tape recorder away in his top shirt pocket.

"I need you to take that back out and open it up, so I know it is not recording secretly," said Blackie.

Arnold did as he was asked.

"Thank you," said Blackie, with a sly grin on his face.

Arnold grunted.

"Problem, my man?" Blackie asked.

He then turned his attention toward Deuce and asked again, "How may I help you two gentlemen?" waving his hands between the two, while taking a seat on his orange-colored leather lounge chair.

"We have some questions to ask you," said Deuce.

"Are you an owl? You have already said that. Get to the point. Why are you here? No bad news, I hope," Blackie said, sarcastically.

A low growl could be heard coming from Arnold.

Deuce tapped him on the knee.

Blackie saw the exchange and figured out who the boss really was. A lot of times law enforcement introduced themselves incorrectly to fool the person they were interrogating.

"We need your help," said Arnold.

"You are the kind of help I don't need," said Blackie.

This was going to be hard, the men realized, but Deuce needs this guy, so he was going to keep trying or haul his ass into the station for a work over. He hoped it didn't come to that because he had to answer a lot of questions from his boss and fill out a lot of paperwork when he brought in a criminal. One needs fake charges, among other things. He was not prepared to do that today, but he had shown his hands by coming here today. When they left, Blackie could potentially go underground and not be found. He could not take that chance.

"Have you been watching TV or reading the papers?" asked Deuce.

Looking annoyed, Blackie said, "The point, my man?"

"The point is, one of our best agents was killed and left in a river. We need to know if you know anything?" Deuce asked.

"The word on the street is you know everything," said Arnold.

Knowing what those words meant, Blackie jumped up out of his chair and said, "Look motherfucker, don't come on my property and fuck with me. I am not saying another word without my lawyer," then folded his arms across his chest.

Arnold and Deuce rose up along with Blackie. This could turn into trouble.

Holding both arms up in the air with his palms facing Blackie, Deuce tried to calm the environment. "Blackie, look, sometimes we men say the wrong things," Deuce said, looking at Arnold, who had one arm behind him ready to reach for his weapon.

"You have a gun? A gun, man?" Blackie asked, pacing in front the men.

"Blackie, he is not going to use the gun," said Deuce with a stern look on his face, looking at Arnold, who hadn't taken his eyes off Blackie. "Put it away now and calm down, Arnold."

Arnold relaxed his arm, still looking straight at Blackie.

"He can let go of the attitude too," said Blackie with a smirk on his face.

Deuce grabbed Arnold's arm to make him sit back down with him to get Blackie to calm down.

"We just need to know if you know anything," Deuce asked again.

"You guys are pitiful. You can't even question anyone. I bet my good life you two are desk clerks," said Blackie, needling them.

"We are not desk clerks. We are the top brass of the law," said Arnold, indignantly.

"Just like I said. Desk clerk. A street cop would never come at me like that," said Blackie with a frown on his face.

"Blackie, look, I have been kind to you. Don't make me take your ass down to our street," said Deuce with a grin Blackie knew well.

"Okay, I don't know anything about your agent who got killed. Anything more?" Blackie asked.

"It's my understanding that you are aware of some undercover agents that are working with a top-level official," said Arnold.

Looking blankly at Arnold, Blackie asked "Any names, my man? I see and talk to a lot of people. They don't introduce themselves as undercover agents."

Deuce didn't understand why Arnold asked that question.

'What was he after?' He would go along until he could talk to Arnold alone.

"Frankly, that is what we need from you, Blackie. We are asking with whom you are working?" says Arnold.

"Man, you are blowing me. I need something to help you," said Blackie.

Arnold opened his brief case that he had with him, pulled out a photo, and passed. "Have you ever seen or talked to this person?" asked Arnold.

"Hey Arnold, that is your name, correct? The next time you pull something out, announce it. I don't want to pull a cap off in here by accident," said Blackie.

Ignoring that statement, Deuce said, "Do you know, or have you talked ever to this person in this picture?"

Looking at the picture that Arnold had dropped on his glass table, Blackie said, "Never, ever, seen or talked to this person. She is a hot mommy. Who is she?"

Hoping this would help Blackie to trust them, Deuce answered, "She is a top official in the agency I work for."

"And that agency is?" Blackie asked.

"I am sorry, Blackie. I can't divulge that kind of information. But we need your help if you know this lady," Deuce replied.

"Sure, my man, but I have never seen or talked to this lady. Can I least have a name?" Blackie asked.

"Can't say," said Arnold.

"Oh, I see. You can ask and expect answers, but I am not allowed to ask and get answers. Gentlemen, that is not how the game is played," Blackie said.

"This person is extremely high in our agency. We can't just give out this information without cause," said Arnold.

'Pussies,' Blackie thought.

Stretching his neck and rubbing it at the same time, Blackie said, "Okay, I will bite. I assure you I don't know her. Do you have anything else?"

"Yes, I do. She is working with undercover agents and by any chance have you talked to them or know them?" asked Arnold.

"Since I am not aware of her, I am lost in answering your question, gentlemen," Blackie answered.

Blackie's mind was racing the whole time this conversation was going on.

The men got up and asked Blackie to contact either one if he had any information on that topic. Arnold dropped a business card on the glass table. Blackie glared at him. Arnold smiled arrogantly like, '*now you jump, and I will have your ass downtown before you can fart*'.

Blackie left the card where it had dropped. Deuce pushed Arnold toward the door. He was tired of the two trying to see whose dick was bigger. Nothing was accomplished today, and he was not pleased.

"Goodbye, gentlemen," said Blackie.

He closed the door behind them and watched as they walked down the hall.

He then went to his window and watched as they entered the beige Accord.

Blackie wrote down the license plate numbers for future reference.

He then picked up his encrypted cell phone given to him by Teg and called the girls.

The first thing he said when Tyson answered was, "Girl, shit is about to hit the fan."

He started telling Tyson what had just happened.

***

In the Accord, Deuce turned to Arnold and asked, "Why did you show Tex's picture?"

"I think she is up to something," Arnold said.

"What makes you think that?" Deuce asked.

"Just my instinct," said Arnold.

"Next time your instinct flairs, you talk to me first. I am the boss here," said Deuce.

"Yes sir," Arnold answered.

CHAPTER TWELVE

The girls were in the middle of finalizing their plans when Blackie called Tyson.
Tyson hung up her phone and went to the girls. Her cell phone rang when she was in the kitchen getting snacks and drinks for the group.
The Tomboys were deep into their mission and working on what needed to happen next, looking at surveillance pictures they got from the game.
Tex had recruited another agent named Walker to get information about the 'cave' Blackie spoke about. Asked him to see if he can plant a camera somewhere for her to get some intel on the area, it contained a secure microwave link that would go unnoticed to the untrained eye.
The link was encrypted when sending images. The images only became clear once it was opened with special software that Bonnie had in her computer. Walker had done this delicate work for her years ago and was remarkably successful. Getting into that 'cave' was going to be difficult. With Bonnie's help, she decided to try it out, only after being reassured that if it was found, it couldn't be traced back to its origin and it was hard to detect.
Tex received an encrypt message from Walker while the ladies was going over the game footage. "Yes', she said after reading it. "Ladies, we are at the 'cave.'
Looking at the footage being sent from the camera; the ladies didn't know anyone shown coming and going from the area. Pictures taken were ran through the computer face recognition software to see if anything matched. Nothing.
Bonnie had noticed that Tyler resembled one of the maids who cleaned the main house and came up with the idea to plant video cameras and bugs inside the main house.
The lady could be falsely arrested for a few hours while Tyler took her place.
All assumed the place would be swept for listening and video devices regularly, so a plan was hatched how and where Tyler would do the planting.
"With a wig and some make up, you can pass for this woman," said Teg.
"Tyson and I will be in charge of collecting the lady for a few hours," said Travis.

"No, someone else, Travis. It will put you two out in the open," said Tex.

"We don't know much about this lady, who she knows, and who knows her," said Bonnie.

"I am going to have regular cops pick her up the legal way. Bonnie will put in a fake order. By the time they figure out it was a mistake, this mission will be over," said Tex.

Upon entering the secret room, Tyson said out loud, "I just heard from Blackie."

"Any good news?" Teg asked.

"I am not sure. He says two guys named Deuce and Arnold just left his place asking questions about us. He also said they showed him a picture of a lady. He described the lady and it resemble Tex to me. I will take a picture to him later and ask him if that is the same person," Tyson said.

Bonnie looked at Tex, who said, "Deuce and Arnold are fishing, but they are not a problem now. I have someone keeping tabs on both."

"We can't have unwanted guests in this. From what I have sensed, Jordan's have spies everywhere.

Someone at the agency might tip him off about Tyler and she could get killed," said Teg.

"They don't know about you ladies, Tyson and Travis go and see Blackie". She didn't like that Deuce and Arnold, were showing pictures of her around town.

Tyler, Teg, and Bonnie will continue working on how to get Tyler in as a maid.

"Yes boss," said Travis.

Travis and Tyson went to the garage underground, hopped into a silver Corvette, drove the half-mile leading to the main road, and zoomed down the road.

Tyson reached over to the dashboard of the car, turned down the music, and said, "let me finish telling you the conversation with Blackie."

"Okay shoot," said Travis.

"He had me laughing. You know Blackie, always trying to be tough. He claimed he was about to pop off a cap in Arnold, who I sense he didn't like on introduction."

"Should have, I heard he was a total shit ball."

"A total dickhead."

Travis laughed.

Tyson said, "He was afraid of two things: one, they were asking him point questions and two, they would be back.

"The agency would have fried his ass on the Brooklyn Bridge on CNN for killing two officials." Said Tyson.

"He is right about that," said Travis.

"Yeah, then he talked about their clothes. You know Blackie, he is a dress freak. He says it was total agency. Those guys tried to be cool by wearing regular clothes. He said only a few can get the dress right and them two didn't have it. Just cheap and babble, babble…."

Travis was half-way listening to Tyson. She had another thought on her mind.

"Ty, I am wondering how they knew about Blackie," Travis said.

"They have informers on the street. Also…maybe someone just threw his name out there and they jumped," said Tyson.

"A big fucking leap, Ty," said Travis.

Shaking her head and sighing, Tyson agreed and said "Blackie has to move. He will not like it,".

Looking at Tyson, while waiting for the red light to turn green, Travis said, "Let's have him go under cover. He would love that," said Travis.

"Yeah, the bugger has been begging us for a while. What will he do?" Tyson asked.

Smiling, Travis said, "We will think of something."

"We, the twins, always do," said Tyson, as she reached for the radio knob and turned it back up. The Corvette sped down the road.

***

Bonnie had received the call she was waiting for. The maid loves to go out alone on Wednesday nights for dinner. She knew someone at the restaurant who could drug the lady's drink. A hostess from Bonnie crew will wait on the lady and will drug something the lady orders. It settles within eight seconds with no taste After ingesting the drug, it would take about two hours for it to come into effect. The person would have stomach pains. If the lady goes home or heads towards the hospital, she will be arrested as planned.

Bonnie had also called her makeup artist friend, who was ringing her doorbell. It was especially important that Tyler was ready when the drug had been administered to the lady. Dash entered the room and kissed and hugged Bonnie.

"Hello my friend. It has been a long time," said Dash.

"Too long," said Bonnie.

"You look great. as usual."

"Flattery will always get you my jobs."

"Peachy," said Dash.

Bonnie pointed to Tyler, who was standing by, waiting to be introduced.

"Girl, you are gorgeous," said Dash.

"Thank you," Tyler said, shyly.

"I promise to do her justice," said Dash.

"Just a little is needed," said Bonnie.

She then gave Dash the picture of the lady he needed to make Tyler look like.

"Oh, you are right. They are almost identical twins. Not much work is needed," said Dash, smiling as he looked at Tyler, who smiled back. "Well, let's get started," he said as he put down his makeup bag on the table. He looked toward Tyler and said, "Honey, I need you in this chair."

Tyler went to the chair to which he was pointing and sat down.

Dash took her face in his soft hands and rubbed her skin lightly and said, "So beautiful."

"Thank you," said Tyler. She was getting a little nervous because no one ever told her she was as beautiful as Dash was claiming, but she sat still and let him start to work his magic.

Within one hour, with the makeup and wig, Tyler looked exactly like the lady in the picture. Dash pastes it on the wall behind Tyler's head, so he could see her and the picture at the same time.

Bonnie was impressed, as she knew she would be. Nobody was as good as Dash when it comes to doing disguises. No one.

Tex had arrived at the house and had walked into the secret room as Dash was putting on the finishing touches.

"Hello, Dash. I see Bonnie has called you into service," said Tex.

"Always the best," said Bonnie.

"Stop. No, don't stop. I love compliments," said Dash grinning.

All laughed.

"Tyler, how do you feel?" Tex asked, as Tyler was checking herself out in the mirror Dash had passed to her. She was turning her head to the left and to the right, examining her looks. She couldn't believe how much she looked like that lady in the picture. The wig felt light and the makeup was flawless.

Tyler answered, "I feel wonderful. The work is supreme."

"Thank you, honey," said Dash.

Tyler rose from the chair and went into an adjoining room. She reemerged ten minutes later and was wearing the uniform that the maid wears when cleaning the house.
Everything looked authentic. Bonnie had done a marvelous job in getting the uniform made. She had some stains put into the uniform, so it wouldn't look brand new.

The white shoes' bottoms had been scraped in the dirt to make them look like they had been worn for over a year, at least. The utility belt had the necessary items like a dust rag, a scraper to remove things like gum from areas, a medium-sized duster to run around the furniture, gloves, a can of regular freshener that was actually a special spray that can only be detected with special eye wear, that will come in handy later in the mission.

Tyler was examined from head to toe to see if anything was missing or out of place.
Tex did notice that the shade of stockings was off slightly. The others agreed, and Bonnie took note to get another pair that was a little lighter. Everything else looked good.

Dash packed his makeup and carrying bags and left the house.

Teg, who was in the other part of the house, still trying to match faces with names and personal information, returned to the room where Tex, Bonnie, and Tyler were starting to go over the equipment needed for Tyler to plant in the house.

Teg reported, "I have two matches that are going to be a great help. Wow Tyler you look great".

"Thanks" said Tyler back.

Tex said, "Go ahead and tell us. We about to go over the last part of Tyler's mission and this might change things."

"I need you all in the command center," said Teg.

Everyone came into the command center. Displayed on the big screen TV were two pictures of the surrounding area of the "cave". The still picture was of the two guards who were guarding the entrance of the main house. The pictures were so clear one could see the stubbly beards on the men's faces. The pictures showed the type of weapons the men were carrying and the moves they took to guard the entrance.

Teg moved the mouse, and the picture became live with the bodies moving.

They were talking and laughing amongst themselves. The conversation was about the club they were going to this weekend. They were glad they didn't have to work because they were the seniors of the group and get weekends off. Two new guys, low in seniority, have to work. The group was happy to hear that piece of information because that went along with how the maids always come in on Sundays. They could come in around 7am and had to be finished by 9am exactly.

"I like this. This new crew don't really know the cleaning crew well," said Tex.

"No doubt given pictures to compare, but Tyler looks good," said Teg.

"If need be, I can use my charms," said Tyler.

"Don't spook them girl, you look good." said Bonnie, laughing.

"I try not to," said Tyler, proud of how she looks.

Tex was smiling. The mission was finally coming together.

Bonnie turned toward Tex and both said at the same time, "Walker."

"Who is he?" Teg asked.

"An undercover agent who can replace one of those guys" said Bonnie.

"I will contact him now," said Tex. She moved over to a laptop computer and cut it on. It fired up in seconds. Tex signed in and sent out an email. Within two seconds, he replied.

"He will be here tomorrow at 4pm. I will meet him at the Hilton hotel in Santa Barbara, California, far away from here, so no one can connect us," said Tex. She pointed to the two guards and said to Teg, "Give me some hard prints from as many angles as you can. Walker will need the Intel. Also, I need some personal information on those two guards."

"On it, boss," said Teg, passing her two folders each with the guards' names on it and their own personal background.
The folders are labeled "Guard # 1 Pete Brown nickname Pie" and folder # 2 was labeled "Guard #2 Rodney Moss nickname Radio".

Tex took the folders and put them along with the still pictures, a copy of the video into her specially made briefcase only she could open. She would deliver it to Walker at the Hilton hotel. She couldn't wait to see him. They had kept in touch by special emails and phone calls. He was so undercover the agency never brought him back.

"Tell him hello for me," said Bonnie.

Tyson and Travis returned to the command center.

Tyson took one look at Tyler and said, "Who is this, pulling out her gun?"

Tyler, who was packing, pulled hers out at the same time. Both were pointing their guns at each other. Travis had a puzzled look on her face, but at the same time, she was alert for danger.

Tex said, "Girls, put the hardware away! Tyson are you crazy! We are in the command center. Who would dare bring their ass in here? And do we look like we are under attack?"

Teg and Bonnie started laughing. Bonnie said, "I swear to God, you four are going to kill each other before this mission is over."

Still laughing, Teg said, "I am going to stay out of the way of you three. I would love to live through this."

Bonnie shook her head and sighed.

"I was just playing. You asked us to get along," said Tyson.

"Sick game ... and dangerous!" said Tex, annoyed.

"She does look different," said Travis.

Looking at Tex, Tyson said, "I am sorry, Tex".

"Always sorry. I can't keep forgiving you because you say you are sorry."

"Technically, she never says she is sorry," said Travis.

"True that," said Tyson, hunching up both of her shoulders.

Even Tex had to agree with that statement. She just said, "Cool it from now on, starting right this second."

"The day has been long and fruitful. Let's call it a night. We all are tired," said Bonnie. All agreed. The equipment was powered down, the lights in the command center were cut off. The security sweeper was cut on until the next day.

CHAPTER THIRTEEN

The ladies woke up the next morning and were at a table eating breakfast. There was a buffet containing different types of eggs, sausages, bacon, grits, pancakes, french toast, biscuits, and fried potatoes with fried onions. Coffee, tea, cocoa, and water were available. The sounds of forks, spoons, chewing, and sipping could be heard as the ladies went back over what they had learned the day before.

Tex repeated information to Tyson and Travis about the two bodyguards and Walker who she was going to meet later that evening. Tyson told Tex what she didn't want to hear, but knew in her heart, that the picture showed to Blackie was of her.

"Oh my god, what are Deuce and dick brain up to?" Tex asked.

"Dick brain, always up to something" said Bonnie.

Tyson laughed because no one seemed to call Arnold by his name. It was always something else.

In between eating her scrambled eggs and sipping her tea, Teg said, "I have thought about a way to get in touch with Sharron Cox. She goes to fashion shows. A friend of mine sent me some pictures of her fashion show and I saw Sharron in the front row. I emailed my friend and asked if she knew that lady in the peach dress with four-inch peach pumps. She emailed me back and said, yes, that lady was at all her shows and was a good buyer. So, I sent an invitation to my pre-show lunch. I am waiting for her to respond."

"Good work, Teg. Watch your back because you never know who is watching her. Remember, she was with Paul," said Travis.

"Okay, Teg is on the hooker...," said Tyson.

"Tyson...," said Bonnie, annoyed.

"What...what did I say wrong?" Tyson asked hunching her shoulders.

"She has a name...Sharron" said Bonnie.

"Again, while Teg is interrogating the hooker, Travis and I will get Blackie ready for his mission," said Tyson.

Bonnie sighed and took a sip of her coffee. Tyson will be Tyson.

"Has anyone thought that maybe the other cleaners might realize the switch?" Travis asked.

"That did cross my mind last night" said Tex. "The get up is good, but she might have certain traits that others might notice that we missed."

Tex took a sip of her coffee and then said to Tyler, "Get away from the others as much as possible and talk little. Hopefully, she wasn't a talker."

"I got it, Tex. I will use an excuse that something is on my mind or something...," said Tyler, waving her hand around.

Tyson asked softly, "Teg, what do you know about hooking? I am not saying you can't handle this job, but those girls are hard and street smart, they have to be to survive that world."

Chewing on her toast, Teg answered, "I did go undercover about ten years ago as a street hooker. It was scary as hell, but I made it through the mission."

Looking at Tyler, she continued and said, "Tyler, you will help me?"

"With anything you need, girlfriend," said Tyler.

Travis and Tyson said simultaneously, "So will we."

Tex and Bonnie loved this moment of unity.

"Set," said Tex.

"Oh, I'd like to state that this mission is freaking me out because I can't figure out why Jordan would do this," said Tyler.

"Jesus, me too. I don't understand the logic behind him," said Travis.

"I need to know to keep this straight in my head," said Tyson.

"Yes, what is his reason?" Teg asked.

Lowering her head and sighing, Tex answered, "I don't know."

"We are fucked," said Tyson.

Bonnie said nothing. She couldn't figure out Jordan's reason either. The room became deadly quiet.

***

The front gate of the main house opened, and the cleaning crew entered. There were two guards waiting in the driveway. One was checking identities while the other was watching the group. Both were armed. One had a sawed-off shotgun visible, so it would scare anyone who decided to get out of line. The other, who was checking IDs, had his Colt pistol on his right hip for easy withdrawal. Tyler was the fourth person in line.

She was not nervous at all because she couldn't be. After all, she was a professional. The guy waved his hand to her indicating to come forward. She did and gave her ID to the guard. He studied it carefully by looking at her and back to the ID many times. Finally, he was satisfied and waved her on. Tyler thought, *number one on the list checked.* Entering the house, another guard watched one's every move. Tyler took note of where he was stationed. He pointed for Tyler to go to the left and start in that room. She went to the cart that was already in place, she was surprised she wasn't patted down before entering the house. They might have found the special spray she had hidden in her undergarment. The guard was guiding the others, so Tyler took this time to add her special air freshener. She picked up the duster and started dusting the furniture.

The guard looked her way to make sure she was doing what she supposed to be doing. Everything looked okay, so he turned back around to guide a big guy who was there specifically to help move some furniture the boss wanted moved to another room, it was Walker, the undercover agent there to help Tyler, if need be.

Bonnie was an incredibly careful person who arranged for him to be there. He was strictly instructed not to let her know who he was or why he was there. He was on a need-to-know basis and was told his assignment just the night before.

Tyler picked up the special spray and started spraying anything that was made of wood and started buffing it down. The items would shine, but the special ink would not brush off with a regular rag, and it can't be seen by the naked eye. She worked fast because she didn't know how much time she had in the room.

The guard watching her cleaning so fast said, "Slow down. What's the rush?"

Smiling Tyler, replied, "Just making sure I do well, sir."

"You are okay. Don't hurt yourself," the guard said. Secretly, he always liked the lady. Today she seemed different, nicer, unusual, not uppity.

Tyler asked, "Where is the next room I will be cleaning?
The guard said, "It is upstairs," grateful she was smiling and talking to him today. Maybe he could ask her out before she finished today.
Tyler smiled back while spraying her special spray at the same time.

The guard smiled back and was interrupted by his walkie talkie going off. "Ben."

"Come upstairs".

"On my way".

Tyler took this opportunity to spray more areas in the room. The room looked like a place that they hung out in. Walker and another man were in the next room, moving the furniture they were told to move. It also helped that he had a good view of Tyler.

The Tomboys, Bonnie, and Tex had thought carefully of items that could be switched by replacing them with bugs shaped like the item. Tyler had the task of matching the bugs per room. She lucked out in the first room. She could replace at least three. One, she put in a lamp with a bejeweled base by adding a bejeweled shaped bug. The second was placed in a wooden doorknob. A wooden door is found in most homes. For the third, she planted a small gold-colored circle at the bottom left-hand corner of a picture frame with gold designs of intertwined circles around the edges that contained a picture of an incredibly beautiful woman.

The bugs were satellite operated. No wires were needed. This was good because she would not have been able to run any wire. She noticed the big guy who was helping move the furniture in the adjoining room was watching her too. She figured he was somebody watching Ben's back.

"Hey," came from Ben, which brought Tyler back to the moment.

"You need to go to the next room upstairs," he said, pointing upstairs.

Tyler ran over to her cart and put her materials back.

She started pushing it toward Ben. The cart was sticking on the carpet.

A hand came from behind her, which startled her, and grabbed the cart to help her push it. It was Walker, who was stronger.

Tyler said, "Thank you," when the cart reached the marble part of the floor.

Walker said, "You are welcome."

He smiled at Tyler, and then turned around toward Ben, who was watching and said, "What do I do from here, man?"

Ben smiled at Walker and said, "You go upstairs also. More things need to be moved. Oh, by the way I like your T-shirt. I am a fan of the Georgetown Hoyas".

Walker replied, "They are *the* best college basketball team on this earth."

As Walker passed Ben, he offered a high five, and Ben returned the action.

Walker helped Tyler take her cart upstairs to clean another room. Another guard was on that level. Both took note. The guard told Tyler, "The room to the right." Walker was told to go to the left. The guard who had watched the exchange from the top level of the house, looking down, smiled at Walker, and said, "I love the T-shirt too".

"They are badasses," said Walker, who then walked toward the room he had been told to go to.

"Excuse me, I'm having a hard time getting the cart across this carpet," said Tyler.

"That's your problem," the guard answered.

Walker, looking at the guard, said, "Come on, man. What happened to chivalry? This is a woman."

Putting both hands up in the air the guard said, "Right man, forgive me, miss. This job can be hard on the manners. Let me help you." He walked over to help get the heavy cart across the carpet.

"Damn, this motherfucker is hard to move," said the guard.

"I don't know how I would have ever got it in here," said Tyler, breathless.

"No problem. Call me when you finish. I will help you back downstairs," said Walker.

"And your name is?" Tyler asked.

"Walker."

"I am Maria."

"I am Mac," said the guard.

"Hi, Walker and Mac" said Tyler. She started dusting the furniture, looking for more places to plant bugs. 'Check' she said in a soft whisper. She emptied the trash and grazed her duster lightly over the electronic equipment.

***

Back at the command center, Bonnie was in heaven. She was already getting images from the bugs, making still pictures of the images being created as they came over of the people and rooms, diagramming the location.

This was the best intel they had gotten so far. Tex will be pleased. Teg, who was a genius at fashion, was also a genius at electronic software. Teg can create and use software for anything one could need, just like she can draw fashion designs.

"This is very good," said Teg, pressing all kinds of buttons on her keypad.

Tyler sent back pictures of each room she entered with her special camera hidden in her wig.

The special software used could remove any item it was asked to, just leaving a skeleton of the area. The software could rotate the skeleton to different angles of the rooms, so the ladies could study the exits and entrances of each.

They noticed one room had a separate guard and a keypad that signaled a special alarm on the door. It was black, six-by-six in size, small pad with only two green lights blinking left to right on rotation, located on the right side of the door. Between Tyler and Walker, they received about fifty percent of the diagram of the house. A special duster was used to scan papers that Tyler saw in the rooms.

Bonnie says, pointing at the screen, "That is Walker" when he came into the picture and that assured the girls that Tyler was safe.

Tyson said, "Oh my god, candy."

Travis and Teg agreed.

Bonnie smiled. She had tasted him and yes, he was delicious.

They also saw the images of where all the guards were placed and, most importantly, the alarm on Jordan's master bedroom door. The video came through with great images. The ladies could see entrances, exits, windows, how the rooms were decorated, what they contained, and crucially, how the inside was guarded.

The group, including Tyler, had been lucky.

Unbeknownst to them, Sharron was upstairs in a bedroom with a head cold. She was in bed and didn't venture out of her room. She was in a bedroom that was guarded by another guard who really was guarding Jordan's room. No one was allowed in that area without permission. One was shot on the spot, no questions asked.

Tyler finished her room and was guided back downstairs where the other cleaning crew are standing ready to be guided out to the front gate to go home.

Tyler got lucky because as she reached the bottom step, Jordan, Rodney, and Pete came through the door. They paid no attention to the helpers; they just walked into the room that Tyler had cleaned earlier.

Tyler's video camera in her wig recorded the whole scene.

Back at the secret room, Bonnie gasped, "Oh my god, that is Jordan!"

"He's dead" said Travis.

"Yep, Tex is going to kill him for real" said Tyson.

"Bar none" said Bonnie knowing her friend.

All were looking at a dead man walking.

Tyler and the other helpers walked out the door and headed for the main gate.

Walker stayed behind. He was talking to Ben about getting a job at the location on a regular or part-time bases.

CHECKMATE.

CHAPTER FOURTEEN

Jordan and his two personal bodyguards entered the room, unaware the room had been bugged and sprayed down. He was getting the particulars of the plane crash that he had ordered. Rodney and Pete relished telling the boss how they had accomplished the job.

Back at the command center, the ladies were watching and listening.

Jordan asked Radio, "Who did we hire to handle the bomb?"

Radio said, "It was a guy who worked there and knew planes inside and out. He is, or was, a gambler who needed the money because the mob was on his ass."

Looking at Rodney, Jordan asked, "Is, or was, a gambler?"

Pie answered that question by saying, "We left behind no witnesses, boss."

Jordan understood and went to the bar to fix himself a drink. He was a handsome man, about six-foot-three with a six-pack to kill for. He was a health nut who only put good food into his body. He loved clothes so much he hardly wore anything twice. His dress was always immaculate, nothing out of place. The clothes fell on his body like a male model. When he walked, it was with authority and charm.

He favored slacks and silk shirts, sometimes wearing a blazer or sweater, but never jeans. His hair was worn short to the scalp and he had a five o'clock shadow.

"Something is on the horizon. I feel it in my bones. I need you two to really keep your eyes and ears to the grind. Check with the other guards and see if they've heard or seen anything unusual," said Jordan, taking a sip of his orange juice.

"You got it, boss," said Pie.

Pie and Radio left the room to do as their boss wished. They were obedient like that. Never question Jordan, just do as told. Jordan stood before the large-paned one-way window. One can see out, but no one can see in and it is bullet and blast proof. He was sipping his drink and thinking. Jordan had chosen Pie and Radio himself. They were trained to be ruthless killers on command. They were young petty convicts when he first met them. He had been at the police station when both arrived for different offenses. He recognized something in them that the others at the police station didn't. They were a perfect fit for his project, they were renegades and expendable. When they were released from jail about six months later, he had Paul pick them up and persuaded them to go to his camp.

When they arrived, Jordan walked into the room and the two convicts, along with six others, came to attention. They saw that this man carried authority with him, and they sensed he was not to be toyed with.

He talked to them about a special program that he is running. He needed to recruit some new blood for the project. He explained that he worked for a special agency that he was not at liberty to divulge the identity of at the moment, but if they pass the camp and were hired, they will know more later on.

Jordan's project had nothing to do with an agency, he needed fresh and unknown people to get it off the ground. The top level contained his people that he had known and trusted for years.

He told the recruits the program would pay for their board and a paycheck would be deposited automatically into their bank account every two weeks. Participation in this program was twenty-four hours, seven days a week.

"I will personally pick two of you as my personal bodyguards who will be paid extra."

He had all eight men's attention. Jordan was not giving them much information, but they liked this program so far. They could see and smell the money surrounding this guy in front of them talking. What they didn't know was they were disposable, and if they get out of line and needed to be taken out, the money went back to Jordan.

Radio asked, "What will we be doing?"

"Mainly protection work. We need bright young men and you eight fit the bill. We have done background checks on all here and like what we saw. Over three hundred people were considered and you eight made the final cut."

All eight men smiled, some nodded their heads and two high fived each other.

Jordan and Paul, watching the action, knew they had hit a home run. Young people were so easy to persuade.

One of the guys sitting down asked, "How we were put on the list?"

Jordan smiled and said, "You all have criminal records. I used to be a police officer. Now I do work I can't explain right now. Paul and I looked over all your profiles and with some guidance you eight will be great for the jobs."

Shaking his head and sighing, Rodney said, "I don't work for the government. I don't trust them."

"Trust me, not the government. After all Rodney, I will be your ultimate boss," Jordan said with authority.

Rodney shook his head *yes*. He didn't want to confront this man. He sensed he would regret it later.

All accepted and entered the program.

A guy who was standing at front, not saying a word, began passing out forms that had to be signed.

Paul said, "Starting right at this moment, no one can be told about this project. No family, friends, or any passerby who you happen to come into contact with can be told."

All had just started their undercover careers.

Jordan looked around the room with an approving look.

Jordan and Paul selected well. They all loved the cloak, dagger, and the secretive nature of the program. They felt like James Bond or Jason Bourne.

Each guy was given a package that contained where they will reside, bank account information, and new personal information.

Training started at the same secret location the next day. Pete and Rodney turned out to be the golden eggs, as Jordan predicted. They took to the training like ducks in water. They relished their duties. They will and would kill on demand with no hesitation. They were exceptionally reliable and there was no threshold of atrocity beyond which the two would not go. They were ruthless soldiers. He made them his personal bodyguards. That made them happy. The other six wished they had been chosen but accepted that the money was good and at least they were still part of program. Their Achilles' heel was their youth. Like most young ones, they act, before they think. They were cocky, arrogant, and were pompous asses. Traits just like Jordan had. They listened only to Jordan, Paul and the other men be damned.

Deep down, all were afraid of Jordan.

They had discussed this amongst themselves since they were roomed together and got to know each well during training. They heard from one of Jordan's men who worked for him for over ten years how Jordan had skinned a man alive who betrayed him with no remorse. They said he loved to torture the betrayers himself.

Pete (Pie) and Rodney (Radio) didn't like that type of scene. They'd prefer to just take someone out and move on to the next. The internal workings at the "cave" were on need-to-know. It was particularly important that the new bloods and others didn't know the real reason behind the project. Jordan, along with Paul's help, in over five years, had stolen over twenty-five million dollars' worth of weapons, drugs, and cold, hard cash from the bureau through fake missions. Jordan and Paul kept the project compartmentalized.

Kings of wicked, both will become....

***

The "cave" community was located high up a mountain forest in Herr, California.
The weather was around seventy degrees all year round, with some rain around January and February of every year. The headquarters was on twelve acres of land. It was a walled compound with three townhouses located on each side of the street and the main house was at the end of the road. A tall tower was erected on the property for guards to see the surrounding area clearly. The main house and townhouses couldn't be seen outside the compound. It had only one road in and out. The road to the camp was four miles long from the only main road, which was another two miles out. The road was heavily guarded. Every mile, guards were stationed with sawed-off rifles and pistols of different types.

There were four rotating video cameras at various locations within a mile radius that sent back video images, but only to the main house. The room to which those images were sent was in a special area in the main house that only Jordan, Paul and the technicians who worked the equipment had access to. It required a code and fingerprint to enter.
A gate was positioned at a three-mile radius that one needed to pass through to continue toward the "cave". Booby traps were planted in the forest at different intervals. There were some even the guards were not aware of. Jordan's level of trust was generally low. Six miles away from the "cave" was a little town with a population of about twelve thousand people.

The community boasted one four-room movie theater, one post office, two grocery stores, including two all-night convenience stores, a fitness gym, three schools for different ages, four department stores, three gas stations, and one police station. Homes, apartments, and condos were scattered within two miles of the downtown area. Most people just walked to the stores. Cars were not really needed unless the citizens ventured outside their community. They had riding vans to help people get around running 24 hours, seven days a week.

Many people in the community had heard about the "cave" but knew not to ask further questions. They were aware there was some type of operation that was going on up there. They kind of loved the idea because they felt more security in their small community.

    Their community are rewarded with generous gifts and they didn't want to push over the apple cart by asking a lot of questions. The mayor interacted with the citizens on a regular basis. He ensured his people that they were in good hands.

CHAPTER FIFTEEN

The ladies were at martial arts training, discussing what to do next with the information they had compiled. Travis was with one of the instructors, doing high kicks.

Tex was on the kicking bag, which weighs seventy pounds and is fourteen inches wide by forty-two inches in length. She was side kicking it to practice on her kicks. She was also wearing quick-strike gloves to do hand smacks. "Tomboys you ladies are doing great work" said Tex in between breaths. "You should be able to make an entrance to the "cave" soon. We do have one problem. The equipment that was planted will be no good if someone redecorate, our eyes or video is blocked. We really need to get someone on the inside to help, the higher up the better. The audio and video bugs will be found out. That is inevitable. Jordan didn't make it to the top by being stupid." She stopped talking and took another swipe at the punching bag.

All four Tomboys are practicing defensive protection like physical defensive moves. Their mission depends on them being fit, furious and dangerous. Pulling weapons was not good in some cases, like when innocent people were around.

Bonnie, a former agent, who now is Tex right hand behind the scenes is jumping rope in between listening and answering questions.

Tex continued, "When the equipment is found, it is important that our person already be inside the house. The first thing he will do is investigate the last few people who joined the group."

"What about Walker?" asked Tyler.

Sighing, Tex said, "He is on his own."

"Jesus, we can't let that happen," said Tyler.

"He is a big boy. He knows the consequences," said Tex. She went back to kicking the bag.

Tyson, who was practicing with two sai, which looked like a long sword with a pointed arch, located on each side the center blade. She was swinging them with fast precision, turning and spinning at the same time.

Travis was beside Tex, working on kicks on a lower hanging bag called a teardrop bag that is used for knee strikes and clinches. She was wearing quick-strike gloves that were in her favorite color, silver.

Teg and Bonnie were doing sit ups on the floor mat together. Their hands were behind their necks and their legs were up a few degrees and they rose up and down, crunching their stomachs.

Tyler was working with nunchucks that are eight inches long with a one-inch diameter width. Nunchucks are wooden sticks connected by a swivel ball bearing chain in the middle for easier and faster rotations.

Bonnie stopped her exercises and said, "Look ladies, Walker is good. He applied for this position. He got the job because it seems like the guards that Tyler encountered liked him and the guy who held that position before is no longer breathing. They might not suspect him at first. That will give us time to help him."

"Unless it's lights out fast," said Tyson.

Everyone turned to look at Tyson. They knew what she meant. They didn't want to be the ones to help an agent lose his life.

"Ouch," said Travis.

"By the way, thanks for the backup," said Tyler to Bonnie.

"Anytime, baby," said Bonnie.

"Teg, you need to step up on Sharron," said Tex.

"I am going out tonight on that business," said Teg.

"Let's hope she has had or has access inside the main house. If she cooperates, she will be a big asset to this mission. Women who are beautiful, have good communication, and good pussy skills go far in this world," said Tex.

"Skills do count for something," said Tyler.

"That's a skill?" Teg asked.

"One that comes in handy now and then," said Tyson.

"I second that," said Travis.

"Case closed," said Bonnie. Everyone laughed.
"I have used those skills myself many times to get me out of hard situations," said Tex.

Everyone snapped their heads towards Tex.

"Whoa Tex, I always knew you were bad. Go girl!" said Travis.

"An ultimate lady at all times as far as I can remember," said Tyler.

Tex looked back and said, "The unexpected always works. In the final analysis, it was me against them."

"I heard that before," said Tyler, looking puzzled, trying to think where and when she had heard it.

"President John F. Kennedy said it during the Vietnam War," said Travis.

"Not quite in that way," said Tyson.

"The meaning is the same. The beginning justifies the end," said Bonnie.

"When it gets down muddy, everything counts. That is what I love about you five. You are willing to get down and dirty," said Tex.

"Okay, we are ready to launch the plan," said Bonnie.

Tex removed her gloves. With towels all started wiping themselves down as they walked toward the back of the training room. Standing around Tex.

Tex clicked on her laptop in front of her, bringing up pictures and notes.

"Let me tell you more about Jordan's personal bodyguards. They are ruthless as hell.

They have no problem using violence as a way of negotiation if necessary. Travis, I need you and Tyson to handle this one.

I found a disc Jordan left behind that had fallen behind his desk. He had been watching these two guys for some time. That tells me he has been planning this move for years," Tex said with an angry look on her face.

"Years?" said Tyson.

"For years," Tex carried on. "They had spent six months in jail and Jordan kept up with them. He even had them released and no one at the station knows where they went".

"A little birdie would say he had stashed them away, cleaned the files, and trained them. That is what most agents do when they need help with a mission, undercover or illegal," said Bonnie.

"I agree," said Travis.

"All is correct. He had their backgrounds erased like they were never born. The only way I know their names is because of this disc. The pictures you see are years old and now they look like this. Thank you, Walker. I need a good informant who can go into the community quietly, and I do mean quietly, to snoop around to see what they can find out. Any ideas, Travis, or Tyson? This is your mission," Tex asked.

Tyson and Travis looked at each other and Travis said, "Yes, we have someone who can be discreet and will fit right in."

"Who?" Teg asked.

"Blackie," said Travis.

"Blackie, you are sure, Travis," said Tyler.

"Sure, as apple pie" Tyson answered. "He is perfect. We have known him for years and he can get the job done, we promise," said Tyson, pointing her finger between her and Travis while she is talking.

"I agree with Tyson and Travis. He is a little off, but I feel he will be perfect for the job. He seems to be able to handle himself," said Bonnie.

"He handled Deuce and tight--ass Arnold," said Tyson.

Agreeing with the ladies, Tyler said, "That he did."

"Okay it is settled. Tyson and Travis will go to Blackie. Teg, you will visit Sharron and Tyler and Bonnie will be at the command center in case you ladies might need help.

I will go into the office to look like I am trying to ease back into my job. Deuce and Arnold smell something and are snooping around and you know the old saying "where there is smoke there is fire" said Tex.

The Tomboys and Bonnie left the room.

Tex stayed at the table thinking with tears in her eyes, *'that coldhearted bastard never loved me.'* Admitting that she was a sucker all those years was hard. She asked herself why. She had no power or upper-level job that could help him advance when they met. She kept asking herself *'why her?'* She promised herself she would find out and then put a bullet straight through his skull.

Bonnie was hiding behind the door, watching her dear friend suffer.

She said to herself, 'Don't worry, my friend. Jordan is going down no matter his reason. I am going to instruct the Tomboys when it is feasible to take him out.**

CHAPTER SIXTEEN

A man was sitting on the last seat in the last car of the metro train. No one noticed he had been riding for hours. A lady entered the train needing to know the time and noticed the man was wearing a watch on his right wrist. She walked over to the man.

"Sir, may I ask what time it is?" the woman asked.
No answer came from the man. Something looked strange.

The woman noticed that his eyes were closed but her instincts told her to check him. She reached over and tapped him lightly on the shoulder. The man's body fell forward with blood oozing out of his neck. She let out a loud scream. His work ID fell out of his front pocket shirt.

His name was Jake Dexter. It was not a name that would cause alarm to the people at the metro station…

A woman's body was thrown from her balcony. Her husband had been tortured in the house and his body was lying in a pool of blood on their living room floor. Her body hit the cement ground with a loud thump. She had been thrown from eighteen floors above from her and her husband's condo balcony. Her husband's dead body followed her within two minutes, after it was clear no one heard or saw her fall to her death.

Their names were Alice and Rob Adams…

Lying in an alley where people were walking back and forth on the sidewalk was a body that had a cutthroat from ear to ear. No one noticed the body because it was around 11:30 PM and it was dark outside. The man's name was Matt…

***

In a convenience store, Noah was picking up beer for the card game back at his friend's apartment. He had lost the bet and he had to pay the next round. He had a case of beer in his arm when a shadow came from behind him and shot him in the neck. The case of beer dropped from his arms as he went down. Knowing he was being attacked, he didn't make a move. He just hoped the person that shot him would think he was dead.

A few seconds passed before he heard footsteps moving away from him. While on the floor, he was praying to God that he didn't stop breathing. The assassin used a silencer, so no one heard a shot.
Outside the store, two men in a kale green Challenger were laughing and sped off down the road.
No one was a witness to the shooting because the cashier was in the back getting supplies. He knew Noah like a brother and asked him to watch the store.

He always gave Noah a discount on the beer since he bought so much. He had teased him that he needed to stop betting because he always lost the bets. The cashier came back from the storage area and looked for Noah.
"Noah! Noah!" the cashier yelled.

Getting no answer, he started walking around the store and looking. He knew Noah would not have left with stolen beer.
Hearing his friend call his name, Noah felt it was safe for him to move. He got up with blood running down his neck. The cashier stopped in his tracks because before him was his friend coming toward him with blood gushing out of his neck, running down his shirt.
The cashier was in shock.
"What happened?" he asked, breathing hard and looking around to see if the attackers were still in the store.
With heavy breaths, Noah said, "Nothing, and you haven't seen anything. Understand?" Holding his hand up to his neck where blood was running between his fingers and onto his shirt, he continued, "Look, I need something to wrap around my neck."
In shock, the cashier didn't move.
"Hey!" said Noah as loud as he could.
He paused because that hurt his vocal cords. Bending down a little on the counter, Noah gently pulled his head up. He was breathing deeply now. With his eyes, he told the cashier to please help him. The cashier snapped to attention and ran to the back of the store.
He returned in seconds with a sheet he and others used to take naps in the back.
With all his strength, he tore the sheet one long strip, so it could be wrapped around Noah's neck. The cashier couldn't believe that this guy was not dead from all the blood.
After tearing the strip, he helped Noah wrap it around his neck, the cashier said, "Man, I have to call the police, or my boss will get me."

Grabbing the cashier's arm with all his might, Noah gave the cashier a hard look and whispered, "Then you will die."
Pulling loose from Noah's grip, the cashier understood.

Knowing not to ask any more questions, he told Noah, "You need a doctor".
He watched Noah leave his store and get into his car and drive off. How he was driving was beyond him.

He ran to the front door and locked it. He went back into the storage and went to a secret room. He pushed a button and rewound the security tape. On the tape, he saw a man enter the store in all black. The man was looking around and stopped when he saw Noah getting a case of beer out the cold storage area through the store mirror. He walked really fast up to Noah's back and pulled out a gun and shot him. He looked at the body for a few seconds then quickly walked back out of the store. The body was left bleeding on the floor. Next, the cashier saw himself walk from the back and yelling Noah's name.

'Holy shit' the cashier said, sighing, as took out the disc and slipped it into his shirt pocket. *'Evidence to save our lives'* he whispered.

He reached over and grabbed a hammer that was sitting on a shelf. He lightly and carefully broke the machine. With no machine working, no taping could have been done.

He then went over to the sink and cut on the water. He next grabbed a bucket, some Clorox, and some cleaning liquid to clean every area where Noah had bled.

Back in their Challenger, Pie and Radio were happy with their day's work. They had contacted Jordan with the news.

Pie smiled and said to Radio, "That was invigorating."

Radio smiled back at Pie and gave him a high five and said, "You forgot one thing."

"What?" asked Pie?

"The beer, dawg," said Radio.

"Damn." Pie made a sharp left and their bodies turned to the left in the car. Straightening up from the sharp turn, he said, "On me, dawg."

"Look, a liquor store in front of us," said Radio.

Pie slid into a parking space to get the beer and snacks.

***

Tex was in her kitchen with Bonnie cooking some fried chicken, mashed potatoes, collard greens, and biscuits. Both had decided they were going off their diets tonight.

The news was playing in the background while they were sitting at the table sipping wine. The newscaster was talking about two bodies found outside on the sidewalk in front of a condo complex. The newscaster said the male body had been tortured before being tossed off the balcony. The woman seemed to have died from the impact of being thrown off the balcony. Behind the newscaster was a video showing one body at a time being pushed into an ambulance in body bags. Their names were Mrs. Alice Adams and Mr. Rob Adams.

When the names were said, Bonnie jumped up from her seat and went to the folders that were on the counter. She flipped through them fast. Suddenly she stopped and turned to look at Tex, who had been watching her, and said, "Damn, houses are being clean. Those two people were at the poker games at the main house."

"Damn," said Tex. "We have to move faster."
The newscaster moved onto the next story. *'A body was found in an alley near the intersection of Coaster and Flock Streets this morning by a person walking their dog. The man's throat had been slit. There was no identity at this time.... A fourth fatality this evening occurred when a body was found shot in the throat on a metro train. It seems that the man had been riding for some time before it was noticed that he been shot. Per his ID, the man's name was Jake Dexter. This has been an unbelievably bad night in our town. Moving on to better news...'*

"I can only guess they were at the poker games?" Tex asked, sipping from her wine glass.

Bonnie just stared back at her, telling Tex she was right.

"OMG," Tex said, bowing her head. "Pass this on to the girls. We can cross their names off the list."

Bonnie came back to the table and pulled her cell phone out of her purse and sent an encrypted message to the Tomboys.

***

The music at the disco was pumping. Sweaty bodies were everywhere. The drinks were flowing like crazy. At a back table, Tyler and Tyson were watching the action in front of them.

Tyson was on edge because there were so many different flavors of candy in there. She couldn't decide who to approach first.

Tyler surprised her by saying, "Don't fret, just go for one and if he doesn't work, try another flavor."

Tyson was beginning to really like her. She gave Tyler a huge smile.

Travis was on the dance floor busting moves with a guy.

Teg was at a separate table with Sharron. She lucked out and realized that they both had the same hairdresser. Sharron had come into the salon when Teg was getting her hair done.

Her hairdresser Tim introduced them, and they began talking like they had known each other for years. Teg told her about her fashion shows.

Sharron squealed and said, "I knew who you were the moment we locked eyes. Oh my God, I am meeting THE famous designer!" She latched onto Teg like she would to any big or famous person.

When Teg's hair was done, she stayed behind to talk while Tim did Sharron's hair. "I have a ticket for front row seat at my collection in New York in February. Would you like to go?" Teg asked.

Thrilled, Sharron almost fell out of the chair.

Grinning, she answered, "I would love to go. Yes, yes, yes!" pumping both of her fists in the air.

Tim, the hairdresser, put his hand on his hip and looked at Teg.

Looking at him, Teg said, "Tim, you are invited every year automatically, so do not look at me like that."

Looking hurt, Tim said, "I would like to be invited like everyone else, dear."

"Tim, would you like to go to my February show?" Teg asked.

"Yes, yes, yes!" said Tim, running around the chair holding Sharron.

Teg and Sharron bust out laughing.

"You are so stupid, but I have to go," said Teg.

With glee, Sharron returned the favor. "Teg, would you join me at Club Barney tonight?"

"Love to," said Teg.

Looking back at Tim, Sharron said, "Sorry, I know you have a hair show and need to get ready love. We can meet up another time," pointing toward her and Teg.

"Yes darling, and the party will really start," said Tim.

Shaking her head and leaving, Teg said, "Bye! Sharron, come to my place so that we can dress together. I have some samples at my place that will look good on you."

Happy, she asks "What time?"

Teg answered, "Around 9 PM, I'll text you the address." Kisses was thrown as Teg left the salon.

Sharron, who had been sick lately, was glad she decided to pull herself out of the house to get her hair done. She had met a famous designer.

Outside the salon, which was located in a mall, Teg called Bonnie.

When she answered, Teg said, "Bonnie, I need an apartment with some clothes because I invited Sharron back to try on some of my creations".

Bonnie said, "I have an apartment located at 4400 Flour Court, Condo number three. What time will you be arriving?"

Teg said, "Around 8 tonight."

"That is short notice. It is about 5 now," said Bonnie.

"Tell you what, I will suggest some dinner and that will give you about another two hours," said Teg.

"Okay, 10 tonight. I am on it," said Bonnie.

Teg hung up her phone and turned to go back into the salon to tell Sharron to meet her at a restaurant first. She stopped in her tracks because she was right behind her.

Smiling, Teg said, "How about we get something to eat before we go back to my place?"

"Okay, my favorite restaurant over there, "Sharron says, pointing to her left.

"I have to go to another appointment first. Let's meet around eight tonight," said Teg.

"Eight tonight is fine. I can't wait to wear one of your creations," said Sharron.

Smiling, Teg answered, "Everyone does, my dear," and walked away.

Sharron was tickled pink standing there and watching Teg walk away, as happy as a little lamb. As she was walking, Teg realized that since she didn't resist, she didn't hear the conversation she was having on her cell phone. *'Close one'*

***

Later that night, they were sitting at a table at Club Barney and having a blast.

Teg was wearing a silk white and red dress. The dress was mainly white with a little red in the design. She had on a ruby and diamond pin, shaped like a starburst. The ruby was in the middle with the diamonds surrounding it. The ruby was really a video and audio device that would send information to the computer at the secret room and other places if asked. Sharron commented on the loveliness of the pin. Teg told her it was a birthday gift from her ex.
She had chosen a purple wrap dress from Teg's collection that gathered at the waist. On each shoulder was a design of purple studs. her black hair up off her shoulders, held up with large purple barrettes. Each lady had on four-inch shoes, Teg's red and Sharron's purple. Teg loved it when the body wore the clothes and not the other way around.

Teg did the usual girl talk to ease Sharron into a state of confidence. Teg had told her about the no-good man she threw out of her life about a month ago.

Sharron couldn't believe a famous woman like Teg would have man trouble. She soaked up everything that was being said. She would have to repeat it to her other girlfriends when she saw them. Right now, they were all envious of her being with Teg but could not come.

After a couple of drinks, her tongue became as loose as Teg wanted. She started weeping talking about how a dear friend of hers had been killed in a plane crash.

Teg reached over and put her arm around her, telling her, "It will be okay."

"It will never be okay. I think he was murdered."

Looking surprised, Teg said, "Didn't you say he was on a plane?".

"Yes, him and over three hundred other people,".

"Girl, my head is a little woozy here tonight and I'm not comprehending what you are saying. somebody took the plane out,".

"Yes".

"Oh my God, who would do such a mean thing?".

"A very mean man,".

"You know him?".

"Yes, but I am afraid of him and will never say his name in public. He has spies all over the world,".

"I don't think he has spies here".

Putting up her hands in a stop action, Sharron, pointed at a waitress and said, "That can be a spy for him."
Teg looked at who she was pointing to, then turned back around to nod at Sharron.
It became too painful for Sharron to continue to talk, so she just sipped her drink.
Teg decided she had made some good leeway and would not push more tonight.
"I am sorry you are afraid of this person. I can assume that you can't get away from him?" Teg asked.
Shaking, she answered "Not breathing. No one leaves this man and lives to talk."
Teg shook her head and took a sip from her drink.

Travis returned to the table where Tyson and Tyler had been sitting, catching a glimpse of what was going on at Teg's table. The lady seems upset, but Teg seems to have it under control".
Tyler and Tyson moved to the bar, when two guys sitting there were looking at them hard.
One said, "Hey baby, would you two ladies like the company of real men tonight?"
Tyson looked at Tyler and said, "Did he say 'heeye' like horses?"
Before Tyler could answer, one of the men came closer and said, "Baby, I have your horse," grabbing his jewels.
Tyson looked down at it and said, "Looks limited to me."
"Puny," said Tyler.
Indignantly, the guy said, "This is prime meat, ladies."
Laughing, Tyler and Tyson grabbed their drinks from the bartender and began to leave the bar area.
The guy didn't give up so easily. He said, "You two ladies sure you don't want to taste?"
Tyson turned and said, "Bug the fuck off!"
His friend at the bar, who was on his sixth drink, said, "I told you them bitches are getting brave since those two damn men named Tyler Perry and Steve Harvey start telling our manly secrets."
"I hate the both of them," his friend replied.
"I have to admit one thing. They are getting filthy rich off our asses," said his friend.
Sipping from his drink, his friend nodded in agreement.
"But some things need to be kept secret. We had those bitches right where we needed them. *"Controlled"*.

109

His friend again nodded in agreement. Finishing his drink, he waved to the bartender for another round.

Tyler and Tyson arrived at their table where Travis was waiting.

"Problems, ladies?" asked Travis.

Giving Travis her drink, Tyler answered, "Nothing we couldn't handle."

"Those two guys looked pissed when you two left the bar," said Travis.

"Assholes," said Tyson.

"Okay, I see Teg and Sharron at four o'clock" said Tyler.

Travis and Tyson looked at the table. The lady is wiping away tears, all wonder what was up. They would ask Teg later.

A guy walked up to the table and asked Tyler to dance. She accepted the invitation and left the table. The music was bumping, and the floor was crowded.

Guys came up and asked the ladies to dance. Sometimes girls came up to the table to try to join or ask them dance. Tyson had no problem dancing with a couple of ladies. While they had no problem with this, Travis and Tyler preferred just men. They never let their dance partners join them at the table, telling them straight out "no".

Most understood and the ones that didn't received the brush off with a hard look of some kind by whomever was at the table at the time. Getting the message, they moved on.

All were having a good time.

Back at the table, Travis was asked by Tyson, "What is the temperature on the floor?"

"A hundred and eighty degrees," Travis said.

"Burning up?" said Tyler.

"On fire," said Tyson.

All giggled.

"I wonder is Teg getting any Intel?" Tyson asked.

"I'm sure, she is working it" said Tyler.

"The table is looking like they are the best of friends" said Tyson.

All looked at the table.

A handsome guy walked by the table. The Tomboys all watched him pass.

"Sweet cheeks," said Tyson.

"Small waist and heavy in the front," said Tyler.

"Girls, girls, eyes on the prize at the other table," said Travis.

"Uh hum," Tyson and Tyler said at the same time.

Ignoring Travis, they cracked their heads to see the guy stop at the bar. He went to another guy and kissed him on the mouth.

"Bite me," said Tyson.

"Oh well, he was just going to be a plaything," said Tyler.

Travis and Tyson turned to look at Tyler. She just hunched both her shoulders up signifying *so what* and took a sip from her glass.

Travis had met a guy who was nodding *let's go* in her direction. Travis turned to Tyler and Tyson and said, "Ladies, I am done for the night. See that nice piece of candy at the bar?" pointing to a guy who was about six-foot-two with a six-pack showing underneath his shirt, hazel eyes, golden brown skin, and white perfect teeth. "Well, I have not fed my nest in a long time. I asked him to keep his snake in the cage and I will be right back after telling my girls I am leaving. So, bye ladies," she said, as she downed her drink and got up from the table.

"What about Teg?" Tyler asked.

Looking over at the table, Travis answered, "Looks like she is okay to me. Bye!"

Tyson grabbed her arm and said, "Travis, give me some facts like ingredients in a salad in case I don't hear from you."

Travis said, "Shaun White, 555-222-2323, 824 Running Pl, six-two, about two hundred-forty pounds, and expensive chocolate."

"Good girl," said Tyson.

Being an agent did have some perks. She had looked him up while in the bathroom around an hour ago. Today's world information comes instantly.

Travis turned to smile at Shaun at the bar and mouthed, "Two seconds."

Shaun gave thumbs up.

"Looks freaky to me," said Tyler.

"Hey, I love freaky" said Travis.

"Does he know that?" asked Tyler.

"Since when do that matter? He's just candy," Tyson replied.

Shaking her head, Tyler said "It never does".

Teg looked at the table that Tyler and Tyson were sitting and took her thumb and smoothed down her left eyebrow, which told all is good.

Checkmate

CHAPTER SEVENTEEN

    Blackie drove along the highway in his orange 1959 Electra 225 Buick car, also called a deuce & quarter, on his left was a breathtaking ocean. The road ran ten miles before crossing the main bridge into Herr, California. The water was clear blue, like you would see in magazines and brochures. The bridge was two miles long with large, rocky cliffs blocking the view of the ocean. At the end, there was a big sign on the right that says, "Welcome to Herr, California. Population: 48,000." On the left, was the first building in the town that had a large display on top that showed the time. Underneath, the display showed a weather forecast: 72 degrees with light winds. Next door is a warehouse where people worked to make pillows, stoves, and all kinds of paper goods. The town was supported by these human-made goods, which were shipped all over the world.

    About a block of land separated the next sets of buildings, such as car repair shops and hardware stores. It seemed like the townspeople liked to keep the noise and stink far away from the civilized part of town because one had to go another ten miles before hitting civilization.

An orange "deuce and a quarter" with four donut tires containing silver, spiked rims on a special, levitated lift, pulled into the Herr community. Townsfolk were looking at the car as it slowly moved down Main Street. It was odd to see a car like that in this area.

Blackie was inside with all four windows down, rocking to music on the radio. He smiled, waving to the people he was passing by on the sidewalk while singing the words to the song that was playing on the radio.

    He mostly waved at women. Some waved back and some just giggled at him because of his car. Most were curious who he was. Blackie pulled his car to the curb and parked. He got out and started walking around the town's Main Street, taking test pictures. He needed to send images back to Travis and Tyson, so he was equipped with a special camera on the bling necklace he was wearing. He wore an emblem in the shape of a large king's crown that held eight diamonds, two rubies, and two navy blue diamonds on a large silver rope around his neck.

    The two navy blue diamonds contained equipment for video and audio recording.

    Knowing that people's eyes would automatically go toward the rare blue diamonds, the twins knew they could get close-up shots of faces, so they could be identified and cross-checked.

He walked slowly like he was sightseeing, sending back the town's sights and people.

After about two hours of walking, he had worked his way back to where he parked the car. Blackie was dressed in all white. It was what he called his friendly color. He had on an all--white light towel cloth jumpsuit with a white T-shirt underneath and white sneakers. Underneath the large silver rope was a medium length silver chain, about two inches thick, around his neck with the letter "B" hanging from the bottom of the chain. It was a prized gift that was given to him by his mom before she died. A white baseball hat topped off his outfit.
Blackie was hungry from all that walking and saw a restaurant up to his left.

He walked into the front door of the restaurant and stopped to look around. It was half-full, from what he could see. A hostess came up to him and asked, "How may I help you?"

Blackie had seen her from out of the corner of his eye and said, "You can go out with me or better yet, have my next baby."

The hostess laughed at the stranger.

Blackie laughed and said, "Sorry. Seriously, you can guide me to your best table."

Smiling, she replied, "This way, sir."

She turned to guide Blackie to a table with a great view. He could see down Main Street and the entire restaurant's interior. Blackie, wearing the special equipment, was now sending images of the inside of the restaurant back to the computer.

To the right of him, about three tables down, sat Pie and Radio, who had been flirting with the ladies who worked there, while having a meal. They didn't notice Blackie. Blackie did take notice of the laughter in the distance, two punks who didn't know how to treat ladies. The guys were openly tapping the waitresses on their buttocks as they passed by their table. The waitress jumped every time and the two guys laughed with glee.

***

Back at the Command Center, all eyes were on the guys. Blackie had just sent them some good information. They kept their eyes and ears open on Pie and Radio.

"Nasty little bastards," said Tyler.

"Well, the ladies aren't fighting hard," said Teg.
"Maybe they leave good tips," said Travis.
"Or they know their reputations," said Bonnie.
"I wouldn't give a fuck. They would have been slapped," said Tyson.
"We need Blackie to follow them to see where they lead him to," said Tex, ignoring the conversation just spoken.
Tyson pulled out her cell phone to text Blackie.
"Wait…, I have another idea. Bonnie, text Walker. He is better trained for them two monsters," said Tex.
Tyson put her cell phone down and Bonnie picked hers up.
Bonnie sent a text to Walker instructing him to follow Pie and Radio, along with pictures, location of the restaurant, and a warning that they were extremely dangerous.
Within seconds, Walker texted back, "I love danger. On it."
Bonnie laughed and told the girls, "Walker is worse than you four Tomboys. I promise he will go down fighting."
"Yes, my son after four girls," said Tex, smiling.
"Goodie, a brother!" said Tyson.
"Older or younger?" Tyler asked.
"Does it really matter?" Teg asked.
"Yes," said Tyler.
"I want to know if he is blood related," Tyson asked.
"Ladies, eyes on the prize, remember? And no Tyson, he is not candy to lick and throw away," said Tex.
"Bummer," said Tyson.
All laughed.
"What is Blackie's cover?" asked Bonnie.
Travis answered, "Blackie's cover is a salesman for the new cable company. Bonnie, when you told Tyson and me the town was so old, they are just getting cable and internet service, we told Blackie to apply for a salesman for the company."
"Yeah, he impressed the hell out of the recruiter. He was hired on the spot" said Tyson.
"That man can sell a heater to anyone in Arizona," said Travis.
"It was a perfect fit," said Tyson.
"He knows how cable works and can hook it up because he's been stealing it for years," said Travis.
"Per Blackie, his boys taught him how to reconnect and not be noticed by the company if caught stealing," said Tyson.

"Blackie will only sale the products, not hook up the service" said Travis.

"Good. Then he will sound legit in case someone gets suspicious," said Tex.

"Yes, a lot of people are going down fast, Tomboys," said Bonnie.

"No shit," said Teg.

"The couple thrown out the window, the metro rider, and the guy in the alley," said Tyler.

"And more that we probably haven't heard of yet or haven't been killed yet. I want everyone in here be on their 'A' game," said Tex.

***

Six blocks down the street from the restaurant, Noah was hiding out with his friend Akers.

Akers knew a doctor who did house calls for a fee.

Noah had not been able to talk for about two weeks and had to be fed intravenously until his neck healed. He figured out who shot him because he had been watching the news.

He put two and two together because the other people who had died were at the poker game parties. He knew he was in great danger.

Pie and Radio were not happy to hear he was not dead. They had gone back to the store to search for evidence of the shooting and the body. A different cashier from the other who found Noah was in that day and was shaking in his pants. He had no idea what the two guys who were pointing guns at him were asking.

"What happened to the body?" Pie asked, pointing his gun at the cashier's cheek.

The cashier answered, "I was off that day and didn't know about anybody or who worked that day."

"Look motherfucker, I know you heard about the shooting, so what happened after the police came?" Radio asked, putting his gun by the cashier's other cheek.

Scared to death, the cashier slowly explained by saying, "It is hard to keep workers, so my boss can hire someone on the spot and put them right to work. I don't know everyone who works here."

Pie and Radio believed his story. The guy was shaking so bad, not to mention he was pissing in his pants. He couldn't be lying.

Radio asked, "Is there any video equipment?"

The cashier said, "Yes, in the back," pointing to a door.

"Show us," said Pie, using his gun to point toward the door.

Radio and Pie, guns still drawn, walked toward the door with the cashier. The cashier was walking slowly. He didn't know if they were going to kill him in the back of the store, but he followed instructions. He hoped someone came into the store to save him. Normally, the place was visited every five minutes, but not today. *Damn.*

They went through the door and to the right was the video equipment. The cashier pointed toward the video equipment.

Radio kept his gun on the cashier while Pie examined the equipment.

Pie turned to Radio and said, "It is not operational."

"Sure? Or we will be damned?" Radio asked.

"Sure. It is broken like someone cracked it up," said Pie.

"Maybe the person who was here broke it and has the tape," said Radio, pushing his gun at the cashier's head.

"No, someone robbed us three weeks ago and the owner hasn't had it fixed yet. Remember? It was all over the news," the cashier said, stuttering his words.

"Wait, I remember the incident," said Pie.

Silence fell on the back room for a few seconds.

For the cashier, it felt like it was several minutes of torture.

Quietly, Radio and Pie left the area.

The cashier stood there for a few minutes, shaking. Looking down, he noticed he had pissed in his pants.

***

Blackie finished his meal and left the restaurant. He got back into his car and drove to the hotel to check in. He was given a key to room 330. Entering the room, he noticed the curtains were open and light was filling the room. He dropped his bags and walked toward the sliding doors and looked out. He had a spectacular view of the whole town and the clear blue sea that stretched from one end of the town to the other. The town was surrounded by an eight-foot-high brick stone wall to protect it from floods. The hotel was located at one end of the town. When he opened the door, and stepped out on the balcony, he felt a cool breeze.

Blackie put his head back, closed his eyes, and let the breeze entice his body, making a mental note to himself. *'Later, get my favorite drink and come back to this balcony and enjoy this great weather.'*

This was a small town, so the hotel had only ten floors with about ten rooms per floor and it was quiet. He had time to sleep for about four hours, then he got up, showered, and put on a brown suit with a beige shirt, brown tie, and beige loafers.

Blackie was a five-foot-nine, one-hundred-and-sixty-pound, brown-skinned man with black hair kept in a short perm that laid his hair down towards his shoulder. He had expressive black eyes and beautiful white teeth with a killer smile.

He added the final touch to his outfit. It was a silver tie pin, two-and-a-half inches wide and two inches long, and a copy of his favorite silver chain given to him by his mother, but this one contained the video and audio equipment. He shook his head about the way the undercover world could film and tape you with all kinds of tricky equipment. He will never trust anything people were wearing ever again in his life. He tested the equipment, as he was taught by Tyson by sending a code through his cell phone. He received a return text message saying, "Happy birthday." He knew everything was okay.

He left the hotel room and went to his orientation as one of the new salespeople in the area for the new cable company.

Blackie arrived at the new cable headquarters and was directed by the receptionist to the conference room where the new recruits were waiting. He walked into the room and there were several people in the room. He introduced himself to the ones near him and they introduced themselves. He found out that one lady was the person who would put in the orders as the salesmen call them in. Two guys were in charge of making sure the cable signal frequency was correct by flying over areas of the city because a high signal would interfere with other electronic equipment like planes.

Another lady was a salesman for the business division of the cable company. Blackie would be doing residential work. The last lady in the room was there just for orientation. She will be working in another part of California as a manager of the call center.
They all introduced themselves to each other and shook hands. They all passed the time talking about how great the weather was in this part of California.

Blackie told them about the food at the restaurant and they all vowed to go together for lunch or dinner before the training was over.

At that time, the instructor came into the room. He introduced himself as Clayton Deeds, a representative of the new cable company. He was there today to go over their job duties. Another guy walked into the room with a laptop under his arm and a briefcase in his other hand.

Clayton taking a seat, looked up as the door open and said, "This is Len."

Len waved to everyone.

Clayton continues "He will be helping out today. We have a long day ahead of us, so let's get started."

Each new hire was given a notebook with a lot of information including important numbers that would help them.

Clayton said, "You can read the notebook's contents at their leisure, they all would start on their jobs within one week". He stopped and asked, "Is that a problem with anyone here?"

No one said no.

Shaking his head signifying *okay*, he continued with his speech.

"Len is passing out information you will need...," said Clayton.

Len started passing out notebooks with each person's name on the front, along with two pens and a notepad for notes. When finished, he continues to setup the laptop to show slides.

Clayton said, "Hold on a moment, folks."

Blackie, who was sitting to Clayton's left, opened his notebook and flipped through it casually. Others did as well because Clayton was referring with Len.

Commission only, no salary, damn, if nothing else, he was a great salesperson. He had done it all his life to survive since he had no parents or family to help him since the age of fifteen.

He could sell ice to an Eskimo if need be.

Clayton returned his attention to the people sitting in front of him and started talking about the history of the company. "This company started in 1948 in Pennsylvania by two ambitious men who were tired of looking at regular TV...."

***

All of this was translating back to the computer, which was being watched closely by Bonnie, giving her ideas. The guy sitting to Blackie's right looked familiar to her. She was thinking hard... *Where...?* She jumped out of the chair as if it were jet-propelled and went toward the file cabinet. Flipping through folders, she stopped at the one labeled "Poker Players" and pulled it out. She flipped through the pictures, then stopped and pulled one out. She put down the folder on the table and went for a magnifying glass. She waved it over the picture. *Bingo.* His name was Akers, a friend of one of the pokers players still alive. She needed to get a message to

Blackie. She picked up her cell phone that was on the desk by the computer and called Tyson.

"Tyson, we need to get a message to Blackie. Watching the feed, he was in the room right now with Akers, and he needs to befriend him, he is one of the surviving poker players friend," said Bonnie.

"On it, Bonnie. Sending the text now," said Tyson.
Tyson texted Blackie. She hoped he followed instructions and cut off his cell phone, so the beep couldn't be heard.

Bonnie watched the action on screen. She noticed Blackie didn't blink, nor did anyone else in the room. *'Okay, he will get the message when he cuts back on his phone.'*

The orientation was over around one o'clock.

It has been a long day, so everyone went back to their hotel rooms. Blackie cut on his cell phone when he reached his room.
"Oh shit," he said.
Befriend a guy name Ackers, Why? He will follow Tyson's instructions. *'That guy is cool, a little reserved, but hell that is nothing'*, he thought.

He talked to him more than anyone else in the room. Akers suggested they go to the restaurant together. Blackie was glad he agreed. That will give him time to sound him out.
Blackie went to the phone on his room's desk and ordered a bottle of Hennessey. After all, it was on the house. He liked it on the rocks, cold.

After hanging up the phone, he pulled out his notebook to go over the material because he decided the day's events would be a go-to for starting a conversation with Akers, and then he could ease into his personal life. He had least one-week time to get next to Akers before his new job shipped him out to another location. Blackie picked up his hotel room phone. "Akers, let's meet up around four o'clock."

"Great, I am bored," replied Akers, who was also afraid to be in his room alone.

A cool, beautiful night at the restaurant, Blackie was wearing a pair of gray jeans with a dark gray casual sweater that zipped down the middle. The sweater had a design on the left side of the chest of a fish hanging downward like it was jumping in the water. The fish was silver, in a side view that showed one diamond eye. The diamond eye was the camera and video feed for the main computer. An extra piece of material surrounded the area to hold what was a slightly heavy camera compared to that type of sweater material.

Blackie ordered two glasses of Hennessey. He explained to the waitress he had a friend coming and she could direct him to the table when he arrived.

The waitress said, "Okay," and left to fill his order. Blackie took the time to survey the area. Everything looked and smelled okay.

He was glad he could order his favorite drink. Normally, restaurants only had wines or champagne. Both made him gag. Akers was coming through the door when his drink came to the table. The waitress was guiding Akers toward Blackie's table. He was wearing loose blue jeans with a white T-shirt with a blue check mark on his left shoulder, along with navy blue high-top sneakers with the laces untied. He smiled when he saw his new friend. He liked Blackie from the beginning and thought he was funny. He liked to be around positive people because negative people put him in a bad mood. His best friend Noah had been like that since he was shot.

Akers reached the table, Blackie got up, and both greeted each other with a handshake.

"What's up, my man?" said Blackie, who sat back down.

"I am doing great. I have a job, finally," said Akers, as he pulled out his chair to sit down.

"Yes, I like everything about this company, hey, look man, I ordered you a drink," said Blackie, pointing to the other Hennessey.

Akers took a sip and smiled. "It is my favorite too".

"Mines too. So, you will be flying a plane for the company? What is that all about?" Blackie asked.

"Well, I don't actually fly the plane, I'll just be sitting there working some equipment," said Akers.

Looking puzzled, Blackie said, "Equipment? What kind?"

Taking another sip, Akers said, "You see, by law any company that depends on signal frequencies has a level of signal they can send out."

"What does that matter? It doesn't interfere with human ears," said Blackie.

Laughing and taking another sip from his glass, Akers said, "You are funny Blackie, but it is important that other devices like planes, radios, and protection equipment can do their jobs without interference. If the frequency is too high, they will not work or go off prematurely."

"Damn a bomb can get a wrong signal and take off?" Blackie asked in a panicked tone.

Putting one hand up in a "stop" motion, Akers said, "Slow your roll, my man. I believe our government has a safety net for something like that not to happen."

Indignantly, Blackie said, "You don't know your government well, some people working for them have a degree but no brain".

Akers laughed. Blackie joined him.

The waitress came by the table. "Would you two like to order?"

"I recommend the veal and spaghetti," said Blackie.

"I will take that," said Akers smiling.

Blackie went back to Akers, asking, "Who is flying the plane? Maybe he will let me go up. I have been interested in taking flying lessons."

"Really don't know him, we meet for the first time at our orientation. I will see him tomorrow to go over details, so we can tighten up the procedures. My understanding from him is that there is an area that we can fly over only one time per the owner's permission. The company had to fill out special papers to get a special permit to fly over this area.

The pilot says the owner is some big man and the Mayor, who is his friend, was the only one who could persuade him to let us fly over".

"I don't understand the reason behind the Mayor's involvement?" Blackie asked.

"Man, these people who have money and what they call power don't go by our rules. They have their own," said Akers.

"Yeah, I agree. I have my own too," Blackie said, smartly.

Akers laughed.

***

At the Command Center the whole conversation was being listen to by everyone.

"He is good," said Tyler.

"I have an idea. Why don't we hook up a video camera to the plane and when he goes over that area the owner had to give special permission and take some aerial pictures?" said Travis.

"I bet that special place is the cave" says Bonnie.

"You think he is talking about Jordan's place? Teg asked.

"Yes, he would be the only one who will object to aerial flyover," said Travis.

"I agree, but how will we put the camera on the plane without Akers and the pilot knowing?" Teg asked. "Wait a minute; we need one of them to click the button for the camera to start.

We can't do an automatic start," said Tyson.

"We can program the camera to automatically click the moment the plane takes off. We can separate the good from the bad after we get the film," said Travis.

"I have a feeling about this guy Akers and been watching him with Blackie. I have a feeling we can trust him," said Tyler.

"NO, we can't take the chance and involved other people" says Bonnie.

"Agree, let's wire another camera to automatic take pictures," said Tyson.

"Walker, who is in place, can handle that," said Bonnie.

"Akers will never know" said Teg.

Attentions went back to the talking on the live feed.

***

You live alone?" asks Blackie.

"No" said Akers.

"Noah, my best friend, lives with me and needs a job. He did get a called back by the company, but he had to turn them down," Akers said.

Blackie looked at him in puzzlement, then asked, "Why are you staying at the hotel?"

Akers waved the waitress over and said, "This round on me."

Blackie didn't object. He liked free stuff.

Akers gave the order to the waitress, "Two more Hennessey's on the rocks."

The waitress said, "Back in a jiffy."

Both smiled at her.

Behind the waitress, another one was coming toward their table with their food.

They waited until the food had been delivered before continuing their conversation.

Blackie brought the conversation back while he started cutting his veal.

"Why are you staying at the hotel if you live in town?"

Looking serious and playing with an empty glass, Akers said, "Because I am afraid to stay at my own place."

Blackie lifted his left eyebrow, signifying *what?*

Akins didn't touch his food. Deep down, he was not hungry; he just wanted to drink his problems away.

Being friendly, Blackie asked, "Anything I can do to help?"

"No one can help with this. One day I get a bloody friend show up at my doorstep and I'm afraid for my life."

"Life is a bitch," said Blackie.

"Up one moment and down the next, man. I don't know what to do," said Akers.

***

Everyone back at the secret room, loved this conversation. They couldn't believe that the only person Blackie befriended was one of the surviving poker players friend.
"Where is Noah?" Tyson barked at the screen.

***

On cue, Blackie asked Akers, "Where is your friend Noah?"
"Hiding for his life, but I can't tell you where man, for two reasons. One, I shouldn't be talking about this and two, it will get both of us killed."
Looking at Blackie for the first time since he had been talking, Akers was about to say something else, but the waitress came back with their drinks.

***

At the Command Center, Teg said, "What fucking timing."

***

The showman side of Blackie grabbed the waitress' hand, smiled, and said, "Keep them coming, darling." She felt the paper against the palm of her hand and understood the request. Nodding her head, she said, "Sure sir," and left the table.
Blackie turned his attention back to Akers who was sipping his drink and said, "You were saying?"
"No more, man," said Akers.
Blackie decided not to push.
He said softly, "Everything is going to be okay, man. You believe in a higher up?"
"Yes, I do," said Akers, taking another sip of his drink.
Blackie felt sorry for this shaking, nervous guy in front of him whom he noticed had not touched his food.

***

Back at the Command Center, the Tomboys were brainstorming.

"We need Blackie to get that guy to give his location so we can see if his friend Noah has any information," said Tyler.

"Or we can have him followed. He needs to go home sooner or later," said Tyson.

Looking at Bonnie, who was sitting in the room with the Tomboys, Teg said, "Looks like another job for Walker since he is in the area."

"Acknowledged, will send him a message now," said Bonnie, who left her seat.

Tyler said, "I will help get the right equipment for the flyover ready and will look up the hanger that supplies the planes and see how the equipment can be attached to the plane without notice."

"Travis and I have to visit Herr to see Blackie, so we can get more information on Noah and Akers" said Tyson.

"I will inform Walker of you two visiting and what I need him to do," said Bonnie.

Tyson sent a message to Blackie saying, "Call in as soon as you can, Travis and I will be visiting soon."

Blackie excused himself from the table by saying to Akers, "Man, I need to empty my snake. Be right back."

"I will be here, not going anywhere," said Akers, who was on his third drink.

In the men's room, Blackie called Tyson back.

"What's up, lady?" Blackie asked.

"First thing, Travis and I will be there in two days and second, a man named Walker is going to come up to you and pay for your dinner," said Tyson.

"Why? And who is he?" Blackie asked.

"He is someone working on another part of this mission," said Tyson.

"Why would he be paying for my dinner?" Blackie asked.

"He needs to see Akers to get a read on him and you need to know what he looks like so when or if he is nearby you know you are safe," said Tyson.

"But…" is all Blackie got out before Travis took the phone from Tyson and said,

"Blackie, we know you can handle this, but this guy has more proxy to do many things you can't. Don't go local on Tyson and me."

124

Tyson took the phone back and said to Blackie, "You are doing a great job, trust us."

Another man came into the men's room, so Blackie said only, "Okay, see you in two days," and hung up the phone.

"He hung up on me," said Tyson.

"Not possible. Maybe someone came into the bathroom. Blackie knows the consequences of that action," said Travis.

"Right," Tyson said, smiling.

Blackie returned to the table.

Tyson and Travis left the room heading toward the supply room attached to the Command Center.

The Tomboys were always amazed with the spy equipment Tex and Bonnie had collected over the years. Every piece of electronic equipment you could think of was there, old, and new ones. It reminded them of the scenes in the James Bond movies with the character named Q.

Tyler and Teg stayed at the computer to research the company who would handle the flyover job. The website gave them plane information, owner information, how to apply for leasing of the planes, and much more information.

A smile came on Tyler's face. She had an idea.

She turned to Teg and asked, "Can you fly these planes?"

"Yes, all of them," said Teg looking at the models on screen.

"Why don't we lease a plane and check it out in person?" Tyler said.

Following Tyler logic, Teg said, "Then we can figure out what kind of equipment we need and where to have Walker attach it to the plane."

"The twins can take over from there" said Tyler.

"We are beasts" said Teg.

Shaking her head and smiling. "Yes, we are" said Tyler.

They both did the secret handshake.

Teg signed up to lease the plane similar to the one being used in California for the fly over for two days, using an untraceable credit card.

The confirmation came back thanking her for using their service and that they would be glad to meet her in two days. A confirmation number, 8844220011, was given along with a leasing date of August 26. Teg had another date with Sharron, so she bid Tyler and others goodbye and left.

***

Blackie and Akers walked out of the restaurant with Akers' food bagged.

Blackie was holding on tight to Akers walking out of the restaurant, who was drunk from all the drinking and not eating.

He will drop Akers off in his room along with his food and a bottle of Hennessey. After all, you never take a friend away from a man in need.

A man was watching the whole scene.

When Blackie got to the cashier's counter, he parked Akers on a chair by the counter while he pulled out the money to pay the bill.

The man, who had been watching Blackie and Akers, suddenly approached Blackie.

"I got this," said the man, who gave the cashier one-hundred-dollar bill.

He then turned to Blackie and said, "Hello friend, haven't seen you in a long time."

"Been like years, um, um…," said Blackie, pointing his finger at the stranger like he was trying to remember his name.

"Walker. How is Tyson doing?" Walker asked.

"Just talked to her about five minutes ago," said Blackie.

The cashier was handing Walker back his change. "Keep it for a tip," said Walker.

"Thank you, sir," said the cashier, who put the change in a tip jar by the register.

Akers was sitting down with his head leaning back, drunk, not noticing the scene.

Understanding who this man was, Blackie asked Walker, "Man, what time is it?"

"It's around nine at night," said Walker.

"No sir, it is eight o'clock," said the cashier.

"Oh, you are right. Seems like a lot of time has passed," said Walker, smiling at the cashier.

He turned back to Blackie and said, "Looks like we're working together at the new cable company in town."

Blackie knew that was a lie.

The cashier, who was loving having cute guys in her presence, said, "You work for the new cable company? I signed up right away when the person came to my door."

Blackie, who was not stupid, chimed in with, "Well I missed a lovely sale already."

The cashier blushed and giggled.

"Nice weather here," said Walker, raising his right eyebrow four times.

Blackie knew that was a sign and said, "See you later, my man, as you can see," pointing toward Akers, "I have a friend in need."

"Need any help?" Walker asked.

The cashier, following what the two guys were saying, asked, "Is he okay?"

"Yes, he just lost an aunt, he is taking it bad," said Blackie.

Looking at Walker, Blackie said, "Man if you can help me get him to my ride, I would greatly appreciate it."

"Sure," said Walker, as he walked toward Akers' left while Blackie was on his right.

Akers was a little man, so the guys got him up and out of the restaurant with a quick pull.

At the car, after Walker and Blackie got Akers in the front seat, Blackie closed the passenger side door and walked around to the driver's side with Walker following him.

Walker whispered to Blackie, "Meet me at 5419 Main Street at eleven o'clock," and walked away.

Blackie got into the car, started it, and drove off with Akers out cold drunk.

Walker watched from afar and picked up his cell phone to text, "Mission accomplished."

CHAPTER EIGHTEEN

Blackie was at the location Walker was going to meet him ten minutes early to check out the area. Walker had been there thirty minutes before to make sure Blackie was not tailed. 5419 Main Street was an old building located outside the city limits. It was made into a YMCA for all sexes with rooms for exercise, cooking, sewing and pottery. The weather was around seventy-two degrees with little sun.

Blackie was instructed by text to wear exercise clothing, so he would blend in with the crowd. Loving to dress, he came in a black sweat suit that had a gold strip down each leg of the pants. He had on black high-top sneakers with the laces loose and open at the top. He wore a black T-shirt underneath with a gold baseball hat and no jewelry.

Walker had on a navy-blue pair of sweats with a white T-shirt and white high-top sneakers. Both men looked great in their outfits. Women were checking them out from head to toe. Walker hoped this would not be a distraction. He loved women like the next man, but he was working now. He avoided their eyes.

Walker had instructions for Blackie. He arrived beside Blackie and said, "Hello."

Blackie responded with, "Hello."

Getting to the point, Walker said, "Blackie, the mission is getting tight and we need to get Akers to tell where Noah is and see if Noah will be cooperative enough to give information about The Cave. Noah is one of the surviving person who was at the poker games more then one time and he has been shot, left to die."

Blackie was now getting the picture as to why Akers was afraid to talk much about his friend. "The guy Akers is on bad nerves, my man. It is going to be hard to get him to talk. He is afraid for him and his friend's lives," said Blackie.

"Well, I heard from Tyson and Travis you are good at your job, so I know, my man, you can get him to talk," said Walker.

Blackie was happy to hear that the girls were speaking highly of him and answered back, "I will get him to talk."

Walker and Blackie were now at a stand that sold drinks and snacks.

Walker asked the cashier for a ginger ale along with some peanuts and Blackie asked for some chips and a Coke. Walker waved off Blackie from paying; he paid for the drinks and snacks. Blackie smiled. *'Cool cat and not tight fisted with the money'*, he thought.

Walker, using his agent senses, could tell Blackie was a good man and a street guy with brains. Taking their drinks and snacks with them, they walked away before resuming their conversation. He needed Blackie to tell him if he feels Akers can be trusted to not ask questions if he is asked to do something out of the ordinary.

"Blackie, you are safe. I and others will have your back as long as you don't do anything stupid. If you do, we have no choice but to let you fry to keep the mission on track," Walker said softly, as not to offend Blackie. Walker stopped walking, turned to his right and smiled at Blackie, saying, "But I know that will never happen."

"You bet your sweet ass. I am not trying to get killed and, if I can be frank, I would love to work closer with the ladies." Blackie tapped Walker on the back and gave him that look of you *know what I mean*.

Walker, catching the drift, smiled back, and said, "Those girls will lick and eat you up alive."

"Exactly what I am hoping for," said Blackie, smiling, showing all teeth.

Taking a sip of his ginger ale, Walker chuckled and said, "Yeah, I know they are hot, hot, but be careful my man."

"Oh, I don't mean Tyson and Travis, they are like sisters to a brother, but I know there are other hot babies in the agency, huh?" Blackie asked.

"Hot and lethal, my friend," said Walker.

Blackie didn't miss the word "friend". He liked Walker's disposition and would like to be his friend. "My friend, you have to hook a bro up," said Blackie.

"After the mission has finished, but let's get back on track," said Walker.

Blackie shook his head up and down. They began walking slowly again. Out of the corner of his eye, Blackie saw an outline of a gun strapped to Walker's body.

Walker said, "It is important that Akers doesn't get wind of what we are doing. Keep him in the dark as much as possible. Give him just enough information to get Intel and to get to his friend Noah before the bad guys get him first. I will be installing the equipment myself; I need you to get Akers to tell you which plane they will be using; you know plane tail number and what time he is going up. When he pushes certain buttons to check for radar frequencies, my equipment will automatic snap pictures without Akers or the pilot knowing. The pilot must not get suspicious. For all we know, he might be working for the man and if he is, I promise you this, Akers' body will fly out of the plane."

"Why do they need pictures of a forbidden area?" Blackie asked.

"Sorry Blackie, I can't answer that one for your own safety," said Walker.

Shaking his head, Blackie replied, "I understand, spy shit."

"Then they will come after you, comprehend?" Walker asked, starring Blackie in the eyes.

Blackie gulped.

Walker looked sternly at Blackie and asked, "Can you do this?"

Blackie looked back at him like he had been grievously insulted.

"How will you get the pic.... tures if I can ask? Blackie asked.

Walker smiled, tapped Blackie on the shoulder, and said, "Every time the camera snap, the pictures will go to the ladies, the equipment is a one-time use, that is why it is important our intel is correct.

"But...the equipment will be there for someone to find later."

"Unless they have reason to look for it, it ill never be found because the equipment looks like it belongs there."

"I see."

Okay, be in touch."

"Do that," said Blackie.

With Walker sipping his ginger ale and Blackie munching on his chips, both departed out of different exits from the building to their waiting cars, parked on different levels of the garage, as was instructed. A pair of eyes watched them. Travis and Tyson were in town.

Outside, in Blackie's car, he received a text. Damn, they are running me ragged. I am asking for more money, he thought.

He started up the car, put it in gear, and headed south back down Main Street.

In ten minutes, he was back at his hotel room. Tyson greeted him with a punch in the chest.

"Damn girl be careful. This is prize meat here," said Blackie.

"More like meat that is walking around with danger and is clueless," said Tyson.

Travis was sitting in the chair laughing.

Blackie, noticing her for the first time, said, "Hello lovely."

"Hello Blackie," said Travis.

Hurt, Tyson said, "I am not lovely?"

"You have different ingredients, but are lovely," said Blackie.

Both laughed.

Tyson said, "As I was saying, do you remember these two guys?" handing Blackie two eight by ten color pictures.

"They were in the restaurant on my first day here. Punks, assholes," said Blackie.

"Ruthless killers," said Travis.

Blackie snapped his head up and looked at Travis.

"Man, those guys work for the man. They are his main bodyguards," said Tyson.

"Never. I would have smelled rats," said Blackie.

"You better check your nose. Maybe a sinus problem, stuffy," Tyson said, smartly.

"Ha, ha," said Blackie.

"We need to know, if you saw where they went after leaving the restaurant?" Travis asked.

"No, I left before they did. They were harassing the waitress, but come to think of it, the woman seemed to like it all except one part," said Blackie.

"We need to meet that guy named Akers. Can you set up a meeting?" Tyson asked.

"A double date type of thing. We need to tweak our treat and need some fresh meat," said Travis, joking.

Tyson joined in by saying, "If I don't have an orgasm every day, I can be difficult".

"That's a mine field, not stepping into that one. I didn't just slither out of a swamp yesterday. But what can I say, we men do have the right sauce and I have the perfect place to meet on a double date," said Blackie, arrogantly.

"Good, make it happen fast," said Travis.

"By the way, I just left your friend named Walker. A cool cat," said Blackie.

"Did he give you instructions?" Travis asked, swinging her leg over the chair's armrest.

"Yes, but he was very secretive," said Blackie.

"He has to be. The information on this mission is on a need-to-know basis," said Tyson.

"I get that. Can one of you tell me a little more? After all, I need to get Akers to talk" Blackie asked, walking over to sit by Travis in another chair beside hers.

Pacing, Tyson answered, "Blackie, we can't get into detail, but it is important for our mission to get pictures of a special house that we call a forbidden area, because the owner doesn't want any flyover above his property, but he is a very bad man, and we need some diagrams of the outside property."

"We are going to invade the house and take out the owner," Travis said with a stern look on her face.

Blackie, getting the gravity of the picture now, said nothing.

Tyson continued, "Blackie, is this guy cool or what?" she asked.

"Tyson, this cat is nervous as hell. I'm not sure if he will talk to me about Noah. I am serious, you two gals and Walker are asking a lot," said Blackie.

"He won't talk to you about Noah or what happen when Noah got shot?" Travis asked.

"Well, I think you should think of another way to get your answers. That's what I am saying. The cat is cool, but he is extremely nervous about his friend and the shooting…like…. like maybe they are still after them or something." said Blackie.

"Sounds like a pussy to me," said Travis.

"Not a pussy, Travis. Just a guy who…what I am trying to say is it will be better if you find a plan B" said Blackie.

Getting up from her chair to go to the bar to get some water, Travis said, "We need to meet Akers and Noah if possible. "

Possibly Akers. I haven't met Noah yet. He will not come out of hiding, per Akers, he never leaves the apartment, I haven't had an invite to Akers' apartment. Hell, the man is so scared, he is staying at the hotel here," said Blackie.

With that remark, Tyson said, "He is here? Call him up now."

Blackie opened his cell phone and speed dialed a number. Tyson joined Travis by the mini bar and poured her a small taste of Hennessey with two ice cubes. Tyson was waving her glass, so the ice cubes would get the Hennessey cold before she drank it.

"Hi Akers, this is Blackie. What are you doing, my man?" Blackie said. He had his cell phone on speaker phone.

Akers said, "Well man, I am at a girl's house getting some gravy."

Laughing, Blackie said, "Oh, when will you be back on this end?"

"Not until tomorrow," said Akers.

"Oh, you are out of town?"

"Yes, about two hours away. I needed to get some fresh air from all I have been through you know. So, what better way?"

Tyson whispered to Travis, "I like him already. My kind of candy."

Travis whispered back, "I still need to see him. Sweet candy or not, the package has to please me."

"So picky," said Tyson.

Travis laughed softly.

"Okay, see you when you get back," said Blackie, ending the call.

After downing her drink in one gulp, Tyson put her glass down on the bar and walked away toward Blackie.

"Look, Travis and I are leaving since Akers will not be in town until tomorrow. Make plans for Akers along with Noah, if possible, to meet around twelve noon," said Tyson.

"Tomorrow is Sunday," said Blackie.

"No off days for agents," said Travis.

Shaking his head, Blackie said, "I am on it. How about we three get some chow and watch a movie tonight?" said Blackie.

"We'd love to, Blackie," said Travis, kissing him on the cheek, "But Tyson and I have business, but we can get together for old times' sake when this is over."

Hitting Blackie across the face softly, Tyson said jokingly, "Speak for yourself, Travis. I don't hang out with bums."

"You will hang out with me because I will rock your world. You better ask somebody or better yet, you better know," said Blackie.

Travis hollered heading toward the door. Tyson followed her giggling.

After the ladies left, Blackie smiled and said out loud, "I am going to get Tyson good." He went to the yellow pages and flipped through some pages. Finding what he was looking for, he picked up his cell phone and sent only an address to Tyson's cell phone. She texted back simply, "Got it."

***

When the cab pulled in front of the address, Tyson went off and started cursing, saying, "I will kill the fucker!"

Travis screamed with laughter, exiting the cab after paying the cabbie.

Tyson slid out behind her, angrily saying, "I am going to snap, crackle, and pop!"

The cab driver, who was confused about the scene he was witnessing, said, "Miss, you should not be acting that way while you are about to enter a Holy Temple."

Tyson turned around fast and gave him the finger. He drove off.

The girls started climbing up the steps. Tyson had a look on her face that could kill, and Travis was wiping tears from her eyes from laughing so hard with a tissue.

Blackie suggested they wear nice pantsuits. He knew from experience he could not get them into a dress, and if pushed, it would tip them off something was up.

Travis was wearing a navy-blue suit with the collar standing straight up. Her pants gathered at the waist area to show off her small waist with a darker colored navy-blue silk line running down the left and right side of the pant legs. Her shoes, that were slip-ons that were the same color as the silk lining, were round at the toe area, and had four-inch heels. On her ears were gold earrings and she wore a gold bracelet on her wrist. A small navy-blue clutch was in her right hand.

Tyson was wearing an all-white vest that had eight medium-sized diamond buttons lining down the middle with no shirt underneath, pleated white pants, and white ankle boots with the toes out. The only jewelry she wore was diamond stud earrings.

Blackie really got back at Tyson this time. He got her to the one place you could probably never find her, a **Church.**

Inside, Travis and Tyson saw a small church that held maybe fifty people at a time. The people inside were smiling as they entered and were given programs. They spotted Blackie, who was waving them to their seats. The guys had on black suits with white shirts underneath and black ties, along with black shoes. Blackie had on black suede loafers. Akers' shoes had three strings that tied at the top of his foot.

Upon reaching Blackie, Tyson gave him a dirty look. Blackie smiled back at her and Tyson silted her eyes, not paying attention to Akers, who was beside Blackie. He looked at her with curiosity. Travis, seeing this, broke his attention by extending her hand and saying, "You must be Akers."

"I am, and you are?"

"Travis."

"When Blackie told me two people name Tyson and Travis will be joining us today,

I didn't expect two beauties with male names."

Before Travis could respond, Tyson pulled her gently out of the way, so she could sit by Akers. Travis didn't object. Tyson, who was squeezing past Blackie, kicked him in the balls.   Blackie put his fist in his mouth, so he would not yell. She looked at Akers and said, "We always get mistaken for guys, I hope you are not disappointed," smiling seductively with her eyes.

"No, I am not," said Akers, looking her over, shyly.

Looking in Tyson's pretty blue eyes, Akers was thinking, *Damn Blackie got good taste. These two women are hot, hot, and hot.*

Tyson took a seat to Akers' left with Blackie on her right and Travis was sitting on Blackie's right.

Looking at Blackie, Travis asked, "Where is mine?"

Whispering, Blackie answered, "Sorry, I couldn't get Noah, this is very delicate. Akers is tight lip about his location, I feel he is getting suspicious. He wants to know why I keep asking questions…Maybe Tyson will have better look.

Smiling, he continues, "I got Tyson back."

Patting him on the back hard, Travis said, "You know Tyson is going to pay you back for this and we will help you to get next to Noah."

All in the church rose up. The preacher came to the pulpit of the church and said, "Let's all come and pray."

Tyson couldn't believe what she just heard and had a frightened look on her face.

Akers, looking at her, said, "It's okay."

Smiling, she followed Travis, Akers, and Blackie to the praying area of the church. Akers was a religious man and somehow, they didn't pick that up when they looked into his background. So, when Blackie told him that he and the ladies would meet at his church for a sermon, Akers was delighted.

Tyson kneeled and folded her hands like the others, not knowing what to say. Blackie passed her a piece of paper. She gave him a steamed look. On the paper were prayers and the quote, "I thought you might need some help."

In a bind, she started reading a prayer from the piece of paper. In between lines, she was murmuring "motherf…".

"What?" Akers asked.

Blackie jumped in with a snickering look on his face and said, "Remember where we are, dear."

Travis giggled in her hands with her head bowed. Tyson answered back with a low deep growl. Blackie smiled and the expression on his face indicated '*I got you, I finally got you.*' Akers, who was beside Tyson, eyed her with suspicion. He had never seen anyone read a prayer from a piece of paper, and in such a bad mood.

Tyson, out of the side of her mouth, asked, "What are you looking at? I have certain things I need to get out. Do you mind?"

Not saying anything, he just reverted his eyes down and continued his soft prayer, then got up. Blackie got up behind him, with Tyson on his tail, punching him in the back as hard as she could. Blackie's body was going forward with a smile on his face. To see Tyson in this way was worth the hits. He knew Travis would not let her hurt him too badly, he would live, but in some pain.

Tyson whispered to Blackie, "If it is the last thing I do on earth, you will be got back."

Blackie whispered back over his shoulder, "I know."

All four were sitting in the tenth row in the middle pews. Akers gently reached over and tucked a strand of Tyson's hair behind her ears. She gave him a gentle look. Travis smiled at the exchange because she knew Tyson had her man and he didn't have a clue.

Blackie, watching the scene out of the corner of his eyes, just thought *'that woman is a man magnet. God help Akers'*. He crossed himself in front of his chest and smiling to himself, still smocking he got Tyson.

The pastor walked up to the podium. "We are at a bad time in society today. We all must pick up the mantle and move forward...."

"Amen!" was heard in the crowd. Some were waving handkerchiefs, others were bobbing their heads up and down, some stood up in their pews, and some closed their eyes to pray again, silently.

Tyson was blown away by the scene. She never knew a church could get people in such a frenzy. Akers kept looking at her.

Travis, noticing the look, whispered to Blackie, "When Tyson takes him to bed, it's over."

The sermon was over, and the congregation started filing out of the church, pew by pew, after the pastor. Travis, Tyson, Blackie, and Akers walked outside and headed down the street to Blackie's car. Tyson slowed up to take Akers' arm to talk to him. Travis and Blackie stopped to walk behind the two.

"Akers, what's your game?" Tyson asked with a smile on her face.

Wondering, Akers answered, "My game?"

"Your beef, life, or your pleasure?" said Tyson.

"Oh, I love the Lord."

With a soft snicker, Tyson said, "Okay, I got that one."

"I like sports," said Akers.

"Uh huh, got that one, let's go a little deeper, Akers," said Tyson, who tightened her grip on his arm with another smile on her face.

Not sure what Tyson wanted, Akers just walked.

"Let me get straight to the point. I need to know you better" said Tyson.

Taken back with her bluntness, Akers stopped and looked at her. Travis and Blackie, who were walking behind them, stopped to watch the scene. Tyson seduced him with her pretty blue eyes. A few seconds passed, and Akers softened his stiff body and his eyes.

Smiling, he started walking again along with Tyson.

Travis, and Blackie behind them.

Loving every minute of Tyson seducing him, Akers asked Tyson, "What do you need to know about me?"

"What kind of food you like, do you like to dance, what you drink, you know the normal."

"I love pizza, no dancing…you know the norm, then biting on his lip, Akers became quiet.

Tyson felt his body slightly shaking. He was a nervous guy, as Blackie predicted.

Rubbing his arm with her free hand, Tyson said, "It's okay."

Akers stopped and turned around to look at Blackie, who was walking behind him with Travis.

Blackie smiled back.

When Akers turned back around, Travis said to Blackie, "She has him now."

"Yeah, a cougar jumping her prey," said Blackie.

Akers look Tyson straight into her blue eyes and asked, "Can I have your digits?"

Tyson reach into Akers pocket and pulled out his phone and smiled at him.

Akers knowing what she was asking reach over and unlocked his phone.

Tyson typed in her number and said, "Call me tonight" in a sultry voice".

Akers nodded his head.

Tyson pushes the call button on his phone and handed it back to Akers, while she pulled her phone out of her purse and answered it.

Akers answered his phone ringing, "Hello."

Tyson said into her cell phone, "Hello back."

Both laughed and clicked off.

Akers locked in Tyson's number and said, "I will call."

Getting close to him, Tyson pushed him back against the car, and gave him a slightly rough, long kiss on the mouth. Pulling back, with a little of his lip still between her teeth, she let go and said, "You can call me anytime you are free."

Akers took a deep breath because his friend had just risen up.

Blackie laughed, kissed Travis goodbye, and walked toward the driver's side of his car and got in. Travis held up hand for a cab to take her and Tyson back to the hotel.

Breathing heavily, Akers only said, "Whoa."

Laughing and walking away, Tyson said behind her, "That is only the beginning."

Akers swallowed hard.

A cab came to the curb with Travis waiting inside. Tyson joined her, and the cab took off. Travis and Tyson waved goodbye as it passed the guys.

"Get in, my man," said Blackie.

Akers, who was watching the cab go down the street, didn't hear him at first. He was daydreaming. Blackie blew his car horn. Akers jumped slightly.

Blackie repeated again, "Get in man, we have to go."

Akers got into the passenger seat and said, "Man she is hot as hell. Both of those ladies are hot."

"When it comes to Tyson, my advice is run, my man, run far, far, far away," said Blackie.

Laughing, Akers said, "Man, you are a laugh a minute."

"I am not joking. Seriously, run your ass," said Blackie with an indignant look on his face.

Akers chuckled, then asked, "Why we didn't offer them a ride?"

"No crazy bitches in my car," said Blackie, who put his foot on the gas and sped down the road.

CHAPTER NINETEEN

Laughter could be heard though the car windows. Pie and Radio were on the phone calling an operator. They were behind a pastry truck that had a sign that said, "How am I driving? Call 1-801-711-2639." Harassing the driver, they sped up on the back of the tail of the truck and blew their horn. They were on a two-lane street, one up and one down, with a no-pass double yellow line in the middle. For the hell of it, Pie pulled over, so Radio could talk to the driver of the truck.

Radio yelled out the window, "Man, you're driving sucks! We are in a high-performance car and it wants to perform!"

"Sir, our truck can only go so fast," said the man driving.

"Fuck that, I am reporting as the sign says on the back of the truck. He is not driving fast enough," laughed Radio while Pie was cracking up behind the wheel.

Pie slowed up and got back on the right side of the road, cranking his horn, blowing for the truck to speed up. Nervous now, the driver picked up his radio in the truck while still moving the truck down the road.

"This is driver Mike, number 905. I have a sports car behind me getting close to my bumper and harassing me. I am calling for help, copy."

To Mike's left, he saw a police car parked on the side road.

'Good', Mike thought. '*The trooper will see what is happening and will stop this madness*'. Mike hit the truck gas pedal to make sure he was speeding, and the trooper would come after one or both. Getting close and passing the trooper's vehicle, Mike's heart sunk. The trooper's car didn't move. Mike immediately went back to his radio and said, "A green sports car is riding up on my tail and we both just passed a trooper who I know saw that we were speeding, heard the loud blowing of their car horn, and can see they are driving awfully close to my tail." Mike was rushing with his words because now he felt he wasn't safe.

His supervisor said to him, "Calm down, Mike."

"Don't tell me to calm down. I just passed a trooper who is doing duck shit and I am being harassed. Hell, for all I know they can have guns."

"Man cool out. Hold on, I am going to call the police station. How far are you from the warehouse?"

The driver answered, "About two miles away."

A click was heard on the driver's phone because his supervisor had put him on hold to call the station. Mike sighed. Mike looked into his side mirror at the car behind him and could see that the driver was either drunk or high on something because the car was swaying to the left and right like he had no control of vehicle. He just hoped they didn't hit him. He would have to answer a lot of questions to management about what happened, and he didn't want to deal with that. All he knew was that he was not going to stop this truck until he arrived at the warehouse. He positioned his foot on the gas pedal for maximum speed.

The supervisor came back on the phone and told Mike, "Keep driving, a cruiser is on the way."

"When?" Mike asked back, who by now was sweating with his heart beating fast.

Calmly the supervisor answered, "My understanding, about five minutes away."

"I hope it is not the same fuck I passed about two miles down the road," said Mike.

"My understanding it is a higher-ranking trooper".

"Not here in five, I'm calling back," Mike shouted.

"Okay," said the supervisor, who knew he was lying, but he needed Mike to get the truck and its contents back to the warehouse safe. He was bringing in a lot of money on this shipment. After hanging up the radio, the supervisor started shaking. Holding both of his hands to calm himself down, he thought,' *I hope they don't stop him and realize Mike is carrying around a half million in cash hidden in some pastry tray'*.

The supervisor picked up his cell phone and when the other end answered he said, "We might have some trouble."

At the same time, a dispatcher from the police station radioed the cop who was patrolling that area of the highway and asked, "Car 4424 are you in the vicinity of highway 301?"

The police offer answered his radio by saying, "Confirm, dispatcher."

"We just received a complaint that a truck driver just passed you with a sports car harassing him. Can you confirm this?"

"Yes, I can. That car is under the protection of the Mayor and if I stop and pull it over there will be hell to pay, over."

"One moment please," the dispatcher could not believe what she was just told. A citizen was being harassed and the officer would not respond. After putting the officer on hold, the dispatcher called for her supervisor and told him what was going on.

The officer sat back into his seat in his cruiser. He knew what was going on and knew what was coming next. He just waited for the dispatcher to return, reading his novel he brought with him title **"Ultimate Tomboys"**. It was tedious to sit all day, waiting for someone in a car to commit a crime that required him to pull them over and give a ticket.

Radio was having fun talking shit to the operator on the 800 number, decided to hang up on the operator. The real fun was in harassing the driver.

Crackle. The radio came back to life.

"Car 4424, this is dispatcher 324. Do you have a tag number, officer?"

"Yes, the tag number is BAD*ONES."

"Hold again, please," said the dispatcher.

"Roger," said the officer.

The officer went back to his novel. The chapter he was reading was getting really good. Within seconds, *crackle*, the radio came alive again.

The tone of the dispatcher's voice was indicating '*I can't believe this*' and said, "Thank you officer."

Smiling, the officer said, "Over," and went back to reading his novel after taking a sip of his hot coffee. *Click* went the radio.

Mike could see the warehouse gate in front of him and was happy. No cruiser had shown up and somehow, he was not surprised. Behind him, over the loud roar of the truck and sports car, he could hear words like, "We are going to fuck you up and shove some of those pastries up your ass, motherfucker!"

It was Pie, yelling out his side of the window. Radio and Pie had worked themselves into a laughing fuss, snorting cocaine and drinking beer, loving the fun they were having. Pie saw the warehouse ahead of them and decided to pull over to the left so Radio could confront the driver one more time before he was safe in the gates. Pie was an excellent driver, so he acted like he was going to run into the truck from the truck driver's side. That made the driver of the truck swerve to the right, so he would not be hit.

Laughing, Radio's head was out the window saying, "We are going to shoot you, motherfucker, and give us some of them damn pies! Pull the fuck over!"

"Yeah!" Pie hollered out Radio's passenger side window, not watching the road, "We want the fucking goodies and money you collected!"

With that remark, Radio pulled out his gun and showed it to the driver. Terror came on the driver's face and he sped up the truck.

"Damn, I didn't know that truck could go faster," said Pie.

"Get closer so I can give him one good scare before he hits the gate of the warehouse," said Radio.

Pie pressed down on the gas pedal and moved closer to the driver's side of the truck. Radio aimed his gun out the window and pulled the trigger. Mike slammed on the gas and the truck jerked but kept moving. The bullet hit the side of the truck, as Radio intended. Parts on the truck splattered in different directions all over the highway. Mike looked only forward, adrenaline running high. Be damned, he was going to make it to the gates of the warehouse in front of him.

Both men threw their heads to the back of their leather seats and roared.

Mike pulled the truck to the right and started blowing his horn to get the guard's attention at the gate. He was under real attack now. Breathing hard with sweat running down his face, Mike never took his hand off the horn.

Pie turned the Challenger toward the left and sped off. The roar of laughter could be heard inside the car.

The guard at the gate came out to see what was going on. Mike drives right through the gate, knocking it on the ground, not saying anything. He didn't press the brakes until he was about to run straight into the building where the employees entrance for work. He got out running and didn't stop until he collapsed on the floor in the lunch area. People inside just stared at him in silence. The guard at the warehouse didn't know what to make of the scene he just witnessed, but he went back into his booth and called the authorities as he was trained to do.

CHAPTER TWENTY

"Girl, I was so hot and in need of sex that I had went to the wrong hotel. I jumped into my rental car and was driving toward some serious fucking, calling my man the whole time, yelling, 'Baby hold the juice, Willow here is on fire and ready to be conquered.'" She pointed to her private parts. "Girl, I was sweating because my body was on fire. You hear me. Fire! Here I am driving around in circles. Every time I call him, he says, 'Baby you are going the wrong way. Turn around.' So, I keep turning around but after about an hour I knew something was wrong. I finally called him back and asked for the exact address. Girl you are going to holler when I tell you this.

"I am already screaming inside because I think I know what you are going to say," said Teg.

"Well let's not hold this story up. I have never used a GPS before, but I figured out how to use the one in the car. The first thing it says to me after entering the address was, 'you are ten miles and twenty minutes away from your destination.' 'Good,' I say to myself now, 'I am getting somewhere.' I started calming down. I didn't want to stink when he greets me at the door. As I am getting closer to my destination, the streets and sights are looking familiar."

Sharron stopped to take a sip of her drink. She gave Teg the look *'of you not going to believe this.'*

"When the GPS says, 'you have arrived at your destination,' Teg…Teg you could have knocked me over with a feather. I was back at the hotel I had left from."

Teg put her head back and roared.

"Girl, I was so horny I didn't realize my man had booked a suite at the same hotel I was staying in. All this time I could have been fucking I had been driving."

Teg was laughing so hard, with tears running down her face.

"Girl, when your willow starts singing, your brain goes stupid," said Sharron.

Teg and Sharron were laughing hard. Teg was enjoying Sharron, a great comedian.

After the two had calmed down, Teg slowly steered the conversation back to the other night by saying, "Girl, I know we just met, but I have been worried about what you said the night at the club."

"What did I say to make you feel that way?" She asked, still coming down from her story.

"You know, about the man who frightens you," said Teg.

Sighing, Sharron said, "Oh that. I was drunk and was talking out of my ass."

Looking at her with a film of tears forming in her eyes, Teg said, "No you weren't. We are friends now. Tell me, or I am going to talk about your Willow," said Teg, jokingly.

"Oh please. Don't hold that against me, please," Sharron joked back.

"Alright girlfriend, no Willow talks, but I don't like my friends being taken advantage of. I want to help." Softly, Teg continued, "You will be safe with me."

Twisting her drink in her hand with her head down, softly, Sharron said, "I can't because I like you and they will kill you."

"Let me be the judge of that," Teg said.

A few seconds passed before Sharron answered. "These people are so bad that if I was on fire, they wouldn't even piss on me to put it out."

"What...kind of people are they? People who deal drugs of some kind?" Teg asked. She took a sip of her glass filled with water as she asked.

"Worse. High government officials of some kind. I don't know or want to know the details. You know what I mean, girl."

"Whoa, but I still don't understand how you are a part of it."

"Teg, I am a high-class escort". Sharron brought her head up to look Teg in the eyes to see if she lost her friend with that statement.

Teg gave her a wide grin back that indicated they were still friends.

Sharron took in a big breath and began her story. "I meet men and they pay me to have sex with them. I get paid a lot of money. One night, about three years ago, I met this handsome man with a lot of money. I was tired of going from man to man, so I thought I met what women call their prince on a white horse. So, I dated him exclusively and he paid for my services. I didn't know any of his background and didn't care. He is paying good money to me, and believe it or not, he was good company. We laughed and loved football together. He bought me a condo, mind you, in my name. That is why I still own it."

"Own it. Nice piece of work, my girl," said Teg.

"Pussy is a powerful drug," said Sharron.

"Bar none," said Teg, snapping her fingers twice.

"Yes, I do have a brain, despite what other people think about escorts. I see myself as a businesswoman who provides a service," said Sharron.

Teg shook her head in agreement. She silently waved to the waitress, looking at her their empty glasses. The waitress arrived at the table and Teg asked Sharron, "What will you have? It's on me."

Looking up with sad eyes, Sharron said, "I'm going stronger, double vodka, no cubes."

Teg looked at the waitress and said, "Same for me."

"Why? You don't need a stiff drink," Sharron asked.

"I am a sign of the lion and I feel my blood rising because my instincts are screaming about where this story is leading. So, I need a stiff drink," said Teg.

"Oh, this guy was sweet. He would never ever hurt me. It's his best friend that is the dangerous one."

"Oh" said Teg softly. Glad the talk is going somewhere.

The waitress was back in a jiffy with their drinks.

"Well, one rainy night, I got a call from a strange man who I didn't know. He knew all about me and said two guys will be visiting my place within an hour.

I didn't know what to do, but for some reason I knew to obey because this guy knew, like, my name, address, and some history about me.

"Were you afraid? Teg asked.

"Slightly, but he mentions Paul name, so I did as I was told. I waited for the two guys. Why didn't I say, 'fuck it' and run? The man's tone of voice had such authority, I froze while he was talking to me."

Sharron paused and looked at Teg with watery eyes. "I didn't know what to do. I can't even repeat the whole or some of the conversation he was having because I went into some, some zone," she said, rubbing her two fingers together nervous.

Teg put her hand gently on Sharron's trembling hand and said, "Don't be afraid. I can protect you."

Sharron, sensing the sincerity in Teg's words, knew somehow that she was safe and went on with her story. "The two guys arrived by damn near kicking down the front door. Upon me letting them in, they pushed me aside and started immediate going through my place like a hurricane. I asked them 'What the hell is going on?'

One told me to 'Keep my damn mouth shut, ho,' with such anger it gave me chills."

Teg raised her eyebrow.

Angrily, Sharron said, "Teg, I am telling you they were the two scariest men I've ever seen. I kept my mouth closed as they went through every room and every inch of my place. They didn't put anything back in its place. About ten minutes passed when one of them came back out into the living room area and asked if I had video equipment or a safe hidden. I said no. He looked at me with a killer face and said with a tone of authority in his voice, 'Bitch ho, you better not be lying to me.' I said delicately to him, 'I am not lying to you.' He seemed to believe me and went back to his friend. I can still hear them tearing up my place. I was shaking so bad I couldn't run.

Five, or maybe two minutes later, both came back to the living room and announced I would be going with them. I totally lost it and thought I was going to die. I fell to my knees crying and begging, 'Please leave me alone, I will not tell anyone."

One of the guys said, 'You bet your ho ass you will not talk to anyone, but you are going with us.'"

Teg interrupted Sharron to ask her, "Did they address each other by name?"

"Never in front of me,"

"Okay, go ahead,"

"One of them reached down to pull me up to go with them. I started fighting and he hauled off and smacked me across the face so hard I passed out."

With a look of astonishment, Teg said, "Oh my god."

Sharron, who was relieved to be able to finally tell someone this story, said, "When I woke up, I was in a strange room. Looking around, I saw a door. I tried to get up and run, only to realize I was tied up by my wrists and feet on a table, spread eagle. First thought came to my mind, I am going to be raped. Then I felt the pain on my face from the blow one of them had given me. Not thinking, I tried to touch it, but my hands were tied to the left and right post of some table. So, I just laid there with tears running down my face. I was tormented."

Teg put her hand up to her mouth with wide eyes looking at Sharron. "Can you describe them?"

"For the rest of my life, I will never forget them," She answered.

"Tell me what they look like." Teg had an inkling it was Pie and Radio but didn't let on.

"Both are about six-one or six-two, very tall. Slim build with, I can't believe I am saying this, but it looked like a six pack to die for under their shirts."

"You can see that?" Teg asked.

"Even through my torment," said Beverly, holding her hands up in a motion, '*can you believe it?*'

Teg said, "I know. Some men, good or bad, are just ripped."

"Both had on tight T-shirts and blue jeans. One had a chain hanging down the left side and the other had a design of, or I should say a sketch of, a gun on the side. Both have their guns in their waist in plain sight."

"Any names said by now?" Teg asked again.

"No, wait…uhm…. uhm…I remember one called the other Radio. Maybe they were talking about a radio. I am not sure," said Sharron.

Teg's was no longer wondering. She knew these were Jordan thugs.

My mind was racing tied to that table like that but at one point the man came into the room and took one look at me and whistle. Those two bad men came back into the room. I started screaming. The man came to my side and softly held my chin and said, "Don't be afraid, you are not going to be hurt". He then turns towards the two dudes and scream, "release her you two fuck ups."

One of them asked "What did we do wrong?"

The man slipped him across the face, while the other reach for his gun. The man didn't even look at that guy, just said "Are we jumping today."

The other guy said, "No boss."

The other guy chimed in "She just an ho."

He got slipped again.

Release her for the last time. Follow my instructions to the fullest or be gone. The man then walked out the door with a powerful authority. Teg I don't know what happen next.

"The man?" Teg asked.

"The boss," Sharron answered. He came to my room later that night.

 What did he want?" Teg asked.

"He wanted to know how much Paul had told me. He told me that Paul had died in a plane crash and he wanted to make sure I was safe."

"Did you believe him?"

"Yes, I believed him. His tone of voice was calming and friendly. I told him I knew nothing because Paul kept his private life under wraps. When we were together, we only talked about football, parties, and having a good time. We had a lot of sex. He was a master at making a woman feel full. Of course, I didn't tell the man that part. I have some dignity."

Teg asked her in a gentle voice, "Did they interrogate you?"

"No, but I was crying the whole time. Those two guys were in the room with him.

I overheard them talking about asking the man for me when he finish with me, the whole time licking their lips at me. The man was on his phone. I became hysterically and started shaking so bad, the back board of the bed was bouncing off the wall.

Those guys thought it was funny as shit. Imaging what they were going to do to me made me pass out."

"For how long? Could you tell?" Teg asked.

"Hell no, but I guess only a few seconds because when I came to, I could hear the man ripping those guys to shreds. He needed information from me, and they were coming on too strong. I kept my eyes closed before I let them know I had woken up. I heard him say, 'Call me when she wakes up.' I opened my eyes. I didn't want to be left alone in the room with them two monsters. So, I start moving my head to the right and left, I wanted the man to know I am awake".

Laughing a little, she continued, "You know, you do learn a couple things from the street. I start screaming 'let me go' and the man walked to my left side and gently rubbed my left cheek saying, 'You will be okay. No one is going to hurt you here. We need some information that's all.' I turned my head toward him with tears in my eyes and said, 'I will answer anything you want.'"

Sharron was crying hard now, so not to draw attention, Teg reached over and said, "You don't have to say any more now."

"Teg, I need to talk to someone, or I am going to burst."

Teg reached into her purse and gave her some tissues. "Okay let's leave here, get yourself together," Teg said.

Sharron took the tissue and blew her nose and another tissue to wipe her eyes. She asked Teg if her eyes were red. Ted said "yes" and reached back into her purse and produced some Visine. She threw her head back slightly and put two drops into both eyes. Within seconds, her eyes were back white.

Teg asked the one question she had been dying to ask. "What is the man's name?"

Looking in her makeup mirror to see she looked okay, she answered, "Jordan."

Teg was quiet.

The waitress came to the table and Teg paid the bill. They both left the restaurant, not saying another word. Both ladies waited at the curb for the attendant to bring her Apple Red Cadillac. She would finish the conversation at her condo.

Teg's cell phone beeped to indicate she had a text message waiting. She read the text message. Bonnie had text her to go to the Hilton. She had been listening to the conversation and wonder how Sharron left the 'Cave" without a bodyguard or someone following her. She was wondering the same thing.

Sharron, who was sitting on the passenger side of the Cadillac, had no clue what was going on. She just went with Teg like a little puppy. She was thinking her prayers had been answered and he sent her an angel to get her out of this mess she got herself into by accident.

They drove down the road in complete silence, enjoying the sixty-nine-degree weather, with breeze coming through the windows of the car. They arrived at the hotel. To make things look okay, Teg told the receptionist behind the front desk that she had lost her key. She was told the key would cost twenty-five dollars to replace but they could add it to her final bill.

Looking at the receptionist's name tag on her left shoulder, Teg asked, "Cindy, can the fee be waived?"

Cindy replied, "No, sorry. Management rules."

"Whatever," Teg sighed and asked for another key.

The receptionist was an undercover agent, so she knew the charge would never go on the bill. Cindy handed the extra key card to Teg.

"Thank you," said Teg, as she and Sharron walked toward the elevator.

Entering the elevator, Teg slid the special key card for the elevator to close and go straight to the top floor where her suite was.

When the doors opened, the ladies were in a hallway and there were two doors on the floor. One said A-8 and the other said B-8. She put the key into the door handle and pushed it open. Sharron walked in behind her, looking around. This had to be the most amazing suite she has ever seen. She had seen many with Paul.

Teg didn't waste any time and asked Sharron while putting down her purse on the table, "I need to know. How did you leave that place without any guards? Are you being followed?"

"Jordan trusts me, those two maniacs wouldn't dare touch me" Sharron looked at Teg with a big smile and said, "You know, again pussy is a powerful drug when used right."

"Amen," said Teg.

Sharron was carrying their leftovers in a shopping bag the waitress had given her. Teg motioned for her to come to the table to finish their meal. She went to the bar in plain view and poured each a glass of wine. She returned to the table where Sharron had removed the containers from the bag and placed them on the table. Famished, they each dug in to eat.

***

"She is staying at the 'Cave' says Bonnie. "We have a way to get more intel. Good job Teg, good job. She is more at ease after hearing what Sharron said. Still, she would be on her toes. Jordan is a dangerous person, no matter what that lady thought.

***

"Hey this is not funny. You can't treat your comrade this way," said Blackie.

"He is right," said Travis.

"He fucked me, so he rides in the back seat," said Tyson.

"It's no back seat. We are in a Corvette," said Travis.

Blackie was knocking on the top of the trunk yelling, "Let me out! I can't breathe!"

"He could be in trouble, Ty. We do need him, and after all, what he did was not that bad," said Travis, trying to get Tyson to calm down and let Blackie out of the trunk of the car.

"He has to ride at least a couple of miles," said Tyson, seriously.

"We are out about ten miles from the town already," said Travis.

Annoyed, Tyson looked at Travis, then stomped her right foot on the brakes hard. The car roared to a stop and all three went forward. Travis and Tyson had on seatbelts, but Travis put her hand out on the dashboard to break the forward momentum.

Blackie yelled, "Ouch!"

Tyson jumped out of the car, went toward the trunk of the car, opened it, and pulled out Blackie with a swift, quick move, throwing him on the road. Travis got out of the car from the passenger side.

Blackie jumped up and began wiping off his clothes saying, "Damn, why so harsh baby?"

Tyson, pulling out a gold badge, said, "I have some hardware that says I can kill your ass and get away with it. So, don't ever fuck me again."

Travis, standing by the Corvette, winked at Blackie. Relieved, he pretended to sweat for Tyson's sake. He looked at Tyson and said, "You are wrong, and the good Lord is going to make you pay."

Tyson went down on her knees and said, "Oh Lord, please don't punish me." She then got up and punched Blackie in the stomach. He bent over in pain, biting his lips so he would not yell. Tyson walked back to the car, got in, and drove off, leaving Travis and Blackie on the side of the road.

As the T-top silver Corvette with spiked rims roared down the street with tires spinning, Blackie said, "What a heifer."

"I smell attitude. Are you mad at my best friend?" Travis asked.

Before Blackie could answer, she pulled out her cell phone and made a phone call. Hanging up she looked at Blackie and said, "Well, we have a little wait. They need to locate us so let's start walking."

Not concentrating on what just happened, Blackie said, "Akers really likes Tyson, she should call him."

"We never run after men. They are like subway trains. One leaves, another one is always on the way."

"Cold."

"Real."

Blackie looked at Travis and asked her, "Why do you always take up for Tyson?"

Travis answered, "That is not always true, or I would not be walking beside you."

"Oh, by the way, thanks. I knew she would get me with that church thing, but I also hoped you would stop her from doing too much damage to me. I did realize before pulling that stunt, she needed me."

Chuckling, Travis answered, "It's the only reason you are breathing."

Looking shocked, Blackie asked, "She would have killed me?"

"No" Travis answered laughing.

Blackie chuckled.

Nothing more was said. Travis phone beeped. She opened it to read the text.

"We should be picked up within five minutes. Now the fun begins."

Blackie's eyes were bugging out, wondering what she meant, but didn't ask.

***

Tyson pulled up by the side of a shed. Walker came out, wearing a jumpsuit like the men who work at the airport, and she handed him the equipment. She sped off and Walker went to work. The equipment must be in place when the plan comes together.

***

"Hello Akers, can we meet tonight" Tyson says into the phone.
"Sure, where?" Akers asks.
"Your favorite place, pizza place"
"Ok"
"Around 4pm"
"Be there."
When Tyson arrived, Akers was already there and had order ahead of time.
She greets him with a peak on his cheek.
The hot pizza with two glasses of soda came to the table that was located next to a big glass windows that were open so the fresh air can come in. Tyson hair blew across her face. Akers reach over and pull it behind her ear. She smiled.
"I'm surprise a handsome man like you don't have a lady friend" Tyson says.
"I can say the same to you" Akers replied.
"Lucky for both of us, won't you say?" Tyson smiling.
Akers took a gulp of his soda, thinking *This woman is fine, I'm going to get her, whatever she wants from me, she is going to get.*
"Have any friends in town? Tyson asks.
"Yes"
"She or he has a name."
"Noah"
"Nice name, was he at the church?
"No, he doesn't go out much."
"Why"
"Why are we talking about him?"
"Just trying to get to know you."
"Really….okay….is you and Travis good friends?"
"Like sisters, we were born on the same day, our moms were best friends."
"Cool"

"Yea, everyone calls us THE twins."

Laughing, Akers says "You two look nothing alike."

Laughing back, Tysons says, true I am the cuter one."

Akers throw his head back and laugh out loud.

"Blackie is right, you are nice. Sighing she continues "Why your friend doesn't go out much? Holding up a hand, she adds "If I am not being too intrusive".

Akers looked into Tyson, baby blues, and said, "He…he was shot in the neck."

"Jesus, by whom?"

Picking at meat on his pizza slice, Akers said, "We think the man was trying to get rid of all of Paul's poker friends. Maybe he thought the poker players knew too much." Putting both his hands up in the air, Akers continued by saying, "Noah and I are only guessing."

"Guessing about the shooting or the people who did it?" Tyson asked.

Sighing hard, Akers said, "We don't know, Noah showed up at my apartment one night, bleeding all over the place. I still ask God how he lived through it all."

Tyson, asks softly, "Did he give any names who he thought shot him?"

"No, he didn't see who, he was shot from the back," said Akers.

"I'm confuse, he was shot by bad people and they let him live."

"Noah and I came to the conclusion that they though he was dead".

"Wow"

"Uhm…. we kind of think this guy name Paul was killed on purpose, did you hear about the plane crash?

Tyson looked surprised he put Paul death and the plane crush together.

"Yeah, hundreds of people died, what…. you think Noah shooting and the plane crash go together?'

"Well Noah thinks there is something fishy about that. Paul normally takes private planes but at the last minute he had to take a commercial flight and the sucker blew up."

"That could have been a coincidence," said Tyson.

"Don't think so, Noah and I played poker with Paul. Nice guy, a little braggadocious but nice. One of the poker players told Noah that he overheard two guys talking about delivering the bomb to the mechanic, who placed it on the plane."

"What is the poker player's name?" Tyson asked.

"He is dead, can't talk to him," said Akers.

"Anyone else or something else you can tell me?" Tyson asked, softly.

"Well…Noah did say he heard on the street after Paul's death, two guys by the names of Pie and Radio, who were deathly drunk, was bragging about how they had given the bomb to the guy to put on the plane." Sighing because what he was about to say next was disgusting, Akers lowered his head slightly and looked at Tyson sideways, and said, "They didn't want to have to go out in the desert to kill Paul then spend half the night digging a grave to bury the body, so they decided to take out the plane."

Gasping, Tyson asked, "Damn, harsh, I do wonder why Paul was killed".

"Noah said he did something that displeased the man".

"The Man?".

"I believe his name is Jordan, look I am talking too much. Let talk about something else".

"Okay, Noah, just one more question. What did Paul do?".

"Don't know what Paul did, only that hundreds of innocent people died and that people who were at some of those pokers games are dying. Noah wishes he weren't there to hear the stories; he believes that's why he was shot and we both are in danger".

"But you are out".'

"I not afraid of any of those motherfuckers, I have protection."

"From whom, what?

Feeling he talking to much, Akers bit into his slice of pizza.

Tyson got the drift and bite into her slice.

Both sat in silence just eating and drinking.

Suddenly Akers called the waitress "Check please."

"Are you ok, my word, nothing from me" says Tyson.

"Good, because I like you and probably put you in danger by talking too much."

"I'm a big girl" Tyson said smiling.

"I don't know how but I believe you" Akers snickered.

Tyson snickered back.

Both got up from the table after the bill was paid.

Outside Akers walked Tyson to her car. He will take the bus home alone.

"She rolled down her window and asked, "Is all the people at those poker games dead?"

"No more questions"

"Please one more"

"Tyson, I don't know all the people who played poker, I only went once. Noah went more times, hell I never met the dude name Jordan."

"Or the guys who shot Noah?'

"That's two questions."'

Tyson looked at Akers with her baby blue eyes.

"Never meet them, okay."

Tyson reaches out the car window and kissed Akers on the mouth. "I'm sorry I asked so many questions, but that story is crazy."

"Yea, I know, goodbye for now" Akers wave Tyson a kiss and walked away from the car.

Tyson watches him walk away from her rearview mirror. *'Akers, you have given me a lot of intel. We have to meet Noah. Blackie your turn'*.

CHAPTER TWENTY-ONE

Arnold was at a small diner located in a rough neighborhood that was open twenty-four hours a day, seven days a week. Big, black, heavy steel bars were covering the windows and the door had to be opened from the inside with a buzzer at dark.

The food was delicious, so patrons would wait in line outside to seat to eat or call in their order and wait in their car to be called it was ready. The line could be a mile long some nights, especially on weekends. Arnold was able to get inside at one of the back tables. He was the only one inside besides the waitress and the cook in the back watching tv, waiting for orders.

The location was picked for one reason; one being that no one would expect an Ivy League guy to be there. He was stirring his coffee and waiting for someone to show up.

He and Deuce had been having Tex tailed for weeks and nothing out of the ordinary happened. Both knew something was up but had been unable to find out what. He became frustrated, so he deviated from normal protocol and hired a private investigator. He smelled something was going on and he wanted to be a part of it. He sensed it would help him move up the ladder at the agency.

A large man, weighing around three hundred pounds, flopped down at his table, it brought Arnold back to the moment.

"You rang?" he said, laughing with a deep bass voice.

The P.I. was dressed in the usual flair: a tan-colored trench coat with the collar up high, a belt tied tight around the waist, along with black slacks, a white shirt, and a black tie. The customary black fedora was on his head with the rim nearly covering his eyes.

'A damn comedian', Arnold was thinking,' *all's well if he can do the job*'. He did wonder about that because the guy was out of shape and was breathing hard, sweating bullets simply from walking from his car.

Arnold started the conversation by saying, "Do you need some water?" and handed the man some napkins.

The P.I. took the napkins, wiped his face down, and said, "I would like a tall glass of iced tea, thank you."

A man wearing an apron came over to the table and asked, "What can I get for you two men?"

"A tall glass of tea" said Arnold.

The waitress left the area to get the order.

"What do we have here, bro?" asked the P.I.

"This is strictly on bolt lock down. I…I mean, the agency needs you to trail a higher level official and report back what she is doing."

"Oh, a lady hum pretty hot, I hope. That will make my job easier."

The waitress returned to the table with the drinks.

Arnold exhaled and said, "This is business, not pleasure, you jerk."

"Down, down bro. I was kidding. I take all my jobs serious. It is just a man thing, you know?" said the P.I.

"I am not your bro, this is business, not a man night out" Arnold said,

"Just saying, light up a little bit, ok."

"Of course. I am just uptight on this one. It is someone I know."

"Everything on level bro," said the P.I. He lifted his tea glass and, drank about half of it.

Arnold, watching, thought, *No manners. Why is some P.I.s such slobs?*
He answered his own question. '*I guess because they live in such a dirty world where everything is secret, and there's night work, bad characters, and low pay. This P.I. seems to be making money by the gold Rolex he is wearing.*'

He made a mental note to ask him about that later but now he needed to pass on the information and leave this ratty part of the town before he was seen by someone.

Arnold didn't touch his coffee, the diner looked dirty to him.

He reached to his left side and pulled up a medium size soft leather briefcase, opened it and pulled out a folder that he laid on the table. Not saying a word.

Arnold nodded, "It's okay to look at it."

The P.I said, "I prefer to look at it in a safer place."

Arnold assured him by saying, "It is safe. The place has backup." This was not true, but he felt the asshole didn't know.

The P.I. opened up the folders and began looking the information over.

Arnold asked the P.I., "Do you have any questions? Ask now, because getting in touch with each other later will more difficult unless it's extremely important." He and the agency couldn't take chances on anyone getting a sniff of this investigation. Asses would burn."

The P.I. gave a thumbs-up.

Looking at a picture, he saw a very pretty lady, brown liquid eyes, pretty smile and by the look of her clothing, rich. The whole time he was viewing her picture, the P.I. was thinking,' *she is fucking material. Hell, I better get a grip. Dick Tracy in front of me is a dickhead.*'

157

He moved the picture to the side and scanned the written information on the lady by moving his finger to the left and right and down the page. He flipped a page up and read the second page.

That was all in the folder, one picture and two sheets of paper. He thinks I am an amateur. *'Dickhead, I was doing undercover while he was still pissing in his cloth diapers.* He looked up and said, "Do I get to keep this folder?"

"Yeah, just don't leave it around. Lock it up. Any more questions?"

'None that you would like' the P.I thought. *What I will do for the main killer of all societies: money.*

"No, I will start first thing in the morning,"

Arnold didn't reply, he just rose, left the diner, got into a black four-door, and drove off.

The P.I. drank the rest of his tea.

No names had to be given; each knew each other's background thoroughly.

The waitress showed up. James, the P.I., smiled at her said, "My friend said it was okay to order the steak, potatoes, string beans, and biscuit dinner on him."

"Yes sir," the waitress said, and she turned to place the order with the kitchen.

James hollered, "And another glass of this great tea!"

The waitress signaled *okay*.

She didn't question him because, after all, the other guy tells her at the beginning he was expecting a friend and the tab was on him. He had given her a credit card. She would just run the numbers again. She knew how to manipulate the cash register to add more to the last card it just accepted. What did she care? It was a bigger tip.

Later that night, the P.I. was standing by the window of Tex's home. He took pains not to step on anything that might let off a silent alarm. Trust and believe his every move were being recorded.

Once on the property her four hidden cameras, designed as flowerpots, picked up all activity around the house and grounds.

Peeping inside, he saw six women having some type of party.

A table loaded with different types of food, a tray of varieties of cheeses, crackers, different fruits, finger sandwiches and chicken wings with sauce, made him hungry again.

On one table, he spotted some funny looking cigarettes in a bowl.

'Cool ladies' he was thinking.

158

On another table were two blenders filled with mixed drinks, water, different bottles of liquors and wines chilling. One of the ladies was at the blender putting in fruit, ice, orange juice and some vodka. She put the top on the mixer and hit a button. The ingredients meshed together, making a smoothie. She stopped the mixer after several spins, then took off the top to pour the liquid in a glass. Taking a sip, she gave the thumbs up to the group. Cheering, they all held out their glasses to be refilled. The lady walked around and filled everyone's glass.

Then he noticed the music in the background, it was an Aerosmith song.

Tyson was now singing out loud through a microphone, standing on a couch busting moves.

The ladies were having a girl's night out.

Tyson had on a kale green lacey slip that stopped above her knees. The top was tight around her bust and underneath, a kale green G-string. Travis, sitting in the armchair by her, wearing short, black, silk short and, a top that was netted red with black stripes going down.

Tyler, drinking a strawberry daiquiri is wearing a short silk peach shirt-like slip.

Teg was in a red, lacey, string camisole that was pulled up on the side, exposing her beautiful legs. She got up with her champagne glass, dancing to the song. She was leaning her body over, dancing with her ass toward the window.

Unbeknownst to her, the P.I.'s face is in that window.

He took a deep gulp of air.

Bonnie was wearing a pair of yellow silk pajamas. The top had short sleeves and the bottom stopped at the calves. Tex had on pajamas that were white at the bottom. The top had spaghetti straps and was purple. A karaoke machine was attached to the sixty-two--inch TV with an amplifier and wireless microphones and the words were on the screen.

Travis and Tyler pulled Tyson down off the couch and went to her left and, right as backup singers.

They were in step, swaying left and right.

Bonnie and Tex were hollering with laughter.

Teg got up to join them by grabbing her own microphone.

All four had their own microphones, singing lead, then backup and dancing at the same time.

The P.I. wished he could take pictures for later enjoyment, but a flash would reflect off the glass window and they would become aware they were being watched.

Tyson let Tyler take the lead. She was backed up by the girls.

Tyler was bending her head down, really getting into the song.

She showed the P.I. her nice coffee-colored butt.

He couldn't believe what he was seeing. His right hand went to his private area.

All four were crooning and shaking their butts toward the window.

Tex and Bonnie are sitting to the right to the girls, screaming with laughter, while snapping their fingers to the beat, not noticing the face in the window.

The P.I.'s eyes were bugging out and he was starting to breathe heavily.

Tyler was singing, *"Take me to the other side"*.

The other girls were singing background vocals, *"The other side."*

Tyler was singing lead *"Mom told me…"*

Everyone sang the chorus, *"Other side…"*

Tyson was playing her air guitar.

Travis yelled, "Aerosmith, you are hot!"

Tyson was doing a solo with the electric guitar hooked up to the karaoke machine and the other three girls were doing dance steps to her playing. Heads, arms, and legs were moving in the same steps.

The P.I.'s body was frozen at the window, staring like a schoolboy, moaning.

Tyson slowed down and the girls went into the next song.

"Love in an elevator…"

Travis took the lead on this one, with Tyson still playing her guitar. She couldn't play as well as Joe Perry, but she was good.

"Workin' like a dog…"

"Yeah, yeah, yeah…," sing Tyler, Teg, and Tyson.

"Going down."

The P.I. was rubbing his jewel faster.

Tyson went into a solo guitar playing a melody after a few seconds she starts singing, *"I'm a road runner baby…"*

"Whoa," sings Travis.

The girl's bodies went down and came back up. Their movements were getting dirty.

"A road runner,

The girls jumped in with the chorus.

"Well, we are road runners honey…"

"Beep, beep…"

The P.I. was beside himself and opened his zipper and started rubbing his jewel up and down, moaning deeply and softly.

In minutes, Teg was up front singing her lead.
She was singing, *"My world is empty...."*.
Everyone stopped in their tracks.

Teg continued, *"I find it hard for me to...."*

"Hey Teg, that's a Supreme song says Bonnie laughing.

"I am changing the scene" Teg answered.

"OK, mama do your thing" says Tex.

Boohooing... came from the girls "

Tyson said, "I am gagging," acting like she was about to vomit.

Tyler waved her hands toward Teg as if to say *no way* and rolled her eyes.

Travis said, "Girl, you have just stopped the party. We are doing Aerosmith."

"Come on ladies, I am serious," said Teg.

"So are we," said Tyson, going for another cheese and cracker, washing it down with a Piña Colada.

"That's cold, ladies," said Teg, pretending her feelings were hurt.

"Oh, don't pout. We get to that later," said Tyler, sipping her strawberry daiquiri.

"Much, much later," laughed Tyson, munching on her cracker and cheese.

"Hey, I can't get any love?" said Teg with her arms extended for a hug.

"No," said Tyler, smoking the funny cigarette, laughing.

Pouting, Teg went back to the sofa, sat down, and took a sip of her vodka and orange juice.

Travis put her arm around her to comfort her, gave her one of the funny cigarettes and said, "Next time, the Supremes. Promise," said Travis.

"Promise?" said Teg, taking a puff.
Laughing, Tex put out her hand for the microphone that Teg was still holding.

She gave it up with a sigh.

Tex said to Bonnie, "Let's teach the young ones, shall we, friend?"

With one hand on her hip and her body in a sexy stance, Bonnie said, "Ladies, this is going to be heavy, so we have to pull out the cannons."

Tyson rolled her eyes to the back of her head.

Travis and Tyler took sips of their drinks. Teg smoked the funny cigarette and, tapped Tyson to pass it to her.

Tex got in line with Bonnie and at the same time both did a spin, and the microphones switched to their right hand.

A roar went up in the room.

Tex wearing a G-string was the last straw for the P.I. His body jerk crazy and, he was trying to keep his moaning down. The melody of the song began. Tex gently pulled the microphone up to her mouth,
and started singing the song. Bonnie did backup by moving to the left and, right of Tex's body.

"*What you want? /*

Baby, I got it…"

Bonnie chimed in with, *"ooo…"*

"What you need? /do you know I got it?"

"Oooh…" sang Bonnie.

Their bodies were moving to help emphasize the words.

"A little respect when I get home, *"R-e-s-p-e-c-t"*.

Both sang together, *"Sock it to me…"*

Bonnie stepped up and started singing. *"At first, I was petrified…*

Pumping her fist in the air, Bonnie sang, *"I will survive…"*

The girls whooped and hollered, *"Yeah, go on girl!"*

Bonnie did. *"Oh, as long as I know……"*

Grabbing Tex's hand for her to come in with her, both started singing simultaneously,

"I will survive……"

Their moves were so sexy, the P.I. climaxed and his eyes went to the back of his head. He passed out with his jewel straight up through the zipper in his pants, a large stain was appearing bigger and bigger by the second on his pants.

Tex and Bonnie took their bows with thunderous applause.

CHAPTER-TWENTY-TWO

Akers, who was afraid to go home, called Noah twice a day to make sure he was okay.

Each day, he was able to talk more. After about two or three sentences, Noah just grunted. This was okay by Akers because his friend was alive.

A lady nurse, who was a friend of the doctor, came by twice a day to make sure Noah's IV was working properly, that his liquid food, water was right and to keep him in good spirits. The two realized they both loved old, classic movies and watched one or two a day.

"Noah, I met some good people, I think they know the people at the house, you know where we played poker" Akers said.

Noah gave out a loud but painful mourn."

"Look, man they are cool, the guy name is Blackie, I met him at my job orientation.

Noah grunt again.

Akers can tell by the sound he didn't like where the conversation was going.

Akers put the phone away from his ear, sighed, then raise it back to his ear.

"Noah, we have to trust somebody, how the hell are we going to get information, like are they still looking for us?

Noah didn't grunt this time.

"Good, I have your attention. They want to meet you, is that okay."

Noah answered, "Hell no, no, no"

"Look man, they are not working for the man, they are not thugs, you know what I mean?

Noah answered, "No"

"I'm afraid too, but trust me friend okay, we need help or …. we need to leave town."

Akers could hear Noah taking a hard swallow, then he said, "Let's go."

"Okay, be home soon, we will leave, my friend. Stay calm, no more talk from me".

Noah answered softly, "Thanks."

Both hung up.

Ackers knew it was no use in bringing up Tyson and Travis. He wasn't sure what Noah would do and he couldn't lose his best friend even thou Tyson was hot as a firecracker; hell, so was Travis, but……Tyson.

***

Akers felt he could trust Blackie, so when he arrived at the room, both were sitting on the balcony, feeling the cool breeze coming from the blue ocean. Blackie had his favorite drink and Akers had a vodka and orange juice. This time, he ate food. Blackie had ordered steaks, bake potatoes and salads for both. It smelled delicious.

He needed to talk to someone to help out with this problem. He had only four days left before he had to leave the safety of the hotel room and go back home.

"Yo, man I sense something is crawling up your mind. Talk," said Blackie.

"Thanks, because this has been keeping me up the last two nights," said Akers.

"My man, the area around your eyes is looking dark and baggy. What is keeping you up?"

Blackie asked, grabbing a slice of steak.

A few seconds pass before Akers started talking. Blackie let him take his time.

"I am going to start from the beginning but will skip some things because it is necessary, okay?" said Akers.

"You have the floor, man," said Blackie, chewing on his steak.

Akers bit into his steak and chewed slowly. He took a napkin to wipe his mouth, then a sip of his vodka.

"Man, this shit is so good when you are nervous," said Akers.

Blackie shook his head up and down thinking' *a church man still needs his juice.*'

Akers blurted out, "You can't imagine what goes through a person's mind when they open their front door and your best friend is barely standing up with blood running down his neck, holding some type of material up to his neck, whole torso was covered in his blood.

I went into shock. He pushed me aside and stumbled into my living room and started pacing.

He was afraid to sit because he thought he would die. I didn't know what to do man. I just stood and stared. Since he was shot in the neck, he couldn't talk".

Blackie took a sip of his Hennessey; he already knew this but let Akers continue.

"He was making signs with his hands and I finally figured out he was asking for a pen and paper. I ran to get some. I didn't want this man to die at my place. All kinds of thoughts were going through my head. What will I tell the police? How will I explain why he came to me? Will the police think I did it? Man, I could have passed out."

Akers stopped telling the story to take a folk full of his bake potato and a couple of sips from his vodka glass.

Blackie stayed calm, hoping Akers would not freeze up and stop.

He was thinking, *'I'm glad I remembered to put on this white cap'*. He didn't know where, but he knew he was recording and sending it back to God knows where.

Akers was shaking a little. To calm him down, Blackie said, "Nobody here is going to hurt you. Get it out so you can breathe, man."

Slightly shaking with the vodka glass still in his hand, Akers nodded yes. "My friend, Noah, hangs out with awfully bad people sometimes. They live on the other side of Herr. No one is aloud near that area without permission. He told me one night he was at a club and met some guys. I believe…their names were Radio, and somebody named after something sweet that you eat. Oh…oh I remember, Pie."

'Jesus, that's the two guys from the restaurant', Blackie was thinking, then he said "Uhm…I need to interrupt here. Did you ever meet those guys personally?"

"No, just Noah knows them. He had pointed them out one day when we were in the car and they were in another car. I didn't like the looks of them. My instincts went haywire, signaling, 'you don't want to meet or hang with those guys.' Don't even mess with them. I swear Blackie, they had an aroma that stated 'Danger! Danger!' You know, like that robot on that TV series 'Lost in Space'?"

"Yeah, I liked that show, especially the professor. That man messed up everything. In fact, isn't that why they crashed?"

Laughing, Akers said, "I believe so. I like the whole cast. The daughter was hot."

Blackie whistled.

Akers laughed.

"Akers, you went to one of the poker games, them guys were not there?"

"No, they were other guys, I would have remembered them, Oh, that guy Paul was there. He was nice really. The whole night was fun, but Noah never took me again saying I was too churchy.

"Is it okay if we go outside on the balcony to finish our drinks, the weather is nice?"

"Yea, Akers picked up drink and followed Blackie outside.

"Hole up, let me get our bottles" Blackie went back inside to retrieve the bottles and to make sure his equipment was still working.

Blackie added some water to Ackers vodka because if he got too drunk, he would forget things, or he might break down and stop talking. Blackie decided to go back to Lost in Space. "You know they made a movie of the series?"

"Bro, I didn't like it," said Akers.

"I didn't make it through thirty minutes before I walked out the theater. Never did that before. Wait, that is not true. It was another movie, but I can't think of it now," said Blackie.

"Still hungry, we better order something, it can be a thirty-minute wait because it was the weekend.

Akers replied, "No, this will do."

"Oh shit," said Blackie, who jumped up out of his seat and bolted into the room inside. Akers, not sure what was going on, started looking all around him thinking, should he run too.

Blackie returned quickly with another bag. He said, "The mind can be a terrible waste." He emptied the bag he had forgotten about and pulled out eight buffalo wings with extra blue cheese sauce and cheesy breadsticks.

"Mmm, this looks delicious," said Akers, rubbing his hands together.

"Good," said Blackie, "They are still hot." He passed a plate to Akers, who took some wings out of the container, a blue cheese pack, and two cheesy breadsticks.

"Hot enough. I do have a microwave here," Blackie said.

"Man, your room has everything," said Akers.

Looking puzzled, Blackie asked, "Yours doesn't,"

"Hell no, it has a bed, desk, chair, table, and entertainment stand with just a TV," said Akers.

"No internet hook-up?" asked Blackie.

"Oh yeah there is, but I don't have a laptop," Akers answered.

"My man, I have two laptops. I will give you one, won at bingo," said Blackie.

Joking, Akers said, "Bingo? I thought only old people go to those games."

"Oh, jokes, my man?" said Blackie, laughing with Akers.

"An innocent one, my man," said Akers, tapping Blackie on the shoulder, laughing.

Tapping Akers back on his shoulder, Blackie said, "Man, you are tripping. That is where the hottest women are. They have to bring their parents and grandparents. Nice stock around. Good for pickin', man," said Blackie.

"Really? I'll have to check that out, but would love the laptop said Akers, gratefully.

"Let me clean it up and it is yours," said Blackie.

Akers noticed he used the word friend again and smiled. He liked having Blackie as a friend.

"Hmm, what happened to your friend?" Blackie asked, dipping a wing into a container of blue cheese sauce.

"I ended up calling a doctor friend I knew because Noah was afraid to go to the hospital. Luckily for Noah, the doctor was in his car about two blocks away. I had given Noah some towels and he was holding them tight to his neck, but the blood was running out fast.

I could see he was getting weaker by the moment. His skin was turning a blue color and his eyes were slowly dilating. I tell you Blackie I was sick with fright.

"Man, I'm afraid just hearing the story, but go ahead," said Blackie.

"My high school friend who is a doctor arrives with his emergency black bag and examined my friend. He said that the bullet went straight through him, but he needed to be x-rayed, cleaned up, and stitched or he would die. Noah went off with fear, mumbling, 'no, no, no, no hosp… He could hardly form his words because of the injury. I know one thing. Noah is a brave man because I can sense him fighting to live and to survive. I asked the doc if he could numb him and stitch him up?"
He replied, 'If I touch this guy and he die, I could lose my license."

"Noah reached for the pen and paper and managed to write out a statement that said the doc would not be responsible, but then he threatened to kill him, and stated he had a gun.

The doc and I looked at each other because we knew Noah didn't have a gun. He could barely move. I pleaded with my friend, the doctor. Sighing and looking at Noah, he went back to check out Noah's neck. The doctor was able to numb the area around the neck and clean up the area with iodine. He stated that without any x-ray, he couldn't predict the damage inside the neck.

I repeated to Noah that this was extremely dangerous. Noah wrote on another piece of paper '*not as dangerous as who will find me in the hospital and finish me off. Right now, they think he is dead but will realize later he is not'.*

Looking at Noah, the doc said, "Maybe this will be okay, but Noah needs to have this checked. If he lives through the night, bring him to my office downtown. Come through the back entrance. I will be there around six o'clock in the morning, and don't be late because the office opens at eight o'clock."
I said, "okay."
The doc went to his bag and pulled out a syringe with a small bottle. He put the needle into the small bottle and withdrew some liquid. He went to Noah and pushed the needle into his neck. Noah moaned. Within seconds, he was out like a light. The doc asked me to get some boiling hot water and some more towels.
"I'm out of towels". I said,
"Get me some sheets. I prefer white." the doctor said.
"Don't have any white sheets."
Sighing, he said, 'Anything light colored.'
"I ran to my closet and opened it wide. Searching up and down with my hands shaking, I found some light beige ones and showed them to the doc who was working on Noah's neck.
"Those will do" he said.
"I left them beside him and went to get the boiling hot water. I found the biggest pan I had and put it on the stove. Man, I was sweating up a storm and when I noticed my reflection in the silver pot, I looked like shit and hell rolled up together. Hair was a mess; skin was ashen, blood all over my clothes and hands shaking something terrible. Oh yeah, and I was breathing fast.
I said to myself, *'Calm down, this is going to be okay.'*
"I sat down at the table in my kitchen, waiting for the water to boil. It took just a few minutes because I had the fire so high, the side of the pan was black. Wasn't going back in to see all that blood or the doc digging into flesh. I swear to god, would had passed out.
Seems like a few seconds after I sat down, the doc called for the boiling water. He needed it to clean the area on the neck and he also needed his tools. I took the hot, boiling pot to him. His plastic gloves were all red with blood. He was so calm, but I was nauseated. I quickly left the area and went to the kitchen, leaning over the sink throwing up.
Afterwards, I grabbed a beer out of the refrigerator. My hands were shaking so bad I needed both of them to get the beer bottle up to my mouth. When it got there, I drank the beer straight down, put the bottle on

the table, and lowered my head to get a grip of myself. Seem like seconds before the doc was calling me back in. I stumbled into the room where Noah was still out cold but now had a large white bandage around his neck."

The doc said, "We need to get him down."
We managed to open the sofa bed and prop his head up on a pillow. He reached into his black bag and gave me some pills to give Noah when he wakes.
The doctor then said, "He going to be in a lot of pain. Get him to the office tomorrow at six o'clock sharp. I will inform my nurse and she will come by to take care of him twice a day."
"I was glad to hear that because I knew nothing about caring for someone who had been shot or even slightly injured for that matter. He packed his bag and left the apartment."

"Whoa, that is a lot," said Blackie.

"Man, that is only half of it. Do you want to hear the rest?" Akers asked.

"Lay it on me, man. Wait a minute, you need a refresher?" Blackie asked.

"Yes, bring out more, man," said Akers.

"I think we have to be careful how many open bottles in plain sight," said Blackie pointing to his surroundings.

"Of course. I wasn't thinking," said Akers.

"No sweat, man. You have a good memory," said Blackie.

"Too good, I need to forget some of this so I can sleep," said Akers.

Blackie nodded his head.

"I wish I had more time here to get myself together," Akers said.

"I will be here only about one more week," said Blackie.

"Who is paying for this, the company?" Akers asked.

"No, I am. I wanted to stick around to do some sightseeing," said Blackie.

"Not much to see here, my man," said Akers.

"Yeah, I found that out when I arrived, but it was paid for in advance. Let me talk to the front desk. Maybe they will give me some kind of discount if I reserve your room for a couple more days," said Blackie.

"You would do that? Why? Where are you getting the money? I thought you just started to work. Have they given you a check already?" said Akers, bombarding Blackie with questions.

169

"Slow down, comrade," said Blackie, holding up his hands in a "stop" motion. "My family left me some money and I don't think it will be that much. This is a small town. The cost of the hotel room you are in is around maybe fifty dollars a night," said Blackie.

He rose up and went to his cell phone. He texted a message asking if he could have the extra money wired straight to the hotel and received a message back.

"Okay, only three more days. You need to push Akers and ask to meet Noah," the message read.

He messaged back, "I can't rush this. Akers is tripping and can't be pushed; both need to be moved to a safe house soon."

The message came back, "No can do. They need to stay at Akers' apartment."

Blackie sighed. *'For agents, these people have no sense of urgency'*, he thought. He messaged back, *'Those assassins Radio and Pie will have their nuts for cocktail olives if they are not moved to safety.'*

The message came back, *'You have to meet Noah to question him about the card players for more intel and more about the house. We have only some information. Whole mission could be blown.'*

Blackie messaged back, *'Okay, I will be extra careful, but consider the safe house'.*

The message returned, *'Meet Noah tomorrow.'*

'Jesus, you are being a little pushy,' Blackie messaged back.

Silence

Blackie said to himself, *'That damn Tyson.'*

Blackie returned to the balcony. Akers was eating some more buffalo wings.

"Hey man, I got a great discount, the hotel extended your stay a few more days, but I need a favor from you. Really, I need two favors. Just listen clearly before you answer."

Akers, in between chews, got out a soft, "Thank you."

Blackie said, "We all go through storms in life. How we come out of the storms is what make us better human beings, agree?"

"Agree" said Akers.

"Well, you are in a thunderstorm and I am going to help you get out. I can't go into much detail, but I have friends who can help you, but I need more information," said Blackie.

Akers sighed, slightly mortified. He just looked at Blackie with fear in his eyes and asked, "The government?"

Waving his hand, Blackie said, "Don't be afraid. I am just an analyst who gathers information like the house Noah played card games., the people who live there." Pausing for a few seconds, Blackie continued, "Don't trip, but we believe the man or men who shot your friend Noah lives there. If that is true, then you and Noah are in a lot of trouble because those guys are ruthless killers and don't leave any breadcrumbs behind. As soon as they realize that Noah is alive, they will come after him and whoever is with him and kill all of you. Where is Noah? Is he still at your place?" asked Blackie.

"He is at my place," said Akers, clearing his throat.

"Is he well enough to be moved and can he talk?" Blackie asked.

"Yes, he can be moved, and he can talk a little better," said Akers, still staring at Blackie, trying to make out what he was really saying.

"Akers, I didn't know you were a part of this investigation until you mentioned some information. I need you to believe I really like you and was disturbed when things started to come together, and I wrestled how to approach you. I swear I really did," said Blackie.

Softly, Akers said, "I believe you. My instincts that have kept me alive all these years told me you were okay. What kind of work do you do for the government?"

"I can't answer that question, but Akers, I don't work for no government agency. I've already told you a lot," said Blackie with a sad look on his face.

"Okay, maybe later?" Akers asked.

"Maybe later. It is not up to me and I can never tell you the full extent because I don't even know. This mission is on a need-to-know basis, and Akers, I don't want to know everything. It keeps me and you alive, understand?" said Blackie.

"Understand-...oh, how about those two ladies Tyson and Travis? They work for the government?" Akers asked.

"Uhm.... not really, but I really can't talk about them. Akers, Tyson really likes you, but she has to be careful she can trust you," said Blackie, giving Akers a smile.

"Man, she is hot and I'm getting a hard--on just thinking about meeting her again."

"Again"

"Yea, we meet last night."

"Action"

"Nope and can wait."

"Better than me" laughing Blackie added "Man don't fuck up my chair with stains.".

Laughing, Akers answered, "I have it under control."

"Five thousand dollars can come to you and Noah if he gives us some more information."

"Five grand?"

"Need to meet Noah tomorrow," said Blackie.

"That's okay with me, but Noah might not be okay with this," said Akers.

"I need to convince him it is in his best interest to meet me and don't tell him yet about my other job. I will tell him on my own when necessary. Call him now please," said Blackie.

Akers asked again softly, "Is this for Tyson?

"Yeah," said Blackie.

Akers pulled out his cell phone and speed dialed a number. He put the phone on speaker phone.

A husky voice came on the other line saying, "Hi, my friend. How is the job going?"

Akers answered, "Fine. I'm coming by tonight. We need to talk."

"Ok, everything okay?" Noah asked.

"Peachy my dawg peachy, need to talk, okay?" said Akers.

"See you then," said Noah.

"Bye," said Akers.

Noah hung up the phone and so did Akers.

He looked at Blackie and said, "I will go tonight to prepare Noah for your visit tomorrow. I will convince him, I promise, only because I am afraid, and I think you can save both our lives."

"I'm glad you have faith in me and my friends, Akers. No more talk. I think the football game is coming on. How 'bout we take this inside and order some more food and drinks?" said Blackie.

"Love to. Pizza?" Asked Akers.

"You are on," said Blackie.

Both got up and went into the living room area of Blackie's suite. Blackie turned on the TV, it came on roaring in with the announcers saying, *'This is going to be one of the greatest games of all time.'*

Akers put himself on the couch right in front of the TV. Blackie picked up the phone on the table and ordered pizza, Meat lover pan crust extra cheese, and fresh bottles of Hennessey, vodka, and orange juice. He was told by the front desk his order would be there in fifteen minutes.

Blackie after hanging up the room phone, said to Noah, "People here gives the best service all around, leaving a huge tip for them.". He then turned up the Tv volume.

The announcer on tv is talking *'Players are being introduced on the field, number 88 Pearson, Number 12 Roger'*, crowd was roaring.

Akers was quiet, thinking, *'Deep down, knowing his friend, no chance was he going to meet Ackers new friends. He was just too afraid and had beg Ackers not to tell them anything about him because he knows a slip of a tongue, he would be dead. Ackers promise his friend, he will not say anything, and they will use the money for them to leave town when he gets paid.'*

***

The next day, Akers went out and successfully pulled off his assignment. He pushed the button many times and clicked off hundreds of pictures over the area.

He saw that the tower that was protecting the area had a watchman looking at him through powerful binoculars. Weapons were pointed at the plane.

The pilot did the signal he was instructed to do to let them know who he was. He tilted the left wing slightly, so the plane was riding sideways to the left. He did that for a few seconds and then straightened out the plane. Seeing this, they lowered their weapons, but kept them nearby so they could be fired if necessary. The camera was in the shape of a fuel tank that had no fuel in it. The real fuel tank was underneath. No one notice.

Akers was thinking about his conversation he had with Noah last night. *'His instinct was right, he is not going to meet or talk with anyone about a poker game, his shooting or anything'*.

He said to Noah, Man I trust this people, I think they work for some type of spy service and will protect us".

Noah replied, "No, and he shouldn't not trust anyone, anyone".

Akers tried again, "Noah if I am right about them protecting us, we are safe. I feel safe when around them".

"What you mean around them, thought you were at an orientation for a job?'

"I am, A guy who I befriended....'Akers stop talking.

"Yea, said Noah, "That was a setup, man".

"You probably right, but....

"Akers, a set up, it could be they are working on their side."

Shaking his head, "No, they are not. They want somebody at the place, you played poker at."

"Who? somebody is killing off people".

"What?"
"Some of those deaths broadcasting on Tv news played poker at that house."
Akers replied "What?"
"They are dead, Akers."
Sighing, Akers said, I really, really think we can trust them to help us".
"No, and I hope you not talking".
Ackers backed down and said, "I told them nothing Noah, we are leaving with my sign bonus check.". Akers came back to reality when he realizes the pilot was talking to him.

"Akers, my favorite team had won by a touchdown in overtime. Their running back had broken the defensive line and ran eighty yards for the win. I was running around the house like a chicken with its head cut off. My wife just shook her head in disbelief. My son was yelling with me. Did you watch the game?" the pilot, named Jed asked.

"Yeah, it was a classic," said Akers, concentrating on his job.

"I can still see that play in my head. It was one of the most exciting plays of all time," said Jed, who was wearing the running back's jersey, number 22, in silver and blue colors.

The whole run took about thirty minutes.

When the plane landed, Jed was still talking about the game. He got out of the cockpit and met another one of his friends, who also was wearing the same jersey as Jed.

High fiving each other, they talked about the game and Jed shouted, "Best game I have ever seen in years!"

"Hell yeah!" said the other guy. "We went all the way!"

Both said at the same time, "Super Bowl!"

The men high fived again, this time by jumping their bodies in the air, chest bumping. Landing, they laughed and walked toward the locker rooms. Ackers following them.

Walker, standing to the right of the scene, walked up to the plane casually and removed the camera. The mission was successful.

CHECKMATE.

CHAPTER TWENTY-THREE

On a nice, seventy-four-degree day with a wind blowing, Jordan yelled, "What the hell?! Radio and Pie, get your asses in here!"
When they arrived in the room, Jordan was holding a round metal piece the size of a nickel with wires attached.

He said, "I thought this room got swept twice a day. How in the hell did this get in?! The real question is … how long has it been in here?!" Look you fucks, we have a big mission coming up soon. This is unacceptable, in my fucking house, my HOUSE.

Radio and Pie were speechless. They just looked at the metal thing Jordan was holding in his hand.
They knew it was a bug of some sort.

Jordan broke the silence in the room, which was getting hotter by the moment, and said, "Get the men in here and begin searching the whole fucking room! Matter of fact check the whole fucking house! These things are like roaches, it is never just one!"

***

The whole scene was being observed by the ladies at the Command Center.

'Oops, he found the fake one. Hopefully, he won't find the real one', Bonnie was thinking, looking at the screen. The bug was voice activated once anyone started talking.

***

Jordan knew, this is the agency. No small-time crook could get this special, type of bug.
He began thinking, *'Are they on to me? Who in the agency is on to me?'*

He pulled out his cell phone, speed dialed a number to his mole in the agency. His body was tense, waiting for the person to answer. He got a voice mail.

He left a secret message. *'The cat has caught the mouse and the trap needs to be emptied.'*

Upset he got a voicemail; Jordan threw his cell phone across the room, breaking it into pieces. Then he said, "I hate voicemails. That asshole should have picked up! I know my number came up on the caller ID. Nobody is doing their fucking jobs around here! You two, get to moving!" He pointed to Pie and Radio.

Sharron, who was standing by the wall next to the left of the doorway, went closer to the wall so she wouldn't be noticed. She became afraid because, she had overheard something,

Radio and Pie passed her in a hurry on their way to the guard post.

When the coast was clear, she tiptoed back upstairs to her room, shaking with fear. She jumped on her bed and curled up like a baby, shaking and thinking.

'He might think it was her that planted the bug.
Hell, right now he would suspect everyone.'

In between shaking, she listened for footsteps heading in her direction. After a few minutes, she calmed herself down, realizing no footsteps, are coming her way.

She did hear the bodyguard stationed outside Jordan's bedroom door, leave their post.

She got out of the bed and slowly opened her bedroom door.

Furniture is being moved around.

She tiptoed toward the end of the hall and could hear Jordan downstairs yelling out instructions. "Move over there and put the machine right on it so it can pick up the frequency! Back in the room, he instructed Radio, go downstairs, knock on the security room door, and ask for the visitors log back one month. Tell them I want all video and audio checked to see who has been in here and who came into the house. Tell them to concentrate everywhere, we may find more little birdies."

Radio left the area to honor Jordan's wishes.

Sharron stepped back by the wall, so he couldn't see her.

He didn't even look her way.

She noticed no one else was on the main floor where Jordan's bedroom was. She went back into her room to get her purse and opened it to pull out the special black hard plastic piece that Teg had given her. Breathing deeply and shaking slightly, Sharron went about her mission for her friend Teg, who promised to get her out if she planted this little black box. Teg told her that all she needed to do was push it up over the one already there and she and her friends would take care of the rest.

Sharron asked her, "Are you working for the government?"

Teg answered, "No, I can't say who, for your own good, but you are safe with me."

Sharron believed Teg was telling the truth, so she didn't question her, friend anymore.

She tiptoed back to her bedroom door, listening out for voices and sounds. Sensing all was clear; she opened her door and headed toward Jordan's, bedroom door.

She stopped in her tracks and sigh. Jordan's door was ajar. She had never even seen it unlocked before. She looked up at the security pad by the door and saw two lights indicated it was unarmed. A lucky sign. She pushed the door open using her shirt over her fingers, having been warn not to never leave fingerprints.

Taking a deep breath, she entered the forbidden room and noticed all kinds of security equipment. She saw a 65-inch color tv that was divided into four squares displaying four different areas of the location inside and outside the compound. She looks at the screens, looking for where people are in the house.

Jordan and his poses were tearing shit up. She laughed softly. Whomever Teg and her group were, they are good. They were not finding anything.

One of the TV screens was showing images of her bedroom.

Teg told her that if she saw anything like that, she needed to get the CD of the footage and put a magnet on it to erase the recordings of what she was doing before entering the room. Teg told her Jordan would think the equipment had malfunctioned. She started looking around for the recording equipment, she couldn't locate it, so she decided to go outside the room and attach the special equipment to the alarm box outside Jordan's bedroom. It snaps on perfectly. She went back to her room, where a text was waiting for her on her cell phone. *'Great job'*.

She knew who it was from. She smiled and cut on the Tv to wait for her next move.

The guards in the security room watching the TV screens didn't notice the slight blink she caused.

***

Bonnie is viewing the images of Jordan's bedroom entrance in the Command Center.

Due to Tyler's superior job, she was able to erase Sharron's activities outside her room, Jordan's room inside and out from the main computer in the security room as fast as she could in case the bodyguards decided to look in that area. Sharron had text Teg, job one wasn't successful.

The guard was not interested in Jordan's bedroom at the time because he was following orders, he was given to get the sign-in log and retrieve the tapes from about a month ago to give to Jordan.

***

Furniture was being torn apart because Jordan had gone into a frenzy looking for more bugs. Another one was found inside the lamp. Jordan's instincts told him these were too easy to find. There were major ones, they were well hidden.

Radio returned to the mayhem and said to Jordan, "The guard post didn't see or have any reports of anything unusual."

"Bring me the copies and get a sweeper to check for listening devices, in here on the double," said Jordan pissed.

Radio left to find another sweeper. Pie started looking around the room to see if his eye could catch anything out of place. Jordan put two fingers on his chin and was rubbing it. He snapped the same two fingers and said, "Docket!"

Docket jumped with fear. Everyone was in fear of Jordan when he was in this type of mood. People die instantly with no regrets.
"Go upstairs and check on my room. Run the tapes and check everything," said Jordan,
 with venom pacing the room.

Jordan grabbed Docket by the arm and held it. He looked at him with a hard stare and said with a deep voice, "I mean, check everything."
"Yes boss," said Dockett, shaking in his high-top sneakers.

"Somebody's ass is going up in flames for this! Someone in my organization dropped a serious ball and I will find out whom and they will be dismissed!" said Jordan.

No one said a word.
Dockett reached the bedroom door and paused, the alarm was not on and, the door was ajar.
He pulled out his weapon and looked around to see if anyone was there.
He saw no one and the area was quiet. Only his heavy breathing could be heard.

'Sharron,' he thought,*' that bitch....'* He walked toward her room, turned the knob on the door, it was locked. Her security book light is red. Instantly he knew his thoughts were wrong.

***

Teg, who had joined Bonnie at the Command Center, pushed a button on the keypad, a live feed from Sharron's room began to be shown on a monitor. She is safe in her room.

They can see and hear Dockett in the hallway.

***

Sharron was in her room, looking at the doorknob turning, with her hands over her mouth so she would not scream out loud, praying hard whomever it was would stop.
Her phone beeps. Looking at it, she saw a message from Teg. It simply read, *'You are safe.'*

***

The command center can see Docket's moves, he turns the knob and walked away from Beverly's door. They heard him talking to himself.
'She couldn't know the code to bypass the alarm. 'Shit, I was the one who went into the room looking for XXX movies that Jordan had in his collection to watch with the guys tonight.
I must have forgetting to put the alarm back on when the commotion started downstairs. Damn.

He hurried inside the room to check; he didn't leave anything else disturbed. Jordan could walk into a room and point out if the littlest thing were disturbed. His eyes darted everywhere, and he pulled out a handkerchief and start, going back over his tracks, wiping down everything for fingerprints.

***

Docket went over to the cabinet that held the recording equipment, opened it, and saw that they were recording. He pushed a button for the dvd to rewind, back at least one hour.

Waiting for about five minutes, he saw nothing but static. Confused, he pulled the dvd out, looked at it, and then returned it and pushed play again. There was still only static.

He tried another dvd, static again. He was not aware that every time he inserts a dvd, it automatic erase its contents due to a program that had been sent to the player from the Command center. He did have some luck; A couple of dvd's showed the outside of Jordan's bedroom and the surrounding grounds. Reviewing a few, everything looked normal.

Docket went back to two of the dvd's that showed only static, put them back in and all he saw again was static, like a tv with no cable or antenna. Those dvd's were crucial because they recorded everything from the last forty-eight hours. He checks the connected wires to the recorder, and everything looked on the level and now he had to go back downstairs to tell Jordan.

Docket took the back way to the security room which could only, be accessed from Jordan's room. knocking on the door, he is met at the door, by a technician.

A little out of breath Docket asked him, "Did you have any recordings from Jordan's room over the last forty-eight hours?"

The technician answered, "Look man, we are busy. The boss is barking orders faster than we can handle. I don't know what we have."

"Okay, I know he is barking orders to all of us, but his machine is not working right, and I have no tape of his room area during the last forty-eight hours. Can I come in and check?"

"No can do. You are not authorized and…."

He put his hand up to stop Docket from talking.

"We don't record the boss' room. He has his own recording mechanism."

Shaking his head Docket said, "Damn, I am fucked."

"Look, we are busy. I have to go, man. The boss is making us go back six months. Sorry."

The technician closed the door on Docket's face, he stood there for a few seconds, and then went back upstairs the back way.

Back inside the security room, another technician said, "You just lied to that guy. We do have video of the boss' bedroom as back up."

"It's his ass or ours. Besides, we are the only two besides the boss who knows" said the first technician.

***

"Well, that's not true" said Teg at the Command Center laughing.

"Jordan your stinking ass is going down" said Bonnie, high fiving Teg.

***

Back upstairs Docket sat down on a chair to think. *'So, if they can't video the boss' room,*
and the machine malfunctioning, that is not my fault, and
best part is they could not see me looking for those dvd's.' he was thinking. Scratching his head, he went out of the bedroom door, put on the alarm, and went back downstairs, this time taking things slowly, one step at a time.

180

He would have to structure this right, or his ass is history.
He can still see and hear this guy screaming,
as he was skin alive by Jordan. His body jerked hard with the remembrance.

***

"Good work has been done by Sharron," said Teg at the Command Center.

"Yes, we have to get that poor girl out of there soon before the man trips," said Bonnie.

"I will get her out," said Teg.

A diagram of the floor where Jordan's and Sharron rooms along with escape routes are formed on the screen and was being analyzed from top to bottom by both.

CHAPTER TWENTY-FOUR

Loud sounds were whirling around the room. Bodies going over the room, with a fine-tooth comb.
A tall over six-foot man in the middle of the floor just watching with intense eyes. Pillows were being torn apart with feathers and other materials spreading, everywhere on the floor,
and on people's clothes. Wooden furniture had been hacked apart,
or was being hacked apart,
looking for anything that shouldn't be there.
Jordan was standing with his Ruger P345, a three-dot, precise target, black-handled gun with shiny chrome on top, in his hand, making everyone nervous. He was known for shooting it off anytime he wishes at anyone he wishes.
So far only two bugs had been found.
"Tear this motherfucking room apart!" yelled Jordan.
Couches were overturned. Glasses were broken by guns and smashed up, against the wall.
The place looked like a war zone when Pie entered the room, looking for Jordan.
"Docket did you get the gate footage?!" Jordan yelled.
"Did boss, right here," said Docket, handing a dvd to Jordan.
"I don't want it! Put in the machine and let it run!" Jordan yelled.
Docket turned to do as he was asked.
He had to move around items to find the dvd player,
hoping it still worked, the room is f…up. Finding the player, he cleaned it, and the TV off,
so, the recording could be seen clearly.

***

Back at the Command Center, the whole scene from the "cave",
was being played out on screen,
which was being watched carefully by everyone, who have returned,
including Tex, hoping they wouldn't find the major electronic bugs that was transmitting these images.
The main ones are hidden in the main security room that monitors the whole complex.

Tex banked on that they would examine the equipment, but not destroy it completely. Had something to do about men and their electronic toys.

***

While waiting for the recording to load, Docket walked up to Jordan, took a deep breath, and said, "Boss, the recording machine had a hiccup and didn't record the last forty-eight hours".

Jordan gave him a hard stare, and then said, "That's okay, because no one can get in my room. Go over there and help the guys anyway you can. Oh, where is Sharron?"

"She is locked in her room boss," said Docket.

Jordan pointed to Pie near the entrance door of the room and said, "Bring Sharron down to me, but not to this room. Take her to the game room and then come and get me."

Pie shook his head *yes* and turned to go up the stairs.

Jordan turned his attention back to the room, surveying it, quietly thinking, *'this mission must go through without any hiccups, it the coup of my career, it will make me the king, all my hard work over the years will come to fruition, I WILL BE KING of arms & drugs. No one can touch me NO ONE'.*

***

Sharron was looking at a text, when the knock came at the door warning her Pie was coming up to get her for Jordan.

The knock came while she was erasing the text.

She came to the door and opened it. "Yes?"

"The boss wants you downstairs," Pie said.

"Okay". She had put her cell phone in her pants pocket before answering the door. She followed Pie down the stairs. He guided her into the game room and left. Jordan appeared within seconds.

Smiling he said, "Sharron, you have to be moved from here. A lot of shit is going down and I don't want you in the middle."

"Where will I go?" She asked, softly wringing her hands together.

"You will be taken to a condo I own," said Jordan.

"Okay. Can I pack or what do you want me to do?".

"You go back upstairs and pack for maybe a week. If more is needed, you can go shopping or I will have someone bring it to you,".
"Okay" said Sharron. She left the room to pack.

Jordan smiled at Sharron. He treated her with kid gloves because she reminded him of a special person in his heart. Jordan went back to the boys.

As Jordan passed Pie, he told him to wait for her and take her to the condo. Jordan stopped suddenly, turned around and said, "Take her to my special hotel suite on the Boulevard, she will be safer, no one can get to her."

Sharron text Teg saying, *'I am being moved now, contact you when it is safe'*. Not aware at the Command Center everyone heard and saw the exchange.

She was mostly ready by the time the guard knocked on her door.

She ran to open it and said, "Just a few more minutes!"

"Yes ma'am," Pie answered. Respecting her wishes.

She smiled back at the guard and continued packing.

Pie asked, "Need any help?"

She answered, "Only with the bags."

Pie picked up two of them and placed them in the hall.
Moving towards the door with the bags, Pie mentions "The boss changed his mind and you're going to a hotel suite."

"Why?" She asked, wondering about the change.

Hunching up his shoulders, Pie answered, "He thinks it's safer."

"Okay with me. The boss knows best."

"Yes, madam he does,"
"All finished here,". She grabbed her purse and last overnight bag.
He guided her out of the back entrance to the waiting black SUV.

Sharron got in without looking around. She didn't want to see anything.
Jordan was watching the whole scene from a window in the game room.

Pie put the luggage in the truck of the SUV, and it pulled off toward the hotel. The driver had been instructed by Jordan to let him know when the package had been delivered.

***

Teg was glad Sharron was being taken to a hotel instead of Jordan's condo. She could be watched more closely at the hotel.
Bonnie got on the phone to advise the undercover agent who works at the hotel, of her arrival.
She was told his special suite hadn't been assigned yet by the agent.
He is calling now, get it ready," Bonnie, hung up.
"Confirm" the agent replied.

***

Jordan was on his cell phone, booking his special suite for his guest's arrival. The clerk who picked up the illuminated button on the hotel phone said,
"Yes sir, your special
suite will be ready and waiting for your guest."
Jordan went back to the room to watch the recording that Pie and the others are watching.
No one could see anything out of the ordinary.

The battle is beginning...

CHAPTER TWENTY-FIVE

"What the hell do you mean you have to stop the surveillance on my person? This is priority!" said Arnold.

"Calm down bro, I got a call from the man and he needs his best on the plane crash that went down about a month ago," said James, the P.I.

"Man, I paid you a lot of money and I demand my worth," said Arnold, banging a fist on the table.

James and Arnold were back at the diner, around two o'clock in the morning.

Both were tired because they had been going nonstop for the last eighteen hours.

Holding up his hand to calm Arnold down, James said, "I am not abandoning you. I just need a couple days off, that's all."

"I need my information like last week, yesterday," said Arnold.

Looking around to make sure no one had come up and sat by them at the near tables, James leaned in closer to Arnold and said, "Look that plane that went down last month was taken out by a bomb."

Arnold mouthed the word, "And?"

James continued by saying, "Come to find out, a body that was on the plane died twice."

Arnold looked at him, puzzled.

Loving having Arnold by the balls, so to speak, rubbing his temple with his finger attempting to remember the name, James said, "The guy's name is…Oh yeah, Paul…Paul King. Turns out his real name is Felix Johnson."

Arnold stared at James with his mouth wide open in shock.

"Jesus, did you say Felix Johnson?" asked Arnold.

"Yes, looks like that man died about two or three years ago. I don't have the numbers with me now,".

Arnold looked at James and said, "Go and do what you have to do." Pointing his finger at James, he added, "If you keep me abreast, it is another ten thousand. You hear me?"

"Crystal clear, my bro," said James, who loved money.

Arnold left the dinner in a hurry, telling the waitress as he was leaving, the tab was on him. After all, not his money but the agency money he is using as a mission in Mexico. He sweet talked a clerk to fill out fake papers, who has a crush on him.

James looked at the waitress and said, "Lobster dinner this time, with the entire trimmings, darling."

She smiled and turned to put the order in with the cook.

James was thinking to himself, *'Hands down this going to be the easiest money I have ever made.'*

Arnold reached his car, closed the door, and reached for his cell phone, at the same time.

Speaking into the receiver, he told the person to meet him at his office.

He sat in his car for a few seconds to take in what he was just told.

He was remembering putting a folder on Tex's desk about three weeks ago with information,

and pictures of someone name Felix Johnson.

He knew that Felix Johnson was Tex's husband best friend who died, but didn't know it was a hoax,

And he renames himself Paul King and is dead for real this time.,

He knew he smelled a rat and it just farted.

Arnold put the car in gear and sped off down the road toward his office.

Within twenty minutes, he arrived at his office door. The light was already on and Deuce was waiting for him.

With a cup of coffee in his hand, Deuce said, "Arnold, this early in the morning, it better be damn good," said Deuce.

Arnold blurted out, "Felix Johnson was on the plane that went down a month ago".

"What?" said Deuce.

Taking his suitcoat off and swinging it on the back of the chair, Arnold sat in front of Deuce, looked him straight in the face, and said, "Felix Johnson aka Paul King died on that plane crash."

Deuce raised his eyebrow and said, "I know who Felix is. Go on."

"According to sources, the plane crash was not an accident. It went down with a bomb. The government is trying to keep it quiet until they find out all the information."

"And how are you getting this information?" Deuce asked.

Pausing for a few seconds, Arnold answered, "I had hired a private eye to watch Tex."

"You did what?! She is untouchable!" shouted Deuce.

"Look, the trail was dry, and the agency wasn't getting any new information, that's why I did it," said Arnold.

Pointing a finger at Arnold, Deuce told him, "You are on your own on this one. She will have your liver along with rice if she finds out."

Softly, Arnold, who knew Deuce was right, said, "Maybe…she is part of this."

Deuce just stared at Arnold, not saying anything.

Arnold knew he had to say something, so he said, "A piece of the bomb was found a mile away from the crash. It was still attached to a part of the plane's wing. It didn't go off, so the authorities have some evidence to examine."

Deuce asked, "Arnold, who is your Private Investigator? And does the agency have deniability about him?"

Arnold answered, "Yes, the agency has deniability. The guy does not know what agency I work with and yes, I have used this P.I many times before. He is secure."

"Keep it that way. Anything else I need to know this early in the morning?" Deuce asked.

"Not now, sir. I just thought you need to know. Oh, by the way, by any chance has Tex discussed anything about the folder you asked me to put on her desk about the crash? You know his name was on the victims list?" Arnold asked.

"She discussed a little about how awful the crash was, but we didn't elaborate on it. Why?" Deuce asked.

"Do you think…. she is part of this?" asked Arnold.

"My instinct says no, but let's keep it tight" said Deuce.

Arnold waited for Deuce to say the magic words.

Deuce understood and granted his wish "This is your only project. Give someone else your other caseloads. Nothing Grade Four or For Your Eyes Only," said Deuce.

"Yes sir" Arnold replied.

Deuce got up and left the office.

Arnold went to his desk and began a security file entitled "My Dream". He James to remind him to report everything to him about the crash.

He smiled with a mouth full and said to no one in particular, *"Yes, for the right amount of money, Arnold will get the rest of the information he has, like the employee name who called out sick that day and who placed the bomb on the plane. Really, he does not know who place the bomb, but Arnold will not know that. He had overheard an official at the site telling his boss an employee is being question. It's not rocket scientist to figure out the reason., the bomb, hello.'* He dipped a piece of the lobster tail in butter and bit into it. *"Yummy"*, he said.

***

Later that night, Jordan received some company, a pretty redhead with, an overnight bag.

She was brought in the back way by Jordan's bodyguard, who was glad the boss had some company because he had been riding everyone's ass hard all day. The atmosphere relaxed greatly when she arrived. Looks can be deceiving and this case was no different. She was an agent. Bonnie work.

***

The next morning, Radio and Pie were at the main house, waiting for Jordan to appear in the game room. They had found out some information that the boss needed to know.

Radio said to Pie, "I don't understand how someone had information about where or how to get into the main house unless they have been here. It had to be someone who knew the layout."

"I am with you on that. If someone had snuck by the guards, there will be hell to pay from Jordan," said Pie.

Looking at Pie, Radio answered, "Someone or some people are going to die. No second chances with Jordan. That's the rule."

"That IS the rule" Pie repeated.

"Expandable"

Pie whistle.

Dockett announced on the intercom, "The boss is on his way down" for all to hear.

Jordan appeared in the room with a glass of orange juice in his hand. Radio and Pie watched as he came in and sat down. His vibe seemed to be good.

Looking at the guys, Jordan asked, "What do you want? You've gotten me up from a nice piece of ass."

Pie cleared his throat and said, "Boss, a guy name Arnold is on your trail, told he works for the agency."

Jordan stared at him.

Radio, sitting across from Jordan, was wringing his hands together. At that moment he did not know if he would be breathing in the following moments.

Pie exhaled and said, "I know where he is, and I have a plan to make sure he is taken care of. I just need your permission."

Jordan took a sip of his orange juice.

Radio jumped in and said, "He has hired a private investigator to track you and some dude name Felix Johnson."

Jordan just stared at the guys; how do you know about this" he asked?

"Well, that private investigator, is a sleezy who works for the right amount of money was bragging to someone over a cell phone at a restaurant we were eating at.

Pie, jumped in and side, I thought I remember that name Felix boss, but was not sure where I heard it.

Jordan quiet, knew who Felix was but did not let on, he just said "Go on".

Radio continues "He was saying he knew this guy worked for a federal agency but not which one and he need information on that Felix guy to continue milking him for money".

Jordan sighed.

Radio and Pie said not a word. This was going downhill. Jordan looked pissed.

Jordan got up and said to the two, "Take care of this investigator, get as much information you can before he leaves this world. Arnold, hold on until you get word from me. He is agency, I need to work out things before he goes".

He did not wait for their answer and left the room.

Jordan, passing Walker, said, "Follow them and report everything."

Walker nodded his head.

CHAPTER TWENTY-SIX

"Jordan, we are on our way to the address now," said Pie into his cell phone.

"You and Radio better not fuck this up. I don't give second chances."

"We have this under control, Jordan. Radio and I will get this straight," said Pie.

"Pass the phone to Radio" said Jordan.

Pie handed the cell phone to Radio. "Yes, Jordan?" said Radio.

"You better have this under control, no extra bodies. Arnold is to be taken out only if it's necessary, he is a federal agent for real," said Jordan.

Radio asked Jordan, "How about if he resist or pull a weapon?"

Exhaling Jordan replied, "Believe this, he will be an ass hole, but the agency will come after you and that could lead back to me....and you know the rest.

With a stern voice, Jordan says "Bring Arnold to me incognito".

Click. Jordan hung up.

Driving by the entrance of the apartment complex where the, private investigator lives, they noticed a guard sitting at the front desk in the lobby.

They decided that entering through the front would leave them vulnerable.

Snapping his fingers, Radio said, "I have an idea."

"I hope it's one that won't get us killed," said Pie.

"Blow up the apartment complex, I know a guy who makes bombs."

Pie smacked Radio up against his head.

"Ouch!" said Radio, rubbing his head.

"Jordan will forbid us from doing that and he stated get all the information the guy knows about Felix and Arnold first, then kill him," said Pie.

"Forbidding is one thing, preventing is another", Radio took a big sigh, "Concentrate stupid on how to get pass the guard".

"We are not a welcoming committee with a Bundt cake. Jordan has given us another chance and the first thing you want to do is blow up a damn apartment complex," said Pie.

"Okay, okay ... you are right, just blow up that one apartment," said Radio.

Pie looked at Radio, thinking his friend has lost his mind.

"It…it can be a small one we plant inside to go off at a certain time. Like when we know the investigator is there," said Radio.

"And if Arnold is there?" Pie asked.

"Don't be stupid, and then we will not blow it," said Radio.

"I am not stupid, but I am responsible for your ass and mine, so I am going to ask questions, stupid or not," said Pie.

Softly, Radio said, "I really appreciate you having my back."

Both looked at each other and busted out laughing.

Smiling at Pie, he said, "Remember a new cable company is in town. We can dress as cable technicians coming to survey the wiring for installation or something like that,"

Pie liking the idea, shaking his head *yes* as Radio is speaking.

Laughing, Pie said, "You are a real prize asshole."

"Thank you for the compliment. One does one's best," said Radio.

At the light, Pie took a right-hand turn to head toward the building address.

***

Tyler, who had been tailing them the whole time, made a right behind them. Safely behind, so they would not pick up her trail. Tex had sent her to trail Radio and Pie. In her dark gray slight bent up Volkswagen, she looked like a townsperson and fit right in.

Tyler called Tex and said, "Something is going on. I feel it in the air."

At the Command Center, Tex answered, "Agree. They are discussing blowing up an apartment."

"What?" Tyler asked.

"Back off and go straight to 240 Pilot Street. That is where some investigator lives. Snoop around to see what intel you can get, that asshole Arnold is up to shit and about to get snatch" said Tex, appalled at what she was hearing.

Having Walker bug their Challenger was a genius move on Bonnie's part.

They could not stop the mission because it could become a telltale sign to Pie, Radio and Jordan that the car is bugged, and someone was on to their shenanigans.

Tyler turned left at the next corner and sped toward the apartment complex.

Pie stopped the car about four blocks from where Tyler turned off and got out. It was a plain looking warehouse. The green dot on her screen stopped at the Command Center.

Tex said, "Uhm a warehouse."

Two blocks down parked, is Walker.

***

Within fifteen minutes, Pie and Radio emerged from the building with Radio carrying a brown leather bag on his shoulder. Both got into the car and drove downtown.

With the speed of the Challenger, Pie was at a store quickly.

'Why are they stopping at this address?' Tex was wondering.

She hurried up and typed the address in the system. 'Uniform store, disguises' thought Tex.

Radio and Pie entered the store without the brown leather shoulder bag.

Tyler had arrived at the apartment complex and was walking into the lobby.

Tex had told her to use the cover of cable manager, asking for the owner.

The guard at the desk was more than happy to answer Tyler's questions. He had seen her get out of the car. Looking her up and down, the tiger in him went into overdrive.

Stretching out her hand, Tyler introduced herself, 'Hello, my name Beverly Davis, cable manager'.

The guard answered Dick at your command".

Tyler snickered at the thought.

"Do you know if the Cable Company coming to his neighborhood on Victor Street, would love to watch sports in high definition?

Tyler opened her briefcase, looked at some papers and replied, "Within two weeks a representative will be in your area. Who owns this building?

Closing her briefcase, so the guard could not see she was reading from an old tire replacement slip.

Happily, the guard reached under his counter and pulled out a black folder. He is flipping through pages. His finger stops halfway down a page, he thumped the page and said, "The owner of the building is Webster's, number is 1-800-801-1937, hours are Monday through Friday, eight am to five pm." Tyler was writing the information down.

Looking up and smiling at the guard, she asked, "Is it okay to survey the place? I need to check for special wiring and room for equipment?

"Yeah, do me a favor. See if the owner would go for the counter having a TV," said the guard, winking at Tyler.

Tyler gave him a wider smile, and then said, "It will be in my presentation, my man."

Leaning in closer on the desk, Tyler asked, "Can I come behind the desk to see if it is equipped for cable?"

With a grin as wide as the cheshire cat, the guard pushed out his chest and, moved out of Tyler way.

She sashayed her body behind the desk, the whole time not looking at the guard, but checking the area instead. She bent over and heard a soft gasp behind her.

Tyler ignored the gasp and remained focused surveying the area. She hurried because she did not know if the guys were close by.

Tyler looked at the electric wiring and said, "It is definitely possible if the owner agrees. The setting is right for upgrade and the desk is on the same side of the building as the outside cable box.

"Loving this," said the guard.

"I need to check the rest of the premises, ten minutes tops," said Tyler.

"Sure thing," said the guard.

Tyler headed toward the elevator and went in.

Thinking how to get the guard out of the building.

Ring.

"Tex," the caller answered.

"I am in the building and it is hard to tell how many people are at home. There are about four apartment doors, not counting the ground level in which, by the way, has a guard, a very friendly guard".

"Work the magic, dear," said Tex.

"I did, boss" said Tyler, laughing.

'Click.'

Tyler spotted a fire alarm button, perfect, before pressing the button, she surveys the apartments on that floor. Tyler stops when she sees 'investigator agency' on a door,

must ask guard about this person.

A young man passes by her without saying a word, Tyler notice but said nothing.

***

"Hi Akers, cable, or should I say high-definition cable, is coming to the building."

"Yeah, I know, man. I work for the cable company and had ask the manager to put this apartment complex on the top of the list. Happy to hear they came to survey."

The guard asked, "Do you know a manager named Sherry Davis?"

Putting his hand on his chin, thinking, Akers said, "No not that name, but there are a lot of new people I haven't met yet."

"Well, she is in the building surveying now as we speak," said the guard.

"See you later," Akers said, as he softly pounded the counter with both of his hands.

"Don't touch! She is mine!" Dick hollered to Akers.
Akers gestured with a thumbs-up, walking toward the elevator.
He pushed the up button.
Right when the elevator door closed, Noah came into the lobby from outside.

He waved at the guard but kept walking toward the elevator. He pushed the up button.

A pair of eyes is watching Noah from across the street.

"Holly shit that guy from the convenience store lives here too, that motherfucker lied to us, Radio," said Pie.

"That fucking clerk is going to get his, no one lie to us," said Radio.

Pie, this is delicious we can kill two birds with one stone, handle our problem and Jordan's at the same time. God is good. The Challenger rolled down the street.

Noah changed his mind and came back out of the elevator and went out the side door.

***

Blackie pulled into the gas station parked and went in to buy some potato chips. Another guy was at the counter, talking to the cashier. He asked the guy, "How are you feeling?"

The guy said, "Better than last week."
Blackie grabbed a large bag of barbecue chips, some crab dip, a bottle of beer, and went to the counter. The two guys were still talking when Blackie reach the counter.
He was getting annoyed because he had to leave.

About to interrupt their little tea tart he heard the cashier say, "You know Noah, you should be careful. The world is dangerous."

Blackie paused. *'Oh shit, this is Noah, the guy we are looking for, okay baby,* work you're magic.'

The cashier finally saw Blackie and asked, "How may I help you?"

Noah stepped to the side to let Blackie come up to the counter to pay for his goods.

"I would like to pay for this and man, can I have some double AA batteries? The six pack, okay," said Blackie.

"Sure, just one moment," said the cashier.

Blackie extended his hand to Noah and said, "I have a friend name Akers who says he lives with his friend named Noah. By any chance, is that you? My name is Blackie."

Noah looked at him.

He continued saying "I know Akers told you about me."

"Right," said Noah with a smile.

"I am sorry I had forgotten your name, but he told me about a guy who, umm…works with him at the cable company, right?" Noah asked.

"The one and only," Blackie answered.

"Nice to meet you."

-"I told Akers to invite you over for a game, but he said you are the shy type and don't like meeting new people," said Blackie.

"He is right. I am cautious these days because I was attacked not too long ago," said Noah.

He was pointing to the large white bandage on his neck.

Looking at the neck, Blackie said, "I see, what happened?

"Somebody came up behind me and shot me in the neck. They were robbing the store I was in," said Noah.

"Whoa, talk about being at the wrong place at the wrong time," said Blackie.

"No shit," the cashier jumped in and spoke.

Noah turned toward the cashier and said, "Be careful, my man. I have to go." He turned toward Blackie and said, "Nice to meet you. I will tell Akers we have met."

Noah picked up his soup and went toward the door.

Blackie pulled out his cash.

"Eight dollars and fifty cents" said the cashier.

Blackie paid him while watching Noah out of the corner of his eye.

He received his change and put it in the donation box on the counter that went to help cancer research.

The cashier told him, "Thanks, my mother has breast cancer."

Smiling at the cashier, who had tears in his eyes, Blackie said, "You are welcome and added a twenty to the jar".

He ran out of the door and whistled toward Noah, who was walking down the street.

"Hey man, let me give you a lift," Blackie said.

Waving at him, Noah replied, "No thanks, I like to walk," as he continued his stride.

Blackie, not deterred, hurried up and got into his car, gassing towards Noah. When he reached him, he rolled down the passenger side window.

"Man, you have soup, I know you don't want it cold," said Blackie.

Not giving in so easily, Noah said, "Actually I love it hot or cold."

Blackie yelled out of the window as he was coasting down the road. "It is not safe. What if you pass out with your condition and all? No one will be there to help you!"

Noah laughed at Blackie's reasoning, but kept walking.

"Look man," said Blackie, "Friends don't let friends walk drunk."

Laughing, Noah responded with, "I am not your friend."

Not willing to give in, Blackie said, "True, but Akers and I have become fast friends. I hate to see his friend walk while I have a ride".

"Still walking, Noah says. I am going to walk".

Blackie pressed the gas to move a little ahead of where Noah was walking. Then he stopped the car and got out of the driver's seat and ran to the passenger side to open the door.

"Get in, my man. I will not hurt you. Hell, I just talked to Akers. He is at the apartment. We can go and meet him and all three of us can have some fun."

Stopping at the rear of the orange car, Noah looked it over and said, "Man you are different as Akers said you were. I don't think I could buy a car that color."

"What? A deuce and a quarter are the main ride out here today," said Blackie.

"Hum orange? I don't think so, man," said Noah.

"Lucky for you, I am a Taurus and not easily offended," said Blackie, laughing.

Noah laughed back, got into the car, and pulled out his cell to call Akers.

Into the phone, he said "Blackie and I are on our way back to the apartment."

"Good, bring me some shrimp fried rice and don't forget my egg roll," said Akers.

Laughing, Noah asked "Anything else?"

"Yeah, get a large size ... and some soy sauce, about six packs," said Akers.

"Your order is confirmed, my friend," said Noah.

'Click'.

Noah looked at Blackie and said, "Akers is hungry and wants Chinese food."

"Sounds good to me, these chips and this dip are not going to do it," said Blackie.

"Man turn right two blocks up. They have the best Chinese food that sales liquor. A one stop shop," said Noah.

Blackie laughed.

***

Tyler had installed the equipment for visual and audio recording. Movement in the hallway showed Ms. Rosenfeld getting her newspaper from, her front door.
Her cat ran past her.

"Kitty, you bad cat get back here! Mommy doesn't feel like chasing you today."

Tyler, coming off the elevator, catches the cat.

Ms. Rosenfeld smiled and said, "She is so bad. Thank you, miss." Tyler handed her the cat, and she went back in with her paper.
The fire lever was pulled, within a few seconds, Ms. Rosenfeld opened her door, with her cat.

With a confused look on her face, she looks around the hall to see where the bell ringing sound was coming from.

"Oh heavens, is this a fire drill?" she asked.

"Madam, I think we need to leave just in case," said Tyler, grabbing her by the arm to lead her.

"Wait baby, you are going the wrong way," said Ms. Rosenfeld.

"No madam, this way is faster," said Tyler.

Pulling back with her arm, Ms. Rosenfeld said, "I have lived here over ten years, sweetie. I am telling you; you are going the wrong way."

Tyler was in a hurry because Tex had messaged her that the guys were on their way turned toward Ms. Rosenfeld and said, "Look madam, I used to live here too. This is a back way. Trust me."

"No," said Ms. Rosenfeld, who stopped.

Tyler ran ahead and pulled the lever on a door. When it opened, sunshine came in and Ms. Rosenfeld look surprised.

"Oh, my goodness, I never knew," she said.

"Please Madam, this way. Quick," said Tyler, smiling.

Ms. Rosenfeld did not hesitate. She went toward the door and left the building.

Outside, both noticed that something was going on. Tyler saw Dick at the front of the building looking down the street. She and Ms. Rosenfeld looked in the same direction.

Fire trucks and cars could be heard wailing, with lights reflecting off the buildings surrounding the scene, chatter could be heard.

Fire hoses were splitting out large amounts of water to put out the fire that was spreading. A fireman was headed toward the guard.

'Good, a distraction', Tyler was thinking.

Akers, who heard the fire alarm, ignored it, thinking it was a false alarm. He had just come from downstairs and no fire could have started that fast.

Boom!!!

CHAPTER TWENTY-SEVEN

All heads turned with stone faces toward the loud sound that just went off. People covered up their eyes and ears. In the aftermath, the only noise that could be heard came from the particles raining from the sky hitting the ground. At the end of the street was half of a building, still crumbling.

The police radio broke the silence, the dispatcher heard the loud noise, due to an officer holding his open mic. *'Please officers!'* the dispatcher was hollering. *'Please someone answer, hello! is anyone out there?'* No one answer because of shock and most had walked away from their vehicles; looking for survivors.

Noah and Blackie, who had just parked the car and gotten out when the bomb went off, looked at each other with horror on their faces. Noah's mouth was wide open, Blackie's eyes were big as a saucer. Neither could believe what they are seeing.

A grotesque scene was being played out in front of many people. Debris was falling everywhere, glass was splintered into a million pieces, with furniture of all kinds strewn about everywhere near the site. Heavy smoke was rising to the sky. Suddenly, a nasty smell of burning materials reached the people's nostrils and many put their hand up to their noses and moved back to stop the debris from falling on them. The firemen and the guards were knocked off their feet but survived the blast. All on ground level looking up at the apartment complex with cringed looks on their faces. Breathing hard, their faces and clothing were darkened from the debris and ashes falling from the sky.

'Please someone answer their radios! Officers, officers, anybody!' yelled the dispatcher.
An officer came to his senses and answered the dispatcher,
who by now was at her wit's end trying to get someone to answer her.

"This is officer 33057. A bomb just went off at an apartment building near 4th and 8th; please send extra personnel to site. I'm on my way in to see if anyone is alive and needs help, over."

"Thank you, officer 33057, is anyone hurt near you?"

"People are moving around" officer answered,

"Thanks. Extra personnel are on the way."

The officer put down his mic, climbed out of his cruiser and started walking toward the scene. The smoke had let up, so the site was more visible. Small debris was still falling from the sky, but nothing that would injure him. A firefighter walked beside him. Neither said a word.

"Jesus," said Noah, looking at the building.
"Akers," said Blackie, looking straight ahead at the building.
Saying Akers name made Noah look at Blackie for the first time since he heard the loud noise. Noah pulled out his cell phone and speed dialed a number. Blackie watched the expression on his face and silently start praying that Akers answer the phone. *Ring, ring,* and then *'Hello you have reached Akers, lea....'* Noah tried again. Still voicemail. He left no message.
Letting out a soft sigh, Blackie put his head down.
"Blackie let's go and see if we can find him," said Noah.
Blackie said, "Okay."
Both started running toward the building, still holding their bags.
Blackie was in front, Noah split off and ran to his left, leaving Blackie running by himself.
Tyler and Ms. Rosenfeld were far enough away not to be hurt. Both looked at the building they had just left with Ms. Rosenfeld holding her cat with disbelief.
Tyler pulled out her cell phone, whisper into the receiver, "A bomb just took down the apartment complex."

***

Tex, at the Command Center with Bonnie, couldn't believe what, Tyler had just said.
Tex motion to Bonnie to bring up images Tyler sent.
In the meantime, Tex asked Tyler, "Who was left in the building?"
"Only the guard" I was going back for him, but this happened.
Don't worry, I see him on the outside with a fireman says Tex looking at a monitor.
Bonnie was checking the video feed, rewinding it to see if she could find anything.
Bonnie let out a loud gasp and Tex turned to see what she was looking at. A loud sigh left her mouth.
"What?" Tyler asked.
Tex answered, "Akers was at the guard desk talking with him before the bomb went off."
"Fuck," said Tyler.

201

Bonnie search for Akers, Tex said.

There he is standing by a police car looking daze.

"He's fine Tyler," said Tex, watching the monitor.

Bonnie, go back some frames see what the hell happen.

Bonnie did as she was told.

Tex instructed Tyler leave area now.

"Here we go, look? says Bonnie.

A dark kale green Challenger was in the alleyway by the building.

One man got out, looked around to see if anyone was nearby.

He gave the okay sign with his hand. He got out with a brown, leather bag.

As he was walking, out came a small device from the bag.

When he got by the large trash bin, he put the device down on the left side, out of sight. Then both got back into the car and drove off.

"Radio and Pie," said Tex.

"They just blew up the building. What is Jordan doing?" asked Bonnie.

"That is not Jordan, because that would bring too much attention. He would not okay something like this. This is strictly two fools acting on their own," said Tex.

***

The Challenger was a good eight blocks away when the bomb went off. Radio and Pie were ecstatic their plan went off without a hitch.

They could see the heavy black smoke in the sky with debris still floating, around in the sky.

In their car, both were hooting and hollering with laughter.

"That guy can make a bomb," said Pie, laughing heartily.

With a wide smirk on his face, Radio answered, "A bomb is like a box of chocolates. You never know what you are getting until its shield is uncovered."

Pie and Radio busted into laughter.

The Challenger was weaving on and off the road because of the laughter inside. *'You Dropped A Bomb on Me'* by The Gap Band started playing on the car's radio. Pie reached over, turned the volume up, and both started singing.

"We lit the...., dropped a bomb...

They were laughing so much they could barely sing.

They were in such a zone they ignored what the song really meant.

The song was about a girl who hurts a guy's feelings. Radio and Pie didn't care, the line *'you dropped a bomb'* appealed to them. They continued singing loudly; slightly altering the words as the Challenger drove forward.

***

Walker was standing by a police cruiser when the bomb went off. Pulling out his phone, he dialed Tex.

"Tex, those fuckers have blown up a building."

"I know. Call Jordan and see what you can find out," said Tex.

'Click'….

Walker called Jordan, who answered on the first ring.

"Mr. Jordan, Radio and Pie blew up an apartment complex on 4th & 8th Street."

He asked, "Are you sure of this?"

"Yes sir, I followed them to the bomb maker and the area near the apartment building."

"How come you didn't call me immediately?" Jordan asked.

"Sir, I wanted to see what was going on."

"Do you see Radio and Pie now?"

"No, they are not on the scene."

"Find them and bring those two assholes back to me immediately," he said harshly.

"Yes boss," said Walker. His cell phone went dead.

Walker surveyed the scene to see if he could pick up any Intel for Tex, then left the scene to find Radio and Pie thinking to himself.

'These guys are shitty.'

***

Back at the scene of the explosion, Blackie turn around from running to ask, Noah a questions,
 and he wasn't there. He saw Ackers.
"Ackers" Blackie screamed
Ackers turn towards his name being called and saw Blackie.
"Where is Noah?" he asked.
"Behind me I thought, where you come from?

"I came out of the building, thinking, get some drinks down the street before you, and Noah get here with the food. Then an explosion happens"
"Shit, where you think Noah would go?
"Hey, Blackie, we have to find him. I am sure he is frightened."
"Yeah, he was a little skittish."
"Let go" says Ackers.
Both started walking when a police car went flying by, Noah was inside driving.
"Noah!" he screamed out loud.
"What the fuck is he doing?" Blackie asked.
"Running. He is scared by the look on his face," said Ackers.
"It's that your friend?" a policeman asked.
"Yes sir, please don't shoot. He is scared. I saw the look on his face," said Ackers.
The policeman didn't answer. He pulled out his walkie talkie and said "Police cruiser has been stolen and is going down the 400 block of Pilot Street. Please pursue with caution, suspect is afraid. I repeat, please pursue with caution."
Two police cruisers pulled out behind Noah who was speeding down the street, recklessly.
The siren on the cruiser was screaming and the lights were flashing.
In the police cruiser Noah was thinking '*I am not going to stop until far away from this town. I will explain things to the cops once he felt safe to stop*'.
One of the cruisers aimed his spotlight toward the cruiser Noah was driving. The other officer was on the loudspeaker, asking him to pull over.
"Oh shit, he is losing control," officer said into his mic.
The other policeman slowed down his pursuit, hoping Noah would see this and, slow down.
Cruiser number two cut off his lights and siren to follow suit with the same gesture. Noah, looking into the rearview mirror saw this and pushed on the brakes. He crashed hard into the cement divider and bounced off it. The impact made the car flip over, and over four times before landing on his hood.
The two policemen got out of their cars, running towards the cruiser with guns drawn for safety reasons.
Seconds passed with no sound coming from inside the vehicle.
The siren light had been dislodged and was sitting yards away from the car. Somehow, the lights were still flashing. Approaching the driver's side of the car, the policeman saw no movement except a head leaning toward the window with blood pouring out the side. He put his gun back into the holster to reach for Noah's neck to see if he could feel a

pulse. He withdrew his bloody fingers and put his head down with a frown on his face. He looked toward his fellow officer and motioned his hand across his neck, signifying that the driver was deceased. The other policeman put down his weapon and walked back to his cruiser.

"Dispatcher, we have a decease body and need proper detail help on Route 87 to block traffic," said the officer in a sober tone.

"On the way, officer," said the dispatcher.

People who were driving in the area had stop on the shoulders to watch the action. They began walking closer to the scene. The officer stopped them and asked them to please get back inside their cars. Most did and drove off. With the sullen look on the officer's face, most realized that the person inside the cruiser was dead.

With the loud sound of a crash, Ackers went down to the ground saying, "My good friend is dead," sobbing with his head in his hands.

"No, that loud crash could have been something else," said Blackie.

Shaking his head back and forth, Ackers said, "It doesn't take a rocket scientist to know what had just happened. My instincts tell me he is dead."

Blackie tried to persuade Ackers otherwise and said, "That might not be true."

Ackers, with tears in his eyes, says "He is dead because of me."

"Don't be silly. Noah did this on his own," said Blackie.

Shaking his head, Ackers said, "You don't understand. He thinks that I brought some agency to our door and that the men were using me to get to him to finish him off."

Blackie grabbed Ackers by the arm. "Look man, I know you are upset but you can't say that out loud".

Dazed, Ackers nodded his head. He sat on the curb, put his head down between his legs, and cried for his friend.

Blackie, not sure what to do, sat down beside him.

***

"Officer, can you tell me how a civilian got a hold of your cruiser?" the lieutenant asked.

"Boss, when I arrived at the scene to help, I got out of my cruiser in a hurry, leaving the engine running and the door unlocked," the sergeant answered.

"Sergeant," the lieutenant said.

Softly the sergeant answered, "Yes, sir?"

A few seconds passed, and then the lieutenant answered, "You might face disciplinary action."

"Yes sir. Should I leave now?" the sergeant asked.

"Is other officer on site?"

"Yes sir"

"Return to the station, paperwork needs to be filled out."

The lieutenant hung up.

A voice announced to all at the scene. "The news is that a bomb went off in the building and a man is dead from a crash in a police cruiser."

The place went silent.

***

Blackie's cell phone rang, looking at the number coming up, he roused to answer in private. "Yes," said Blackie.

"Any news you need to share with me?" Tyson asked.

"I think Noah might be dead. He ripped off a cruiser and went speeding down the road.

We heard a loud crashed. I can't talk much because Ackers is a few feet away from me."

"The boy had some balls I see. Collect Ackers and go back to your place. Contact me when you get there," said Tyson.

"On it," said Blackie in a gloomy voice.

Tyson, sensing his mood, said, "Blackie I am sorry about Noah, but I need to warn you.

Shit is about to hit the fan. You and Ackers need to be out of Herr, California as fast as your balls will allow."

'Gee that lady has a way with words', Blackie was thinking.

"How long do I have?" he asked.

"Less than two hours," she answered.

"Not much time. How am I going to do this? He hardly knows me that well," Blackie asked.

"He is sad and confused right now. Convince him that this might have something to do with the shooting and he better leave the area. Advise him he has nothing to lose. His friend is dead," said Tyson.

"Good points. Thanks," said Blackie.

"Blackie, I can't stress this enough. Leave as soon as possible," said Tyson.

"Click".
Blackie looked over toward Ackers, whose head was still down, crying. He walked over to him and pulled him up.

"Man, we have to leave this town. Don't ask any questions, but the phone call I just received convinces me this is no coincidence." Blackie gestured toward the grotesque scene.

Ackers didn't argue. They reached Blackie's car and drove off.

✱✱✱

Tex called Walker and said report back to The Cave.

Next, she called the Ultimate Tomboys and told them to report back to the house.

She turned to Bonnie and said, *"88 tango has begun...."*

CHAPTER TWENTY-EIGHT

Three vehicles came to a sudden stop at the front of Tex's driveway. Tyler got out of the black cobra mustang. Teg got out of a red cadillac. Tyson and Travis got out of a navy-blue Ferrari. The Private Investigator wasn't home, he is parked in the driveway of a neighbor who had left town, watched the scene. He sensed something was up by the way the ladies left their vehicles in such a hurry.

Bonnie was at the door, welcoming them in before they reached the entrance.

Putting down his French fries covered in ketchup, he pulled out his cell phone and speed dialed a number. Talking into the speaker, he said, "You better get your ass on alert. Something is about to go down".

The person asked, "Are you sure?"

"Sure, as my ass is sitting here looking at the scene."

"Find out what it is and call me back," the person said.

Arnold hung up and walked out of his office. He headed straight for Deuce's office. He had a plan of his own. The P.I went back to watching and eating his fries.

***

Arriving in the Command Center with Bonnie, Tex looked at everyone with a serious look on her face and said, "88 tango is a go."

They all knew what that meant. The Cave would be attacked at dawn.

***

Arnold went to Deuce's office door and knocked. He heard, "Come in." Deuce was on the phone, so he silently waved for Arnold to take a seat. Arnold sat down. He was holding a briefcase that contained two thick folders.

Deuce said, "Yes, yes of course. Be right on it."

He hung up the phone and said, "That commander is a pain in the ass. He always waits until the last minute, then starts burning everyone ass on down the ladder to jump so he can look good. Asshole to the nth degree"

Arnold, sitting in the chair, said nothing. He knew to let the Captain blow off steam, and then he will get to why he was there.

With his hands under his chin, he asked Arnold, "Why are you here?"

Arnold got up and went in front of Deuce's desk. He dropped one of the large manila folders on the desk. It hit with a loud thud.

With a sigh, Arnold said, "Jordan is alive".

Deuce looked at Arnold like he had just dropped a bomb.

"What did you just say?"

"Jordan is alive and here are the papers to prove it."

Deuce opened the large folder and started reading the papers.

"Let me help you, boss. There are a lot of papers there."

Deuce stopped reading and looked at Arnold.

Arnold sat back down and said, "Let me start the story with how Jordan has stolen over twenty million from the agency, along with about two million dollars' worth of drugs and guns to resell".

Deuce sat there with his mouth agape. He couldn't believe his ears.

He started to go back to the papers, but Arnold stopped him.

"Deuce, I will leave the papers for you to read later. Let me continue my story."

Deuce waved his okay.

"We need to get a group together fast and take him down. The man is more dangerous than you and I ever thought."

Deuce put up a finger to interrupt Arnold and asked, "How come I am just hearing of this?"

"I needed to be sure of the facts."

"This is unbelievable from such a high ranking official."

Arnold pulled out another manila folder from his brief case and handed it to Deuce. Looking down at the folder, Deuce noticed it was labeled "Airline Crash".

When he opened the folder, there was a picture of a man with two names under the photo.

Deuce gave Arnold a look of *'what the fuck'* on his face.
Arnold nodded his head up and down, confirming that what he was reading was true.

The names under the picture were "Paul King, died this year on 6-10 and "Felix Johnson, died 5-5-99".

Arnold didn't have to tell Deuce who the man was. He knew it was Jordan's best friend.

What the fuck is this?" Deuce asked.

"A man who died twice. The second time, more people died with him," said Arnold.

"Look, I don't need an ulcer. Spill it, will you?" said Deuce.

"Jordan took him and many innocent people down with that plane crash because Paul aka Felix had betrayed him in some way, no Intel on that yet."

"That's awful thin."

"Thin, is my middle name, boss. Do you remember the Thomas case?"

Nodding his head yes, Deuce went back to the folders.

Sighing deep he said, "Yeesh, I am going to need some solid evidence to get a warrant from a judge."

Arnold pulled out the ace he been holding in his pocket. He twisted it in his hand for Deuce to see. It was a dvd.

"No riddles, just evidence," said Deuce.

Arnold rose to slide the dvd into the player, it showed Jordan, live and in color.

Pointing toward the screen, Arnold said, "Evidence number one."

"So?" said Deuce, raising an eyebrow.

Arnold fast forwarded to a grotesque scene with Jordan and, Paul interrogating a man.

Blood was everywhere, and the man's screams were so loud, one could hardly hear the conversation in the background.

Arnold looked at Deuce and said, "I have a technician working on cleaning that up as I speak, so we can hear what Paul and Jordan are saying."

Arnold said, "Evidence number two."

Harshly, Deuce said, "That is what he is trained to do, how old is this?" He did not want to believe that his best friend who was sworn in the same day he was, the friend he cried for in the dark at his home, was such an evil man. He didn't even cry over his father's death. He held his tears as little boys were taught.

"Not sure when this was filmed," Arnold replied.

Deuce sighed.

With his hands up in the air Arnold, pulled out the showstopper. He ejected the dvd from the machine and slid in another one.

The screen lit up with the words in large bold letters: **Property of the Bureau…. Top personnel only.** The TV went dark. You could only hear voices. *'Hurry up, man. We have only a few seconds left.'* You could

hear feet moving, heavy breathing, gun fire and somethings being shoved around. Deuce recognized some of the voices.
The TV was now displaying blurring pictures. Within seconds, the picture became clear, showing four officer's bodies laid out on the floor, dead from gunshots wounds.
Deuce stood up with fury in his eyes.

The room was the evidence room that held everything that was confiscated from the official busts. It held money, drugs, guns, and many items that were needed in court when trials began. A face came on the screen.

"A major mistake," says Arnold.

"That's Felix aka Paul, Jordan best friend" says Arnold, who has removed his mask.
Deuce moves closer to the television to see the face of the man standing by Paul. His face is cover but a small portion of his neck is visibly displaying a birthmark shaped like a crescent moon.

He pushed the pause button on the machine.

Looking at the mark on his neck, Deuce said in a whisper, "That is Jordan."

Deuce stood in silence.

Arnold cleared his throat and said, "Deuce, uhm, Jordan and Paul are stone cold killers. Jordan needs to be handled. Not sure what Tex role is in this, having Intel being done on her now."

With fury in his voice, Deuce answered, "Intel on a ranking official, who gave you permission?" He walked back to his desk with the frame still frozen on the screen and he picked up his phone. He punched in four digits and when the other side picked up, he said, "I have a situation and need the force, stat."
Arnold was standing a few feet away from Deuce's desk, with his arms folded across his chest,
wearing a smirk on his face. *'Beep, beep'.*

Arnold looks at his phone, it reads *'Action has begun.'*
"Who is that" Deuce asked.
"My informer" says Arnold.
"He's off the case, this is an internal problem, no fucking outsiders and another thing, let me make this clear. You never ever do Intel on top ranking officers without my consent. Tex is not part of this. I personally recruited her. Do we understand Arnold?
"Understood."

***

"Okay, listen up. This is how it is going down. Many police divisions are represented at the location. We need to avoid all or most of them. I have a few deep friends that I have asked to wiggle their way into the inner perimeter of the invasion," said Tex.

Bonnie put three pictures on the screen for the Tomboys to see their identity.

Under each picture was a name along with their agency (e.g., DEA, ATF, etc.).

"They will be working close to 'The Cave', so if any help is needed, feel free to ask. They know how to be discreet". Tex continued.

"Candy," said Tyson with a wink.

"Down, twin," said Tyler, winking her eye back.

"Later," whispered Travis.

Smiling, Tyson said, "You bet your ass, later."

"I am betting my ass later," said Tyler, keeping up with Tyson.

Everyone looks back and forth from Tyson to Tyler.

"Going forward there will be about twenty police cruisers on the outer perimeter with about two officers per vehicle. They are just protecting the outer perimeter, making sure no one gets in or out of the area. Sergeants, Lieutenants, and Captains will be on the inner perimeter. They will be nearest to the action. Easy to spot...." Says Tex.

"By the suit and ties," interrupted Teg.

"And the air of arrogance," said Travis.

"They are all candies," said Tyson.

"Tyson, give it a break. Cool down the cat, will you?" Tex said.

Tex held up her finger for silence at Tyson and the others. She didn't want a reply.

Tyson pouted silently.

Sighing, Tex continued, "The chief of the county will no doubt be in on this. He most likely will be at a long lunch getting status updates from the captain."

"The Mayor?" asked Travis.

"Believe it or not, evidence has surfaced that he has been taking a kickback from Jordan, so the chief advised him that if he wants to keep his job, he needs to stay in the background. They really want to keep this under wraps. Jordan was one of them and this will be an embarrassment to the bureau and with all the news reports, the California police tasks forces will look bad to the world".

"Yes, we all remember the bad press the L.A. police division received about eight years ago," said Tyler.

"They deserved most of it, those officers beat that man so bad…. on film. "They were clearly out of control," said Teg.

"A few bad grapes make every officer look bad" said Travis, shaking her head in sorrow.

"Most officials are the cream of the crop and some are my best friends," said Bonnie.

"Yes," said Tex. "I would go into battle with a lot of them. They are good people."

Bringing it back to the matter, Bonnie added "In case Tex forgets, all of them are armed. If need be, they will fire, and none, I mean none of them, are familiar with the Tomboys," looking at all four ladies.

All nodded. The point was taken.

Speaking up, Travis said, "That is a lot of fire power to avoid, Tex, from what you and Bonnie are telling us. How will we get in and out without being noticed?"

Bonnie brought up a skeleton design on the computer.

The Tomboys all had a puzzled look on their faces because the picture was just a dirt road with trees.

"Right," said Tex, looking at their faces. "Bonnie is a genius. Look over by the tree to the right. What do you see?"

"Some kind of steel plate in the ground," answered Travis.

"Right, a drainpipe that has not been used in years. That is our way in," said Tex.

Before anyone could say anything, Bonnie jumped in and said, "I have been down it myself."

All four heads turned toward her in a snap.

"You've…been down that?" asked Tyler.

"Don't look surprised, ladies. I was once an undercover operative, remember?"

All nodded their heads except Tyler.

She said, "I didn't know you were an operative."

"For a while, until she was captured," said Tyson.

"Then Tex came to her rescue with a team of operatives to help her escape from a drug dealer who had tortured her for days and left her for dead," said Teg.

"Yes, Travis and I were part of the team," said Tyson.

"And I will love you three forever for that, I retired after that incident to go behind the scenes to work for my good friend here," Bonnie said, pointing to Tex, with her eyes slightly wet. "The itch was still in my blood, so I asked Tex if I could be the one to test out the entrance. Well, first I sent down a camera to see where it leads and found out that it is an escape route. Jordan or someone had it planted there. Smart move if you ask me. No one will look twice at the rusted, really dirty plate, with weeds all around it labeled as a water drain by the county of Herr; California. They were pushed aside to take pictures of the entrance."

Bonnie pushed a button on the keypad. Up on the screen came the picture she was just describing.

"How wide is that pipe? It looks thin," Tyson asked.

"It is big enough to get a six-three-foot man through," said Bonnie.

Bonnie put up a split screen. One side showed the pipe in detail and the other side showed how it would look when they first come upon it.

She pushed another button, and the screen was showing the Tomboys and Tex the interior of the pipe. Shockingly, it was somewhat clean.

Tyler asked, "Why is it shining?"

Tex answered, "In case someone gets stuck. The slide will help them maneuver down."

"Down, or oh, can they come up it?" Travis asked.

With a small snicker, Tex said, "Right to the left of the pipe on the inside, there are some steps, or I should say, a ladder where they can climb out."

"To another escape route," said Tyler.

"You ladies are smart," said Tex.

Bonnie instantly pushed another key on the keyboard and the screen showed another area around The Cave. This one took them into the main town. The end of the route emptied out inside a building, near an alley, but out of sight so the person could come up and go straight to a car and take off.

"Tex, are the police divisions aware of these escaping routes?" Tyson asked.

"Not sure, but I am going to guess no because I tested my friends at the divisions and none of them mentioned it," said Tex.

"Would they have? After all, these are undercover invasion materials," said Teg.

"To me, they would have," said Tex.

"When is this going down?" Tyler asked.

"Daybreak. Right before the sun comes up. Hopefully, we catch them off guard," said Bonnie.

"Guards? Didn't we see a guard tower in pictures?" said Tyson.

"Yes," all the other Tomboys said in sync.

"They will be the first to be taken out. Remember, we have Walker on the inside," said Tex.

"Walker. Forgot about him," said Tyler.

"We need a picture," said Tyson.

With stern looks, everyone looked at her.

"Come on this time I am serious." Pointing at Travis and Teg, she said, "We have never seen him."

"True," said Bonnie. She typed on the keyboard and Walker's picture came up.

Tyson gasped lightly with her hand up to her mouth.

"So, let me get this straight. Walker, Topher, and Peaches are our only contacts inside."

"You got it," said Bonnie.

"All will be dressed in civilian clothes.

Peaches, she is DEA, wearing a special necklace of a red apple on a gold chain.

The men will have on T-shirts of the Georgetown Hoyas and Dallas Cowboys," said Tex.

"Um, Topher is already there as one of Jordan's bodyguards.

He has already hooked up with Walker.

So those two will likely be the most help," said Bonnie.

"Most importantly, both know of you all and will come to introduce themselves in some way. Follow them if you are lost. But get out after you get Jordan."

"You need him alive?" asked Tyson with a smirk on her face.

Tyler raised an eyebrow at that question.

Travis looked at Tex, contently waiting for her to answer.

Teg shook her head at Tyson, thinking, *'the girl has gumption'*.

"I would like to know why that fucker did what he did, but…if the bottle needs to be dropped…drop it," said Tex.

"You got it, boss," said Tyson.

"Dead" Tyler asked.

"Heaven or Hell, I will apologize when I get there. Any more questions?" asked Tex.

"No" Tyler answered.

"None," said Travis.

"Ditto" said Teg.

Looking sternly, Tex added, "If I call abort, walk away, no hesitation."

"If we see…," said Tyson.

Tex cut her off. "No. Abort."

"As you wish," said Tyson.

"Great, I am going to the gym next door," said Tex.
No one said a word because the ramifications are excessively big this time.
Any one of them could lose their lives.

CHAPTER TWENTY-NINE

Daybreak brought in slightly cooler weather for this time of season, sixty-two degrees, high winds.
It was the perfect weather for an invasion.
Police forces are required to wear certain clothing, that hides their gear and protects their bodies from things like fire or bullets. The windy day was welcomed by all, readying themselves for an invasion.

The Tomboys, along with Tex, were putting on their gear. Bonnie was helping them gather everything they would need for the invasion. She would stay back to monitor the events, run the software for guidance, and give out information to the agents. She gave her long-time friend a look that only Tex could understand. Tex stopped putting on her gear and patted her friend on the back, saying, with her eyes *'Everything will be okay'*.

Appeased, Bonnie went to the computers to make sure all the screens necessary for the invasion were up and running.

"Never look back, ladies, because something could be gaining on you," said Tyson.

Everyone knew what she meant. It was Tyson's way of saying *'Be careful'*.

They nodded *'yes'* and continued putting on their gear.

Tyler made sure she grabbed the keys to the Hummer. She would be driving for this mission. Tex would follow behind in her specially made black Jeep, equipped with a special computer, it could go at high speeds, but cops looking out for speeders would get a reading on their radar guns that she was doing the limit even if their eyes would tell them a different story. She could spot other vehicles in front and behind her before they could see her coming. It would automatically read the tags and report information about the vehicles and their owners to her. She could shoot out tires with a push of a button. She loved this vehicle because it is something out of the James Bond movies.

Tex looked at the Tomboys and Bonnie and said, "Always give your best. Never get discouraged. Remember, others are not used to us. We are a team. Those who hate you don't win unless you hate them, and then you destroy yourself. The finest steel has to go through the hottest fire."

Four faces looked puzzled.

"Oh, Nixon. I get it, boss," said Travis.

"Damn Tex, you and your history lessons," said Teg.

"Lessons that will help you live another day, ladies," said Tex, softly.

"Amen" said Tyler.

"Ladies," Tex said, "I was venting the other day, I was mad, realized Jordan never loved me,

or he would have never tried to kill me. I just need to know why. So just take him."

"What if he doesn't agree to the arrangements?" Tyson asked.

"We will make him," said Teg.

"We will take out Radio and Pie because those two are a menace to society," said Tex.

"Punks, who can be handled by anyone of us one on one. Let the regular officer handle them," said Tyler.

"The Tomboys don't go along with police protocol," said Bonnie.

"Yes, we are above all others," said Tyler.

"I get it," said Tyson, jumping for joy. "You need some action to work off that fucker deceiving you right?"

"You are always one step ahead, Tyson," Tex joked.

"Yea I remember you are the one who corrupted my youthful innocence" said Tyson.

"You did that all by yourself my dear," said Tex.

All laughed.

"This is illegal, and I don't want to end up under a man--made jail with cockroaches as my pets," said Tyler.

At that moment it became so quiet you could hear a rat piss on a cotton ball.

Everyone looked at Tyler.

Teg said, "Tyler, Tex is the A-in alpha and we help our friends, legal or illegal."

"This is not brain surgery. We are going to take out two fools and talk to a dick. Do you mind, Tyler?" Tex asked angrily.

Softly, Tyler said, "I don't mean any harm, but someone has to think logically."

"Point taken and noted, so if you or anyone else has any problem with this mission, speak now or forever hold your tits," said Bonnie.

"I'm a go," said Tyson.

"Count me in," said Travis.

"I already broke a nail earlier. Why not two more?" said Teg.

Everyone looked to Tyler, who had her head down.

Sensing this Tyler raised her head up with a sly smirk and said, "You all said I had no sense of humor, remember?"

Tex reached over and slapped her behind the head for her earlier remark. The others follow Tex's motion and slapped Tyler in the head as they prepared to leave the house.

"Ouch, ouch! I was joking," said Tyler.

"Get in the Hummer. We need to take off," said Travis.

The Tomboys had filed out of the room while Tex looked back at Bonnie, who was standing by a desk.

She said to her "I will be back, because I have my best friend watching my back," as she pointed to the computer, and Ultimate Tomboys beside me."

"Yes, you do, my dear friend," said Bonnie.

Tex left the room, closing the door behind her.

Bonnie went to the computer, typed in 88-tango, and the screen lit up.

"Ready" was blinking on the screen.

***

Deuce was down in the police garage, giving the troops their orders. He advised them, "Be on top alert because this mission is extremely dangerous. These are people who have already killed our kind and will be willing to kill again."

Arnold, whose nerves were getting the better of him, was unable to warn Jordan because once an invasion was on; anyone using any kind of talking device would be arrested. The deputy chief stood by Deuce, with about fifty personnel from the DEA, ATF, and FBI.
The agents that were set to be in inner perimeter were in civilian clothes, and the others set for outer perimeter, police uniforms with mirror shades. All kinds of weapons and survival gear could be seen.
The captain didn't have to give much detail; they had been briefed.

All personnel had been shown pictures of the people they would be going after.

Deuce said, "Bring them in alive, but if necessary, take them out before they cause any damage."

The chief, who was only there briefly, jumped in and said, "Ladies and gentlemen, let's not lose anyone on this one."

All nodded.

The chief patted the captain on the back and walked back to the elevator to go back upstairs. He will handle that dumb fuck of a mayor. Arnold moved to Deuce's right after the chief started walking. The top brass behind Deuce looked at Arnold with disgust. They all knew what his game was.

"The time is now. Set all scanners and let's go," said Deuce, waving his arm up with his finger circling. Car doors were opening and closing with scattered bangs. Engines came to a roar and, one by one, the cars, trucks, and suv's took off out of the garage.

Deuce, walking to his vehicle, was thinking, *'why would Jordan do such a thing when he had a great career and life in front of him?'* He was glad to know that Tex was not a part of the game. He really liked her. Reaching his vehicle, he pulled out his radio and announced, "Put your radios on frequency 8-1-37.

Don't speak unless spoken to. For all we know, they could have a police scanner on them. Be careful all."

Vehicles of all type is headed towards Herr, California.
A shit storm is on its way.

***

Teg pulled out her personal cell phone to call Sharron.

When she answered, Teg said, "Hi Sharron, I need you to leave according to the plan we talked about earlier."

"How much time do I have, Teg?" Sharron asked.

"You have 30 minutes max but move as fast as you can and text me when you reach the destination we agreed on."

"Well, I am already packed, just need to go to the bank."

"The money has been transferred and will be waiting for you at the destination. I left a couple of hundreds in your top bureau drawer that will get you out of the area. "GO Now!"

Guessing, Sharron said, "Shit is hitting the fan, eh?"

"Like diarrhea, it's coming fast."

"Gone my friend. Be careful, see you soon."

"Bye, and don't forget to text me."

"I won't."

Both hung up.

Tyson pulled out her cell phone to see where Blackie was located. When he answered on the first ring, Tyson asked, "Where are you"

Before he could answer, she asked another question. "Is Ackers with you?"

"Yes, and we have left the town on the highway toward home."

"Keep your big ears alert. Company might come."

"Like whom?" Blackie asked.

"Hell, if I know," said Tyson.

"I swear Tyson, you are driving me insane. One day, someone is going to lock you up in the looney bin."

"That's okay. I have friends there."

Blackie laughed.

"Seriously, get moving. You are not safe."

"That's good Tyson, like I don't have enough on my mind."

"Just a heads up, be safe my friend."

"Getting soft on me, I see.""

"Never but be careful."

'Click'

Blackie smiled.

"Who was that on the phone, Blackie?" Ackers asked.

"My friends, telling me to move our asses. Shit is about to hit the fan."

Behind Blackie and Ackers is a Challenger.

***

"Look, there is that orange piece of shit of a car we saw at the gas station! I bet that guy is in the car.
Move up, Radio," said Pie.

"God help them if he is in there. I see two heads. We can take out both. No one is around."

The Challenger sped up to the orange deuce and a quarter. Blackie, looking in his rearview mirror, saw and heard the roar of the engine gaining on his car. When he saw an arm suddenly come out on the passenger side, a horrified look appeared on his face and he stopped talking. Ackers, looked at Blackie to see why he stopped talking, saw the look and turned to look out the right-side mirror. The color drained out of his face.

"Jesus! Blackie put your foot to the petal! Fast!" said Ackers breathing hard.

Blackie pressed the gas pedal down hard. The front of the car leapt up in the air slightly and took off with its race engine.

Radio pressed harder on the Challenger's gas pedal.
"That shit can't outrun my baby," said Radio.

Pie pulled the trigger on his Star Model 30M, a gun with a chamber-loaded indicator and adjustable sights. It was solid steel silver with a capacity magazine of fifteen rounds.
Bullets started flying toward Blackie's car.

Ackers ducked down in his seat. Blackie weaved the car sporadically left, and right so, Pie would not have a direct target.
Pie was shooting bullets wildly at the deuce and a quarter.
After about a mile of car weaving and shooting, a bullet hit the back windshield. The glass splattered all over the back seat of the car.

The sound made the guys cringe. Ackers went lower to the floor with his head in the seat and his legs under the glove compartment of the car. Lucky for Blackie and Ackers, the deuce and a quarter had plenty of room up front and back.

The whole back glass was gone.

"Shit," said Blackie.

Ackers started hollering, "We are going to die!"

"Hold on, buddy. I know many maneuvers that will help us. Just hold on to your butt cheeks."

"Tight as I can, my man," said Ackers.

"Get closer, Radio. I can take them out with the next shot," said Pie. He aimed the gun so when Radio got a little closer, he will have the best bull's eye shot.

Blackie waited to the last second, and then he made a sharp right onto the next highway.

Radio, who had moved closer to Blackie's trunk, didn't expect the sharp right, had to slow down to avoid the exit divider and make the same right turn.

Both Radio and Pie's bodies leaned toward the right and that made Pie lose his great position.

"Damn Radio watch the fuck out!" said Pie.

"I am on this pussy. Just aim and shoot fucker" said Radio.

Pie leaned back out of the car to take aim again.

Suddenly, another car came into play. It jumped in front of Blackie's car.

Blackie and Noah stopped breathing for a few seconds. Both saw their lives before their eyes. The dark brown 300 four door car slowed down a little and let Blackie get to its right.

When the cars were side by side, the blackened window on the passenger side rolled down so Blackie could see inside.

Blackie smiled at the occupant and took off faster down the road.

"Who, um, is that? Ackers asked nervously.

"An angel who is saving our asses, friend," Blackie answered.

The brown 300 car took off to the left, like it was leaving the scene.

The exchange had made Radio and Pie slow down to see who had interrupted their chase. When the car took off, they went right back to business.

"Finish it now before we have any more interruptions," said Radio.

Pie shot a bullet toward the car. Blackie swerved to the left then to the right.

"That bastard can drive, I will give him that," said Radio.

"Yeah, but I am a good shooter and here comes the killer," said Pie.

He aimed his gun toward the back of Blackie's head and started to pull the trigger.

BOOM!!!

The Challenger launched up in the air and landed about twenty feet away, when it came to a stop on fire. Blackie looked in his rearview mirror, Ackers looked in the passenger side mirror, with stunned looks on their faces. Blackie slowed down his vehicle and put it in park.

Ackers came up higher in his seat and sat back down upright.
After a few minutes, he looked at Blackie and asked, "Who was that angel?"
"Bad motherfucker, my man"
Both went back looking at the car behind them on fire.
A sickening smell began to fill the air because the bodies were burning inside the car.
Walker had parked his car and aimed a launcher at the Challenger to take it out.
He opened his cell phone and said only into the receiver, "Tango 88, taken out."
He hung up the phone and went back to his car.
Blackie put his car back into gear and drove down the street.

***

'...At the beep, leave a...' Jordan said, "Fuck."
"I told those boys to always answer."
Jordan hung up and redialed the number.
Ring... *'You have reached...'*
Jordan flipped the phone closed hard. A second later, he reopened his phone to try Pie's cell phone number.
Ring...ring... 'You have reach...'
'Where the fuck could those two be?' Jordan thought while pacing, He cleared his throat and walked over to the table in his room,
pour a glass of orange juice.
Slowly, he sips. The whole time, his mind was racing. *'Something is wrong. I smell something in the air, and it is foul'.* Suddenly, he stopped and reached for his cell phone again and dialed another number.
Ring...ring...ring...
"Walker," said a voice on the other end.
"Are you still trailing Radio and Pie?" Jordan asked harshly, not even introducing himself.
"No boss, I lost them," said Walker.
"Well, find those motherfuckers fast and get the hell back here," said Jordan.
"I will call them right away," said Walker.
Sighing, Jordan said, "I already tried. No one answered."
Walker noticed Jordan's attitude and asked, "Is everything okay?"

"Hell no, I have a feeling something is up, and I need all my heavy guns, Jordan shouted in the phone.

"I'm on it," said Walker, calmly.

"Faster!" Jordan screamed and hung up.

'*Jesus, he is about to bust some arteries,*" *I better let the women know Jordan feels something is up*'. Thought Walker.

"Hello," said Tex.

"Jordan is aware of something going down. How much, I am not sure," said Walker.

"The mayor might have been in touch," said Tex.

"He wants me back at The Cave."

"Go. Back up there already, the Tomboys and I are not far behind. Get rid of your phone after this call. We are going dark. Use the special frequency, only if needed. Jordan is not stupid, and I don't want to lose you. He is bound to find out about Radio and Pie soon."

"I have that one covered. I told him that I had lost them."

"Good, he will think someone else took them out. Wait until clear and leave the area."

"Sure" Walker responded.

'*Click*'.

Walker walked over to a rock and slammed his cell phone down onto it. The phone broke into pieces. He scattered the pieces around.

Walking back to his car, Walker pulled out his special phone, and programmed so Jordan can call and be recorded, then he drove off in his brown 300.

The site where the Challenger blew up was getting attention, a woman has her cell phone up to her ear, other cars have stop to look at the burning car. Sirens can be heard in the distance. Some people were video the scene.

The air was foul and smokey.

CHAPTER THIRTY

"Somebody ratted me out, Jordan. Who the hell knew? My ass is in a sling," the mayor said, wiping his forehead with a handkerchief.

"Calm down. What are you talking about?" Jordan asked, wondering what was going on.

"I got a call from the deputy chief, telling me he had proof that I was getting kickbacks from you and if I interfered with your takedown, my ass would be court marshaled. That is what the hell is up!"

"Only one person can give that kind proof."

Both said simultaneously, "Arnold…"

The mayor talked first. "I told you about that little prick ass kisser."

"We needed someone in the agency. Besides, he is nothing. I'll have him taken out before he can testify or give anything concrete."

"The consequences are dire, Jordan. We need action…Now."

"What do you mean dire?"

"Man, they will be on your ass within an hour. I am out of the loop, but my understanding is the invasion is going down soon."

Jordan reached over and pressed a button on his desk.

Two bodyguards are station at his door.

Jordan got up and went to his bedroom door.

"Mayor, I need you to hold on for a minute."

The mayor, who was furious with Jordan for letting this happen, kept screaming, "I want that prick taken out!"

Rolling his eyes, Jordan walked over and opened the door to tell the guys, "We are on a class four alert. We are going to have some company soon."

"What? Class what?" the mayor asked.

"Mayor, please calm down and give me a second," said Jordan.

The mayor keeps talking…*I need protection….* but Jordan was not listening.

The two guys' faces went ashen, class four meant feds.

Both shook their heads *yes* to indicate they understood and left to deliver the message to the others at the "cave".

Jordan closed his bedroom door, locked it, and went back to his phone, the mayor was saying…." I need protection and a place to hide...".

"Mayor, if we are going to get out of this, you need to get your ass on board."

The mayor tried to interrupt by saying, "What, what did…?"

Jordan continued, "You are a big boy. You knew the circumstances up front. You went into the ball game wide-eyed with glee, so let's play out the ending and stop bitching."

"I dare you speak to me like that."

"Well, stop acting like a bitch and find out what the hell is going on, so we can survive this." Jordan hung up on the mayor.

The mayor couldn't believe what just happened. He was holding the receiver in his hand looking at it. He sighed, hung up the receiver and pushed back hard into the back of his chair.

That guy is going to let me burn. All the work I put in to get where I am is going to go down in flames and I might go to jail, the mayor thought, not liking where this was going. He picked up his receiver to call the chief.

When the chief answered, the mayor said, "What do you need to know? The Cave is getting into battle mode."

Jordan pulled out his cell, but before he could dial, a call came through. Answering it, he immediately started before the caller could say anything.

"I need you to detour and go to the mayor's office. He is tripping. You know what to do," said Jordan.

"Um … boss, Radio and Pie are dead," said Walker.

Jordan went quiet. Moments went by before he spoke again.

"Are you sure?" he asked quietly.

"Yes, I retraced my steps from where I saw them last. There were policemen, ambulances, and fire trucks around a burning car. As I got closer, I could tell it was the Challenger with charred bodies still inside."

Jordan's mind began to race again. *'How much do they know? Who knows what?'*

"Walker, go to the mayor's office and take the fucker out."

A loud explosion rocked the house. With astonishment, Jordan fell to the floor of his bedroom.

Walker, who was still on the phone, heard the noise, asked "What just happened?"

Dazed, Jordan answered, "Someone just annihilated the guard tower."

"What?" Walker asked.

***

"Ouch," said Travis.

Laughing, Tyler said, "That's a bad mother."

Tyson had taken out the guard tower with a rocket launcher.

Teg was looking through her binoculars and told the girls, "Ladies, it is gone."

Bonnie, back at the Command Center, was laughing her head off. She knew the Tomboys were in their element.

Tex and the other police forces on their way to the location saw the dust in the air and heard the loud explosion. The sound caused things to shake within a radius of at least two miles.

'Damn those Tomboys. I told them to start quietly. I'd bet my ass it was Tyson.'

She shook her head and snickered, *"That girl is going to be the death of me one day."*

***

Arnold looked at Deuce and said, "That was a launcher."

"No kidding. Who has one? Get on the phone."

"I don't need to. No task force brought one."

Shocked, Deuce looked at Arnold and said, "Who, then?"

Arnold stretched out his arms and said, "I don't know."

"Whoever it is needs to be found out. It looks like we have company."

The black SUV with tinted windows sped up toward its destination.

Its occupants were dead quiet.

***

Outside the mayor's office building, Walker prepared for his mission. He was putting a silencer on his gun. He was in luck. Most of the building was still empty because it was still early in the morning. He was surprised to hear from Jordan that the mayor was in his office at daybreak. He knew a secret way to get in by passing the guards at the front entrance.

There was a service entrance to the west of the building. He got out of the car and went toward the door, pulled the door handle open, and put his nose to the grindstone to see if anything smelled funny. It was quiet, and the stairway was hot. No air circulated in this part of the building. He proceeded up to the tenth floor where the mayor's office was located. Coming out of the stairway, he looked down the hall. The mayor's secretary's desk was empty.

Walker thought to himself, *'He wouldn't be alone, would he?'* He took a deep breath and took in his surroundings. A door opened to his left. He ducked back into the stairway. He could hear the footsteps passing by the door. Then he heard an elevator door open and close. He waited two minutes before coming back out of the stairway. He thought *'I hope that wasn't the mayor.'*

Walker stepped out further into the hallway, at the far end is the mayor's office. Large black letters on the glass to the left of the dark brown, wooden door announced this to visitors.

A silhouette, in the shape of a body, passed the glass window. Walker froze. He watched as the body was pacing in front of the glass.

He tiptoed toward the wooden side of the door.

Within seconds, he recognized the voice that belonged to the mayor.

"I can get you close, but he is well guarded," the mayor was saying.

'Okay, he is on the phone. Good,' Walker was thinking.

He aims and pulls the trigger. A body hit the floor with a thud, a small hole where bullet enter glass panel was only evidence outside office.

Walker waited only a few seconds to see if it was clear for him to move. Feeling it was clear; he went back to the staircase and left the building.

Outside the building, back in his car, he called Bonnie.

"Parasite," is all Bonnie said with a smile.

Walker headed to The Cave.

Bonnie texted Tex. *'Parasite is gone.'*

Tex texted back. *'Next.'*

***

Arnold, riding next to Deuce, was thinking how this mission will get him that promotion. The mayor would be the sacrificial lamb. All the heat would be put on him. He was a stupid moron anyhow. Clearing his throat, he began the process.

"Hey Deuce, I think the mayor has to be knee deep in this. How can this be going on in his town and he didn't know?"

"Jordan is the one of the best we have at spy games. He could have fooled the mayor."

"True, but the mayor can't be that stupid," said Arnold, needing Deuce to agree to get the ball rolling.

"If he had realized what Jordan was up to, he would be dead. Trust me on that."

With a look of amazement on his face, Arnold asked, "He would kill an official as important as the mayor?"

Looking dead into Arnold's face, Deuce said, "Yes, he would."

Both stared into each other's eyes for a few seconds.
Arnold turned his head and leaned back into the car seat.
Exhaling air out of his lungs, he tried another tactical way to get his point across.

He stated to Deuce, "I will, with your permission of course, take legal action on several accounts against the mayor."

"Arnold, we need to see what the mayor knows first. Jordan is clever. Chill out."

"Yes, sir" Arnold answered. He would try this avenue again later.

***

Four bodies ran through the woods quickly, feet lightly touching the ground. They stopped by some trees that shield them. Male bodies can be seen by them. Slowly, they made their way toward the male targets, who are in groups of two walking, and patrolling the area.

Each had a 9-millimeter KG9 rifle with a magazine capacity of twenty rounds on their shoulder, positioned for action, if needed.

Quickly, Tyson and Travis went to the right. Tyler and Teg went to the left.

"Fuck," said one of the guards, as a shadow move, he readied his rifle and began pulling off shots in rapid fire. Tyson and Travis jumped back for cover, removing their guns, and firing back. The other two guards, upon hearing their comrade yell, went into cover mode.

Luckily for the Tomboys, Tyler had already jumped up in the air and was coming down behind one guard. With two quick slices, she slit his throat from ear to ear. His body dropped in a pool of blood. His gun went off prematurely, shooting bullets everywhere.

One of the guards went for his radio for help, Teg took out the hand holding his radio with a serious blow from her gun.

He fell to the ground, groaning in pain, with his face askew. Tyson and Travis aimed their guns and fired. The body was moving and twisting in ways a body should not.

He was tough and returned fire, hitting Travis in the shoulder. Blood blew onto Tyson's face, which sent her into a manic mode, and she pulled out her second gun, a Heckler & Koch HKP30, with a magazine of fifteen rounds that can be operated by thumb or index finger. Tyson was using her index finger, hitting that man with everything she had. Travis was on the ground, trying to get her wits about her. Her shoulder was bloodied and dirty from the wound.

"Okay!" yelled Tyson, not taking her eyes off the guy.

"Hell yes, just a flesh wound, I think!" Travis yelled back breathless.

Tyler, who saw Travis get shot, came up behind her.

A guard they didn't see was running toward the woods, Teg saw him and climbed a tree, aim her gun that held a sight, turned the level for sharper focus and pulled the trigger, he fell quickly. "Gotcha!"
She came down the tree and ran back toward the girls.

Tyson and Tyler were gathered over Travis' body.

"Stop babying me! I am okay," Travis said.

"Travis, this is more than a flesh wound, be still," Tyler told her.

"She tries to be so tough, but I am not losing my twin today," Tyson said, moving around like a tiger.

Sighing and taking a deep breath, Travis said "Tyson, I am okay. I just should have ducked."

"Not you too with the history lessons," said Tyler.

"History lesson? What do you mean?" Tyson asked.

Tyler stood up and said, "President Ronald Reagan said that to his wife Nancy when he was shot by that Hinckley guy."

"Oh yeah," Tyson said.

Teg, breathing slightly from running, asked, "Is everyone okay?"

"Yeah, did you get the last one?" Tyler asked.

"Blew the fucker away," Teg answered.

Giving her a Tomboy handshake, Tyler said, "My girl."

Travis and Tyson both gave Teg a nod of approval.

Looking at Teg, Tyson remarked, "I have never seen you dirty."

Teg's jeans were dark with stains from the hard bark, and she wiped her hands on her shirt for better gripping purposes.

"You bet that fucker made me climb a tree" said Teg.

"I would love to have seen you climb that tree," Travis said, laughing.

"I hit that motherfucking tree in one-minute flat, like the old days," said Teg, examining her dirty and broken fingernails.

Patting her on the shoulder, Tyson told her, "I will personally pay for the new nails when we get back, my friend."

"I am going to hold you to that." Pointing her fingers at Travis and Tyler, Teg continued, "You both heard that."

Travis and Tyler jokingly looked around like they didn't hear anything.

"Come on," Teg said, laughing.

"Travis, can you continue? Tyler asked.

Travis stood up and said, "Let us soldier on."

"Mighty Tomboys!" said Tyson.

All four ran back through the woods toward their destination.

CHAPTER THIRTY-ONE

The Tomboys reached the entrance to the pipe, a change has been made.

Teg tapped her cell phone open and said, "The entrance has been changed."

"Look around it. He couldn't have changed much" Bonnie suggested.

All checked out the entrance, it did look the same, but something is off.

Nothing looked disturbed.

Tyson motioned for her to hand the phone over. Teg gave it to her.

"Bonnie, we are blind here. Nothing looks disturbed," Tyson said.

The others start looking around the area for traps.

Bonnie's phone beep, a massage from Walker.

"Hold on ladies, an urgent message is coming in," said Bonnie.

'Here at cave. Jordan is aware something is going, be careful;'

Bonnie pulled up the design quickly, saw slight change outside, no change inside.

"Tomboys, we are back in business," said Bonnie through the speakerphone.

"Good, because I am getting a little antsy," said Tyson.

"The air smells funny, ladies," said Travis.

"I think we are just a little off," said Tyler.

"I agree, but the smell is rotten," said Teg.

Bonnie's voice came on the speaker. "Ladies, the lock was change slightly."

"What made them change it?" asked Tyson.

"I'm guessing here, Tyson, it always good to change locks in case someone who knows about it talks" said Bonnie.

"The man is not stupid," said Tyler.

Exhaling, Travis said, "True that."

"Can we still use the same tools to enter?" Tyson asked.

"Feel around, try not to trigger anything, be careful" said Bonnie.

"Big help, Bonnie," said Tyson, sarcastically.

"Sorry, best I can do, you'll pictures doesn't show invisible alarm lines," says Bonnie.

"Right, this old phones technology is gone," said Tyler.

"From now on, I have you link verbal, no more phones" says Bonnie.

233

"Yeah, prayer girl, did you say a prayer before we left?" Tyson asked.

Travis and Teg gave Tyson a look of disgust.

Getting into Tyson's face, Tyler said, "I pray every day, but especially for you because the devil is so…so strong in you."

Getting closer, Tyson said, "The devil can only win if you let him and I don't."

Teg pushed her way between the two bodies and said, "Girls, not here."

"Yeah, Tyson and Tyler, not now," Travis said, angrily.

Travis pushed Tyson back and whispered in her ear, "I love you girl, but cut the shit out".

Teg, standing by Tyler, slapped her against the head.

Travis, standing by Tyson, slapped her against her head.

"Hey!" said both simultaneously.

Muttering, Teg said, "Best of friends, huh?"

Rolling her eyes, Travis pulled out a flashlight to study the new lock.

Teg pulled out a small device used for removing security devices. She moved the device over the lock.

Travis stopped her by grabbing her arm and pulling her back up into a standing position.

"Wait, something is wrong. Jordan would have something securing this," Travis said.

Understanding, Tyler pulled out her device that will detect a motion alert used for sophisticated security devices.

"Where did you get that?" Teg asked.

With a look of surprise, Tyler said, "It is the latest."

"Um, I thought I had that" Teg replied while looking over her device.

The device went off with red lights flashing all over.

The Tomboys all jumped back off the area.

"Just like I thought," said Travis.

Tyler put on special glasses that magnified the area surrounding the system. She knelt to get a better grip on disarming the area. Travis, Tyson, and Teg froze where they were standing. The area could have silent alarms. Travis pulled out her sensory device and moved it in slow motion in circle. Tyson looked through her binoculars searching the surrounding area for any signs of trouble. Working fast, Tyler and Teg were disarming the system.

Travis knelt beside Teg and Tyler to see what they were doing.

Tyson kept a look out for any unwanted trouble.

"How do we open it?" Travis asked.

"I see no pull hatch or anything," said Tyler.

Tyson bent down with the rest and helped them look.

"It has to be some kind of hatch, button, or something to pull," said Travis.

Eight eyes were searching the entry gadget hard.

Finally, Teg said, "No! It can't be that simple."

"What?" Tyler asked.

She pulled out a nail file and used it to flip up a piece to the left of the entry. Up came a lever to pull. She pulled it straight up and the hatch began to open. It slowly began to take another shape, larger than it looked previously.

"Whoa," said Travis.

Shaking her head, Tyson commented, "Yes! A body can get through this."

"I have to admit, this is smart," said Tyler.

Teg pulled out a long wire that at the end, held a camera, aimed it into hole.

Tyler, holding the small screen that displayed images,

pushed buttons to widen the view of the area.

Camera was sending back images of steps and a door at the end.

The image made the Tomboys relax because they were the same pictures that were shown to them in the Command Center.

Travis says, "Tomboys going in."

Bonnie answered back, "Check."

Tyler went down first, followed by Teg, with Tyson right behind, and Travis the last to go down pulling the hatch close behind her. When Travis had reached the bottom step, Tyler already was working on getting through the door. Teg had set the special box left on the surface to give out false images to the security team. Tyson was going over the door entrance with the special device that let the ladies know what type of alarm system it held. The red light on the device was going off like crazy.

"This is not going to be easy," said Travis.

"In our business, nothing is," said Tyson.

"That is why I like this business. It makes you think fast and hard," said Tyler, starts working the nuts and bolts.

"Tyler, is that your blade you are using?" Teg asked.

"Nasty girl," said Tyson, laughing while patting Tyler on her shoulder.

Laughing back, Tyler said, "Opens you *and* kills you."

The three other Tomboys snickered softly.

Tyson hit the last button on her device that disarm the alarm for only thirty seconds, they had to move fast.

***

Watching the scene on her computer via the cameras, Bonnie relayed the information to Tex, "The ladies are going in."

"Good, let me know the moment they have that fucker," Tex said.

"Check," said Bonnie.

Tex had arrived at the observation point with the leaders of the invasion.

Beside her were Deuce and Arnold, along with several other personnel. They were at the inner perimeter with twenty other agents who were about to begin the invasion. It contained a large trailer that had been driven to the location two miles away from the action.

The trailer had two windows on each side of the trailer. In the middle was the only entrance with four steps in front of it. On the left side of the trailer was a long table that contained the coffee, tea, sandwiches, and sweets, along with plates, cups, and the necessary condiments needed, set up for the task force's consumption.

To the right of the trailer was the most important table that contained the equipment needed for the invasion. Two screens were set up with computers, communication equipment, binoculars, cell phones, earpieces, and sunglasses, many types of guns and their bullets, and bulletproof vests. Behind the trailer were two porta-potties for the Task Force and a mid-sized satellite dish, pointing toward the sky.

Information, like a view of the area, could be seen on the screens, and the computers gave and received information. Inside the trailer were four agents, manning the computers that were sending out the Intel to the chief and other leaders. Each task force had personnel inside, to contributed greatly to the invasion. Information was passing back and forth as the invasion got on its way. Four high-back leather chairs had been positioned for the highest-ranking personnel.

Tex was sitting in one of the chairs, drinking from a six-ounce coffee cup, watching the scene before her. In her lap was a small computer screen that was showing her a picture of the Tomboys in action,
sent to her by Bonnie.

Her main and only concern was that the Tomboys were getting in and, out without anyone noticing them, except those she picked to help them. Tex had an earpiece in her ear that gave her audio of the action.

She cannot reply or help the Tomboys in any fashion.
Her chair was facing the action in front of her, looking at the screen and listening, she could only hope that everything would go okay.
On the outer perimeter, twenty police cruisers with about thirty policemen and, policewomen whose job was to strictly not let anyone in or out of area.
The area contained two ambulances and two firetrucks, along with the corresponding personnel that would come in at the end to gather evidence and bodies. Deuce had invited her to the invasion, she accepted the invitation to observe them. Deuce smiled at Tex and got to business by addressing the leaders of the different task forces.
"Advise your people in the inner perimeter to bring out some captives, if possible. Upper intelligence wants to interrogate for information".
He put up both hands with two fingers motioning quotation marks, and laughed and said,
"I mean *chat* with them."
The leaders all smiled, knowing exactly what Deuce meant.
Tex just smiled because she was thinking,' *that is why the Tomboys are the hell out of the system. No bullshit to deal with.'*
Arnold slowly made his way to an area where he could use his cell phone privately. He was calling the Mayor but got no answer.
'Where fuck is, he?' he whispers.'
Arnold dialed another number.
"What the fuck do you want?"
"You should be nicer to a person who is about to save your ass," said Arnold.
"Fuck you, prick! I don't need you!"
"In case you are not aware, the force is on your ass. We are about two miles away from you" Arnold said back, harshly.
Silence from the other end of the phone.
"Good, I have your undivided attention, so I am going to be quick. I will tell you the perimeter locations of our people if you leave evidence the Mayor was the head leader, and you leave the states for good" said Arnold.
The caller started pressing buttons furiously on his console at different angles of pictures, while Arnold was running off his mouth.
A soft sigh of relief came on his face when the image of his escape route came up.
The exit had not been invaded or covered by the force.
Arnold was still talking. "…The account number is 00442277. Oh, Jordan. I need a half million to save your ass."
Looking annoyed, Jordan said, "Repeat the account number, motherfucker."

"Down...dawg. I'm in charge here" said Arnold.

"Just repeat," Jordan said, angrily. "God, I hate assholes."

"I can hear you, Jordan."

"Who gives a fuck?" Jordan answered.

"00442277, it is ready to receive right now."

"I bet motherfucker."

Arnold cringed at being called that name by Jordan.

He thought, *'Maybe I should get my money and still let this fucker go down.'*

He looked over toward the observation area to make sure he was still covered. All clear.

"Done," said Jordan, *'Click'*.

Arnold, hearing the click, pulled the cell phone away from his ear and looked at it and thought, *'the nerve of that man'*, as he made an insulted face, He opened up the web browser on his cell phone and he typed in a code.

He waited a moment, and then the screen on the phone lit up, showing that the money had been deposited. *'Fuck you,'*. He had already made the preparation for the mayor to take the heat. He had given that man a lot of information on his enemies to help him stay in office.

Arnold walked back toward the action.

Deuce was talking to the others. "New Intel just came in; someone has killed the Mayor."

"What? Oh my god," said a lieutenant.

Deuce continued. "We have personnel on the scene. When I get more intel, I will pass it on."

"Jordan did this?" Tex asked.

Exhaling, Deuce looked at her and said, "Maybe."

Both looked at each other, silently.

Arnold was glad to hear this because his plan would work. *'Blame it all on the mayor. After all, Jordan might escape and come after him later, but the mayor can't'.* He smiled to himself.

Deuce, looking at Arnold, said, "Something we all need to smile at?"

"No, boss. I am sorry, my mind is wandering," Arnold answered.

Deuce didn't give up and asked Arnold, "You were smiling when I said the Mayor has been killed. That is not anything I would smile about."

"If a smile came on my face, I assure you it was not because someone was murdered," said Arnold.

Looking at Arnold hard, Deuce said, "Keep your head in the game. What we are about to do is serious and there can't be any mistakes or people will get killed."

"Yes boss," said Arnold.

The others who were listening to the exchange looked at Arnold.

Tex thought, *'He's a weasel in the highest'*.

Arnold bowed his head and walked over toward the food table and pour himself some coffee. In the background, one of the personnel whispered, "That guy is a prick."

The others nodded their heads in agreement.

***

Jordan went to his laptop computer and pulled up a special email account.

He typed a message, telling the person he was being invaded by the force.

If I die these are the people you need to come after. I will not put their names or important information on this email because it is not safe. It can be traced with the right software even if you delete the email. You know where to go.

A manila envelope with all the information will be inside.

I love you with all my heart Kobi.

"Message sent: Urgent" was displayed on the computer screen.

A loud bang shook The Cave's foundation. People were falling everywhere.

Screams could be heard all through the house inside and out on the grounds.

"What the fuck?" Jordan said, looking around.

He looked again to make sure his email was sent. The message read "Email sent." He went for his weapon and intercom at the same time.

***

Teg disconnected the security system, Tyler moved in with her drill removing the nuts and bolts.

Bonnie came into their ears stating, *"Company is on the way and they needed to hurry to get inside and leave the premises."*

Travis says one of the most famous quotes in the world, "Say hello to my little friend," as she blew the door off its hinges. Smoke and debris were in the air when the Tomboys went through the hole.

In front of them was a wall and there was a hallway to either side.

"A guard is coming from each end with weapons drawn.

Teg pulled out her gun and shot the guard straight through his right eye. As his body hit the floor, Tyler took the one on the right.

Travis and Tyson broke off and climbed through the air vents in front of them.

Bonnie shouted to Tyler in her earpiece that another guard is coming her way. Tyler slid close to the side of the wall and waited for him to come to her.

Locking eyes, she made a quick move by jumping in the air, Pulling out her knife and slit his throat with one quick move.

Blood ran down his neck and chest as he fell to the floor.

Stepping over the body, she quickly moved towards the main security room.

Bonnie, back at the Command Center, yelled, "Lethal! Deadly!"

***

In the meantime, Teg came across another guy waiting for a status report. As she got closer, he looked her way but did not even draw his weapon. Teg got into a boxing stance. The guard laughed. She suckers punched him in the groin. He stopped laughing and gave her a good one back. Teg faked her reaction to the blow and went down. When he came to finish her off, she jumped up fast, kicked him in the balls, and when he bent down, she put one arm around his neck and with her other hand, turned his neck to the left and right. *Crack.* His neck broke on impact and his body slid down to the ground. Teg continued toward the master bedroom.

Travis and Tyson came out of the vents and ran into a guard that was 6'4", 380 pounds.

Before he could aim his weapon, Travis shot it out of his hand.

He yelled, holding his bloody hand.

Tyson jumped up in the air and karate--kicked him in the chest. He was pushed back a bit. Travis jumped up and kicked him again. Being so big, he only went backward but didn't fall.

"Shit, we always get the big fucks," said Travis.

"Just the way I like it. The bigger, the better," said Tyson, whose adrenaline was on high. One thing she liked about being a Tomboy, shit she can get away with.

The guard was trying to get his wits about him.

"Let's have some fun," said Tyson.

Smiling, Travis shaking her head answered "Yeeeees".

Both jumped up together, Travis kicked him in the chest and Tyson kicked him in the balls at the same time. The guard groaned. Travis backed off while Tyson just punched him with her bare fists. Blood was going everywhere.

The guy did not have a chance to defend himself because the blows were coming at lightning speed. Travis jumped in and began giving him blows all over his body. The guy was puking up everything he ate today and yesterday. He probably peed on himself, as liquids of all kinds and colors were splattered against the wall, the floor, and his body.

Travis finally pulled out her automatic and shot him in the head four times. His big ass body went limp against the wall.

They headed towards the master bedroom.

Bonnie, laughing, said "Fatal."

***

An explosion came from the main house, everyone in the inner perimeter stood in shock.

Deuce was on his radio, asking, "Have the personnel reached the house already? Agent one, what just happened?'

"Someone blew something up," came back an answer.

Disgusted, Deuce said, "I know that! More detail, agent."

"More detail as soon as I can get closer sir."

Annoyed, Deuce said, "You are not the one blowing up something?"

"No sir."

"Then who the fuck is it?"

"Not sure sir."

"Well find the fuck out and get back, pronto."

"Yes sir."

The radio went dead.

Deuce announced to no one in particular, "What the fuck is going on?"

He shook his head, annoyed.

Tex, who was standing by Deuce, knew it was the Tomboys.

'Good', she was thinking, *'They got in first and will bring Jordan's ass to me.'*

She turned toward Deuce getting his attention by tapping him on the shoulder.

Deuce turned around.

Tex said, "Deuce, tell your people, come correctly or Jordan is going to have their asses. He will take them all out with no conscience."

Deuce gave her a look of agony. A former agent taking out his own was bad.

She continues, by saying "He's not coming out alive, he will go down in a hellfire of bullets if necessary".

Deuce said nothing.

***

Jordan saw on his security cameras the force was coming his way. He started barking protection orders. "Whomever is on the inner perimeters, I need you to get guns and start shooting bastards, NOW!!!"

He notices on his security camera; his outer perimeter was taking over by the police blockade. "Shit"

BOOM!!!

The people who were closer to the explosion that survived went to protect the area. Jordan began reassessing the situation, he knew he was being attacked and, action getting closer.
"Talk to me people, I need to have eyes and ears everywhere, let's start communicating."
All he received back was static, his communication has been taking out. Grabbing his Glock and a pistol, he started moving towards his escape route.

***

-

All hell broke loose. Radios and computers at the inner perimeter were operating on full blast, spitting out information.

***

Peaches, a DEA agent who was secretly working for Tex, went through a window on the side of the house. Her other comrades are having a shootout with the guards protecting the front gate. She was able to slide by through some trees to an unprotected window.

Entering through the window, Peaches was met by two guns, one at each of her left and right temples.

"Comrade?" Tyson asked.

Using the code word Tex gave her, Peaches answered, "Tango 88."

"Good answer," Travis replied, withdrawing her weapon. Tyson did the same.

"First mission?" Tyson asked.

"Yes," said Peaches.

"Nice. Having toddlers guarding a mission," said Tyson.

"I was the top in my class, mama," said Peaches.

Sullen, Tyson looked at Travis and said, "Do I look like a mama?"

Travis looked her up and down, taking too long to answer.

Tyson sulked, putting her hands on her hips. She gave Travis a hard look.

Peaches, not knowing they were joking, froze in place. She was thinking she had just insulted Tyson. She heard of their reputations.

Travis says seriously, "You look all of thirty-two.

Sighing, Tyson pointed her finger at Travis and said, "Quicker answer next time, you hear?"

"Yes mama," said Travis, laughing.

Looking at Peaches, Tyson said, "Don't get yourself killed rookie. I don't want to have to answer to Tex."

"Yes ma…, uhm sure"

Travis chuckled.

Tyson gave her a sharp look. Peaches bent her head down and went past her to take the lead toward the master bedroom.

Travis stopped her by pulling her arm and said, "Look, rookie. Jordan is a gorilla and when you are taking a gorilla down, you hit him with everything, I mean everything, he will do the same, understand?"

"Understood" Peaches said.

Peaches went toward her exit she had been instructed by Tex to protect. Tyson and Travis headed toward the master bedroom.

***

Tyler, reaching the security room, took out the one guard and put an usb in the hard drive and, started typing in codes that will give Bonnie back at the Command Center control of the security systems. Bonnie sent her a hello message.

Before leaving she protected the entrance by adding a bomb that will explode if anyone tries to enter after she leaves. She headed towards the master bedroom.

CHAPTER THIRTY-TWO

Cops at the outer perimeter, the townspeople were aware something was going down. Many got into their vehicles and headed towards the action. Being stopped by copes wearing mirror shades from getting close, they started bringing out chairs, tables, and grills to camp out to watch what was going on. Children were running around like they were at a picnic. Music could be heard in different parts of the crowd.

Binoculars were passed around as each tried to see what was going on, the cops were not talking. Whispered conversations were going around about the man who owned that part of town was a drug dealer and the force was taking him down. Some were surrounding a TV that someone had brought out, watching CNN, which was reporting on the death of the Mayor. Nothing like this had ever happened in the history of this town. This was big, and no one wanted to miss it. Some businesses close shop, others that were necessarily stayed open, sales were high.

This was historical to all.

***

Teg was the first to arrive in the vicinity of Jordan's bedroom. She spotted the two guards entering the room. She came closer with her gun drawn and the sound of clicking locks were heard. Tyler came up behind her, giving her a soft whistle. Teg turned toward her, gun still drawn, and advised Tyler that the guards just moved inside.

"We have to tell Travis and Tyson," said Teg.

"Yeah, we need to change our plans," said Tyler.

"I will reach the girls and you, get Bonnie for video help inside," said Teg.

"Tomboys," said Tyler.

"Yeah?" came back Tyson's voice.

"Have to change plans, two guards just moved inside the master bedroom," said Tyler.

Teg added "It is impossible for us to blow the master bedroom door. It is a bomb proof door, and his bedroom windows probable shatterproof.

"We will go through the air vents in the master bedroom, one moment," said Travis.   "Bonnie, we need eyes inside the master bedroom", says Tyson,

"Travis and I have to go through the air vents."

"No way I can help you, can't see inside the master bedroom, ladies you're on your own," said Bonnie.

"We are blind ladies" said Tyler.

"No shit" says Teg.

"Girls we play this by ear" said Travis.

"Me and Travis are going through the vents, it always leads to somewhere" said Tyson.

"Hope the master bedroom" says Teg.

Softly, Bonnie said" Be careful."

Teg and Tyler took position outside the master bedroom.

Travis and Tyson started crawling to see where it leads.

***

Stricken by how fast things were closing in on him, Jordan told one guard "You watch the monitors, sound alarm if you see anything suspect, position the others guards for protection."

"Yes boss" the guard replied.

To the other guard, "Watch all monitors for where the task forces were located. Use whatever force necessary for us to survive".

"Yes Boss" the guard replied.

Jordan went toward his escape route entrance.

***

Travis gave Tyler and Teg the signal that she and Tyson were in position by tapping her earpiece four times. Tyler tapped her earpiece back four times.

Tyson was watching the action through the air vent. She could see Jordan with his back toward them. The two guards were busy watching the monitors as Jordan was walking towards his escape route. One guard is on his cell phone, barking out orders.

Waiting for Jordan to exit the area, Travis and Tyson blow the vent cage open, so they can go into the room. Both took a guard out before hitting the floor, hearing this Jordan continued his escape route.

Tyson opened the door from inside to let Tyler and Teg in.

Tyson said, "Jordan went that way".

Looking at a computer monitor, Teg said "He sent a message, look."

"Can you tell whom? Tyson asked.

Typing on the computer, Teg says "No"

"Can we give Bonnie access to check it out? Travis asked.

Teg replied "No, he has coded it, can be broke, but we don't have the time," said Teg.

"Send it to Bonnie, anyway, could be useful later" said Tyler.

"True that" said Teg. Typing away at the computer after putting in an usb connection.

"Travis and I are going after Jordan" said Tyson.

"Right behind you, after Teg and I gather some intel said Tyler.

"Be quick, we don't know how many people in the area" said Travis.

Travis and Tyson left the area same way as Jordan did.

While Teg copy intel, Tyler places a bomb on the master bedroom door from within.

***

Jordan turned toward the commotion as Tyson closed in right on his ass, pointing her gun straight at him. Hearing the footsteps behind him, Jordan continues moving as fast as he could.

"Tex" he said softly.

Travis right behind Tyson. "The motherfucker" said Tyson.

Jordan heard a gun clock and stopped.

Looking back at Tyson, he asked, "Where is Tex?"

"You don't ask questions here, motherfucker," Tyson replied.

Jordan kept his mouth shut.

Tyler and Teg had caught up by this time with the girls within the exit route.

The Tomboys had cuts and bruises on different parts of their bodies. Tyler had small bloody circles over her body from bloody spattering from necks she cut. The blood was in her hair and all over her skin and clothes. Teg had black and blue bruises from fist fighting.

Tyson's hair was askew from the sweat and she and Travis had bloodstains all over their bodies along with black and blue bruises from hitting the walls, floors, and hard bodies of the guards. They all have been in combat.

Tyler said into her earpiece, "Package on its way."

"Check," came back from Bonnie.

Peaches, who could hear the conversations, moved towards her next destination.

"Move this way, Mr. Jordan," said Tyler.

"One who has manners," said Jordan.

"Don't mistake my kindness for weakness. You tried to kill my friend, just move," said Tyler.

"Oh, you are friends?" Jordan asked.

No one answered.

Jordan turned around with hands up toward where Tyler was pointing. The others filed behind him with weapons still drawn.

"Tex, the package is on its way," said Bonnie.

"I am moving toward the exit," said Tex into her cell phone.

"I have you all the way, my friend," said Bonnie.

A red light is blinking in the master bedroom.

***

Jordan smiled as he was walking, he was not surprised, Tex is top gun.

Wished she had died that night.

Five bodies were working their way through a narrow, barely light path toward a pair of steps that would lead them to their destiny.

Coming close to the exit steps, Tyler signaled Peaches. Peaches went up the stairs, opened the hatch, peeked out, everything was clear.

She signaled back that everything was clear and waited on the ground for the five bodies to emerge. Tex was already at the location, waiting for everyone.

"Peaches, move" said Tex.

She nodded and moved.

Jordan's face was the first one seen by Tex; it had been a long time. Surveying the area while adjusting his eyes to the bright sun, his body was pushed up by Tyson.

Jordan thought, *' I could kick this lady and make a run for it'.*

Just as he was thinking that he felt metal against his left temple.

"Come on up, Jordan" the voice said.

Doing as he was instructed; Jordan came on up and turned slowly around.

"Hello Tex," he said.

Tex, who was standing straight up with stern look with both hands on her Ruger Super Redhawk revolver with a direct scope said nothing.

The Tomboys, one by one, came out of the opening and surrounded her.

"Nice group you have here. I have to admit, lethal," said Jordan.

"Nothing but the best," said Tex firmly.

The Tomboys stood back slightly. This was Tex's show now.

Tex pulled the trigger and hit Jordan with a bullet through his heart.

He went down fast with eyes wide open, not saying a word.

The Tomboys were silent. Tex, with gun still drawn, went toward the body. The girls moved closer with their guns now drawn for cover.

She let one hand loose from the gun to put on his neck to see if he was dead. Feeling no pulse, Tex rose back up and put four more bullets in his head and the last one through the heart, emptying the chamber. The Tomboys turned around and started walking toward the woods to exit. Their mission was over.

BOOM!!!
Bodies flew up in the air.

***

Bonnie and Walker, back at the Command Center, were suddenly terrified.

"Jesus, what just happened?" she asked.

"I think…think a bomb went off," said Walker, pushing buttons on the keyboard in a frantic way. He was adjusting the camera angles, so he could get a read on what had just happened and what was happening now.

Bonnie, who now had tears in her eyes, was pacing around the area, breathing heavily.

Bonnie asked, "Anything yet, Walker?"

"No, still looking, there's so much smoke blocking the scene," Walker replied, still pushing buttons on the keyboard.

The computer was sending back images of black and grey smoke, no matter which way the cameras turned. He couldn't make out anything.

"Bonnie, we have to wait for the smoke to clear for any indication," said Walker.

"The hell I will," said Bonnie, who picked up her cell phone to dial a number.

Ring…ring…ring…

No answer.

Click.

She tried to get the girls by audio feed.

Tyson…. Travis…. Teg…. Tyler…somebody answer please.

No one answered.

She tried yet another number.

Ring…ring…ring…

Bonnie sat down hard in her chair, let out a heavy sigh.
She is thinking the unthinkable.

***

Groans were heard in the woods. Bodies were turning over, trying to figure out what was going on. Tyson pulled herself up into a sitting position, wiping her eyes to clear the debris from her face, focusing her eyes, she started becoming aware of where she was. Travis, who was knocked right beside her by the blast, was rolling over with both hands to her face, as she laid on her back. Jordan's body was the closest to the bomb and went up in the air and flew into pieces.

His body parts landed in different directions. Some parts ended up about a half-mile away. Teg came up on all fours, getting her wits. Tyler's body laid still.

All bodies were covered from head to toe with dirty debris.

Tyson turned to her friend, "Okay, Travis?" she asked.

"I have a splitting headache and my ears are ringing something terrible, but everything else seems to be moving," Travis replied.

Tyson saw Teg looking at her and gave the okay sign.
A body is still, not too far from the girls. Instantly, without hesitation, Tyson crawled toward the body on all fours.
Turning it over, she noticed it was Tyler, not breathing.

"Teg, Travis! Tyler is not breathing!" she yelled.

Teg and Travis jumped up and ran toward Tyler and Tyson.

Tyson was giving her mouth-to-mouth resuscitation by holding her nose and breathing short breaths into her mouth. Travis had both of her bloody hands on her, counting and pumping her chest.

Teg was beside the others, whispering "Come on, Tyler. We came too far… Come on girl, fight…fight!"

Tyler was not coming around.

Travis' hands started shaking with tears in her eyes. "No god…not this baby"

Teg grabbed her hands and said, "Let me take over, Travis."

Travis moved aside and Teg start pumping Tyler's chest.

Tyson kept breathing small puffs oxygen into her lungs.

Tyler starts moving.

Footsteps came up towards them, Eyes diverted towards the noise, Travis pulled her weapon and moved towards covering the others whose froze.

The voice said, "Are you going to shoot your boss?"

All three said at the same time, "If need be."

250

"Wise asses haven't lost your sense of humor," said Tex.

Looking around, she asked, "Where is Tyler?"

The girls had protected her body with their own when they heard the footsteps.

Teg, Tyson, and Travis moved their bodies to reveal Tyler behind them.

"Tyler, are you okay?" Tex asked with concern in her voice.

"I'm still trying to get my lungs to breathe in sync," answered Tyler.

Tyson reached down to help her up.

Ring…ring…ring… Tex cell phone was ringing.

Bonnie and Walker at the Command Center were ringing Tex's cell phone and calling out to the girls earpieces, simultaneous which by the way wasn't working, but Bonnie and Walker didn't know that. They still couldn't see any images because the smoke had not subsided yet.

Tex answered, "Bonnie, we are okay."

"We, as in…who…how many?" Bonnie asked.

"As in, all the Tomboys and I are on our way home."

"God Bless," Bonnie said with a sigh.

Tex hung up.

Tex walked closer to the Tomboys and said, "You four are the best in the world. Thank you."

"Don't get all sentimental on us now," Tyson joked.

Teg, Travis, Tyler, and Tex all said simultaneously, "Tyson, cut the shit."

# # # #

Ultimate Tomboys is a trilogy.
I am thrilled to be putting out my first novel.
It is a joy and a blessing to represent ladies of all ages and nationalities world over.
Ladies **let's ride and die together.**
Ready!!!!

I found writing about my ladies, very therapeutic and had to continue the story.
Ultimate Tomboys: Saga continues…. will be release next.
Third installment ……. still writing doing this printing.

To order a copy of this trilogy, get information on author, status updates, inquires, questions, comments, or testimonials send an email to
Bunny.Productions@yahoo.com.

Visit my website, **Bunny.Productions.com**
Thank you for reading, ordering, or passing my novel to other readers.

Bunny